TEA AND NO SYMPATHY

"Somebody killed him, Fiona."

She looked startled.

"We assumed he fell in the dark and hit his head."

"No. He was lying on his stomach, and the whole back of his head had been knocked in. There was a big brass lamp on the floor beside him, and it was covered in blood." I started shivering as the images came back into my mind.

"Don't think about it. It will all be sorted out. Come along, drink that tea, and let's hear no more nonsense."

"Is the fire out?"

"Yes, finally. But the cottage was destroyed. Just parts of the wall left standing. It was an awful eyesore, but I suppose a new owner could have made it over into something livable. You can hear the hoses, they're still watering it. I think the whole village is out there watching."

I winced and closed my eyes again. The pain in my burned arm was getting worse, making it hard to concentrate on what she was saying.

"How can these things be happening?" I said. "Two men have been *murdered* in this village, Fiona."

"My dear, what a thing to say! I'm afraid you're rather going off at half cock."

"You don't believe me!"

"Let's not talk about it any more. How about a biscuit?"

ARSON &
Old Lace

PATRICIA HARWIN

POCKET BOOKS
New York London Toronto Sydney

The sale of this book without its cover is unauthorized. If you purchased this book without a cover, you should be aware that it was reported to the publisher as "unsold and destroyed." Neither the author nor the publisher has received payment for the sale of this "stripped book."

This book is a work of fiction. Names, characters, places and incidents are products of the author's imagination or are used fictitiously. Any resemblance to actual events or locales or persons, living or dead, is entirely coincidental.

An *Original* Publication of POCKET BOOKS

POCKET BOOKS, a division of Simon & Schuster, Inc.
1230 Avenue of the Americas, New York, NY 10020

Copyright © 2004 by Patricia Harwin

All rights reserved, including the right to reproduce this book or portions thereof in any form whatsoever. For information address Pocket Books, 1230 Avenue of the Americas, New York, NY 10020

ISBN: 0-7434-8224-7

First Pocket Books printing February 2004

10 9 8 7 6 5 4 3

POCKET and colophon are registered trademarks of Simon & Schuster, Inc.

Cover illustration by Bob Dombrowski

Manufactured in the United States

For information regarding special discounts for bulk purchases, please contact Simon & Schuster Special Sales at 1-800-456-6798 or business@simonandschuster.com

To Robert and Emily, my favorite techies.

CHAPTER ONE

I pulled the car in close to the hedgerow and turned the key, and that amazing silence came down. It was the silence I had been wanting for more than a year, since my husband had left me, since I'd decided my only hope of peace lay in the ancient rhythms of an English village.

I used to wake in our apartment on West Eighty-third and listen for that silence through Manhattan's background hum. Keeping by long habit to my side of the bed, I would see behind closed eyelids the narrow country road and the old cottages with roses in bloom on their walls, as they had been when Quin and I had first come to Far Wychwood.

The village inn had been more affordable than an Oxford hotel when we'd come over to attend the wedding of our daughter, Emily, in Christ Church Cathedral, and we'd loved it so much, we had stayed there again when our grandson was born. The memory had become a refuge after Quin told me he'd fallen in love with another woman, and then through the hard labor of adjusting to life alone.

I closed my eyes and sank into the silence. When I opened them I saw my new home, standing where it had stood since the seventeenth century. Built of honey-colored Cotswold stone, its slate roof thick with velvety lichen, its windows mullioned and diamond-paned, a trail of brown vine by the door with the ghosts of last summer's roses clinging—it looked like a *Travel Britain* poster, and it even had a name, in the English way: "Rowan Cottage."

I had been right to give the realtor an order for "a nice little furnished place in Far Wychwood" and leave the rest to her. She knew the kind of thing we Yanks were looking for.

I stepped out of the little car I had rented that afternoon at Heathrow, on a surge of relief at having made it all the way to Gloucestershire on the wrong side of the road without killing myself or anyone else. It would have been more sensible to have spent the night in London, as Emily had urged me to, but I couldn't wait to see my new home.

I pulled my suitcase and carry-on from the trunk. I had given everything to my friends in New York except a modicum of clothing, and the books, CDs, and photo albums I'd shipped. The rest belonged to the three quarters of my life Quin had shared, and I never wanted to see it again. I looked forward to leisurely days browsing county markets and antique shops for the furnishings of my new, solitary life.

But as I opened the gate and started up the worn brick path, the first pang of doubt struck. Could I be turning into a crazy old lady already, in just the first year of my sixties? It *was* kind of crazy to leave a circle of friends, a long career as a librarian, a whole country behind on the strength of a memory. After thirty years in Manhattan, could I be happy out here in the sticks? Wasn't I liable to go crazy from boredom?

The great adventure I'd been having began to feel like one more example of "going off half-cocked," as Quin called it, that impetuous nature he and Emily found so trying. But I realized I was veering perilously close to self-pity. This mood had to be the result of a drop in endorphin levels from two days without a good long walk, I told myself firmly.

My English realtor, a woman named Eleanor Coleman, had sent me a key. When I opened the door and stepped into the narrow hallway, the musty smell of a long-closed house rose around me. I flipped a wall switch and an overhead light came on. Thoughtful Eleanor Coleman! She'd had the electricity turned on.

I stepped into the room on my right and pushed another light switch. I was in a cozy little sitting-room with bare, random-width floorboards. A sofa covered in classic chintz and a green baize wing-chair flanked a fireplace. The far wall was ridged with empty bookcases from floor to ceiling.

The kitchen, across the hall, was the real English article, with stone-flagged floor, wooden dish rack over the sink, and glass-fronted cabinets. The only appliances were a rather elderly refrigerator and a huge Aga stove that took up most of one wall. I opened a door beside it and started up a steep, boxed-in staircase.

The second floor was tucked under the eaves, the ceilings low and slanted. There was an adequate, old-fashioned bathroom and two bedrooms freshly painted in a nice pale peach color, with good firm beds. The leaded casements of the larger room overlooked the back yard, its bare trees and bushes soft-edged in the twilight. The other bedroom looked out on the road and somebody else's cottage across the way, with one lighted window.

I leaned on the sill and looked out. Whoever lived in that little cottage was my only near neighbor. Woods and fields surrounded us, except for an abandoned building with a fallen-in thatched roof a few hundred yards down on my side of the road. We were apparently the last two occupied dwellings at this end of the village.

My second thoughts were multiplying into third and fourth ones. Everybody had said I was so brave when I'd told them my plans, but could it be that, under the surface bravado, I was really just one of those awful clinging mothers?

Emily had been a Rhodes scholar. As soon as she had finished her Oxford degree she had married her tutor. While I'd felt some regret that she would be staying in England, I'd had my chosen life and wanted her to have hers, too. She'd gone on to qualify as a psychotherapist and found a great job at an Oxford hospital. As it turned out, it was better that she was overseas during the breakup. It had hurt her enough at long distance.

That had all happened while she was still on maternity leave. Only after she went back to work had I begun to hear stress in her voice over the transatlantic wires. A succession of babysitters proved unsatisfactory, the hospital wanted her to take on more patients, little Archie came down with the usual baby ailments. She had sounded so delighted when I'd suggested coming over to live nearby and lend a hand. But how would she feel now that I was really here?

I flashed on her face, younger than her years, the blue eyes going cold behind her glasses. I remembered her voice, that patronizing tone she could assume so easily: "No, Mother, I don't think he needs a little cereal. That's an outmoded idea from your generation. The best authorities say milk is all a baby should have for the first six months, so *please* don't keep on about it."

That had been fourteen months ago, the last time I'd seen her. Quin, as always, had backed her up, and I had swallowed my opinions to keep the peace, hard though that always was for me.

Having burned all my bridges behind me, how would I now stand up to her when she gave me the Look, as sooner or later she would?

You will *not* go on worrying like this, I told myself sternly. I knew I was strong enough to forget the past and deal with whatever dilemmas the future would bring. It only required determination and will, and plenty of exercise. I ordered myself to think about something else—that cottage across the road, for instance, about as old and picturesque as they come.

The little structure had spent centuries settling into its plot of ground, and now it leaned noticeably to one side. There were a couple of broken panes in one of the casements, which must make it pretty cold in there on a March evening like this. The window and door frames hadn't been painted for years, and the yard was such a tangle of weeds, I couldn't see a path. I wasn't going to find any new friends in that decrepit place, I thought glumly.

Then I noticed something grey and wispy, easing out under the door. I peered closer. Yes, it *was* smoke, seeping around the door, blowing through the missing window-panes. As I watched it came faster and faster, and then the light went out.

I ran downstairs and across the road, and pounded on the door. There was no answer, but I could hear somebody blundering around in there, knocking things over.

"Hey!" I shouted. "Your house is on fire! Hello!"

There was still no response, so I turned the knob. The door swung in abruptly, and I was enveloped in smoke. Something black went whizzing past my feet and out the door. I didn't stop to see what it was, but plunged in, holding my breath.

The fire lit up the far wall. I could see the flames rising from a stove, reaching for the rafters. They had begun to consume a curtain above the stove, and a piece of the fabric was drifting to the stone floor, just missing a burlap sack that lay there.

As I came near the fire a shape loomed up beside me, tall and dim in the smoke. It stood there unmoving while I groped for the stove knob and twisted it. The fire died into the burner. I grabbed the curtain rod and jerked the burning curtain to the floor, leaned across to the sink to turn the faucet on full blast, let the water partially fill a battered tin pot, and upended it over the curtains. Then I did it again. The damp smoke gagged me, but the flames smoldered out.

I pressed a towel over my mouth and nose and went around opening casements. In a few minutes the smoke began to clear. Now I could make out that figure by the stove, a tall, thin man with a beard, bent over, coughing spasmodically. Why hadn't he made a move to help me?

As we both began to draw breath again, he spoke. "Annie?" he said in a high-pitched, quavering voice.

"No," I choked out with exasperation, "my name's not Annie!"

I grabbed his arm and pulled him out the door. We stood on the doorstep, dragging in air and looking each other up and down.

The moonlight showed me what a very old man he was. Gnarled bones stood out under the furrows of his face. His clouded eyes were sunk back in their sockets and his mouth caved in on toothless gums. His shirt was a mosaic of food stains, his fly was half unzipped, he wore a broken-down shoe on one foot but only a sock on the other. And he smelled. The odors of unwashed flesh and stale urine floated to me on the night breeze.

He was glaring at me indignantly. "You bain't Annie!" he growled.

"No," I said, much more gently, now I could see the old man must be senile. "My name's Catherine. However did that fire start?"

He glanced back into the cottage, shaking his head of long, matted grey hair.

"Don't know, do I? Just fixing a bit of egg and bacon for dinner, I were, and there the cooker took fire. It's they witches, I don't doubt."

"Right, must have been witches." I felt too sorry for the poor old fellow to laugh. "Well, it's about cleared out, and I'm getting cold, aren't you? Let's go back inside."

He followed me. The inside was just like the outside, cluttered and unkempt, with burlap bags of produce standing around, dry sticks that must once have been herbs hanging from the rafters, food-crusted dishes and pans on the table and in the sink, and under the smell of smoke the smell of rot.

There only seemed to be one source of light, a big brass lamp lying on the floor under the window. Crossing the slanted floor to get to it was like walking up a ramp. It was heavy, and, when I set it on a table and twisted the switch, its light was flickering, inadequate.

The old man went straight to the stove and reached for a box of wooden matches sitting next to one of the burners.

"No, no, no, you're going to do it again!" I exclaimed, pushing in to grab the matches out of his shaking hand.

"I'll have me egg and bacon!" he shouted feebly.

"Why don't you just sit down, Mr.—What's your name?"

"Me name?" He stared as if unable to believe a person lived who didn't know who he was. "Me name's George, ain't it? George Crocker, same as it's been for more nor ninety year."

"Sit down, then, George. I'll fix you some bacon and eggs."

He sank into a chair by the big wooden table, muttering unintelligibly.

"You shouldn't be trying to cook," I said. "Isn't anybody living here with you? Your wife, or a son or daughter?"

"Wife?" He squinted with the effort of remembering. "Died long years ago, didn't she, Emma? A son, aye, I've a son. I've taken gurt care of him. He'll not want after I'm gone, won't Arthur."

"Why isn't he taking care of *you?*" I demanded. "Where is he, while you're setting fire to your house?"

"Arthur? In his home, and that's at Oxford. Did ye think I'd forgot where Arthur lives?"

"Does he ever come to see you?" I asked, already disliking Arthur, as I sawed at a rock-hard side of bacon sitting on an old hutch. "Why doesn't he hire somebody to stay with you, or get you into—" I stopped, realizing I might be treading on dangerous ground.

"A *workhouse?*" He fired up instantly, his eyes flashing back in their caverns. "Nay, Missus, Arthur knows I'll never go to the bloody workhouse!"

"No, of course not. Don't worry about it. They haven't had workhouses for a long time." A vision of the dancing orphans in *Oliver* went through my head. "So, Arthur's your only child?"

"Nay. There was Annie."

He subsided, staring down at the flagstones, shaking his head sadly.

"I'd not mind if she were still here, but she's gone, ain't she? It weren't her fault. She were a good girl, always reading them books. Only a lass she were when it happened. And she made it right in the end, didn't she?" He slammed his fist down on the table, as if I were arguing with him.

I wondered if he knew what he was talking about, any more than I did. The bacon was sizzling now. I filled the tin kettle from the tap and lit another burner with the last match in the box. The room was getting chilly with everything open, and the smoke had cleared, so I shut the windows and went to shut the door. Just beyond the doorstep, a skinny black cat was sitting among the weeds, its tail curled neatly around its feet. It stared up at me, unblinking. As I started to close the door, it sprang up and ran past me into the cottage, as fast as it had streaked out before.

It went straight to George Crocker, sniffed his sock gingerly, and rubbed its body against his leg.

"There, Muzzle, 'twas naught in the end," he reassured it.

"*What's* its name?"

They both looked at me with wary hostility.

"Muzzle's his name."

"What kind of a name is that for a cat? Muzzle?"

"Aye, Muzzle, Muzzle—where the bloody mouse lives!"

"Oh, Mousehole!"

He went back to stroking its scruffy fur.

"He can find 'em out better nor any cat I ever had, and

do for the mouse as well. Do ye see any vermin runnin' about me house? Nay," he answered himself, "Muzzle'd not stand for it."

The cat slunk under the old man's chair and crouched there in lion-position, glaring out at me malevolently.

"Should I open a can of food for him?" I asked.

"Nay, he don't need you to do aught for him, no more nor I do! You go on home and mind your own dinner. Muzzle and me's fine on our own. I'll make the dinner, I been doin' it for fifty year!"

It was no use arguing with him. I looked around at the mess, wondering whether he would have a fit if I brought a mop over tomorrow. Old men were impossible to predict, I knew from experience. I remembered how my father had been in his last years, never as cantankerous as George Crocker, but ready one day to cooperate with anything I proposed, and the next in a feeble rage at an innocent word.

My eye lighted on a wavering line of white paint drawn around the whole room, where the floor met the walls.

"What did you do that for?" I asked, pointing at it.

He stared at me as if he doubted my sanity. "Why, for the witches, bain't it?"

"Oh, come on, George." I couldn't help smiling.

"It don't do to make game of the witches, Missus. They'll not cross one of they lines, everybody knows that. Think I want to be strangled with witch-weed in me sleep?"

It was hard to believe that thirty-six hours ago I'd been

hailing a cab in mid-Manhattan traffic, and now I was listening to a character out of Thomas Hardy recommending the best way to deter witches.

"This were ever a gurt place for 'em," he rambled on. "Tell that by the name, can't ye? That'n's mother were a witch's familiar." He pointed under the chair. "The witch vanished away one day, like they do, with his cat, and left its kitten behind, and I took him in. I reckoned then the witches'd leave me be, and so they have." He chuckled at his own shrewdness.

"Then what do you need the white line for?"

"No harm in bein' double-sure. Not when it comes to the witches. What are ye grinnin' about? Them as don't credit the power of the dark ones'll turn up in the wych-wood one night with a rope of the witch-weed about their neck!"

"Well, Catherine, you were looking for old and quaint," I muttered sarcastically as I turned the bacon and eggs out on a cracked plate.

When I set it before him he grumbled about the way the food was cooked, but stuffed it in ravenously. Finally he set the plate on the floor. He had left one of the eggs, and the black cat crept out and ate it. When I went over to pick up the plate, the scruffy thing drew back and hissed at me.

"That is the meanest cat!" I exclaimed. "If it would act halfway friendly I'd get it some food, but—"

"Forget that!" the old man ordered. "It's got late. I can't be nattering with fools all the night. I'm off to bed."

"Do you need any help?"

"Don't I tell ye I'm fine on me own?" he flared up again. "I've seen the day I could throw the smith over his smithy, if I'd a mind to. You ask folk, they'll tell ye."

I made sure the burners were off before I left. A quick look around had not revealed another box of matches, so I gave myself orders to bring some over tomorrow. I'd already decided to come back and cook him another meal.

Rowan Cottage was cold, and the musty smell was everywhere. I was too exhausted to figure out how the central heating worked. In fact, I opened one of the back windows in the kitchen to air the place out.

Before going to bed I picked up the phone. There was a dial tone, another detail seen to by miraculous Eleanor. I would have to be sure to look her up and thank her for all the extra trouble she'd taken.

I longed to hear Emily's voice, but something told me it would be better not to disturb them so late. I'd call in the morning.

I wandered around the place for a while, turning lights on and off, opening cabinets, the refrigerator, the stove, sitting down on the sofa to test it for comfort. Tired as I was, the thrill of actually being in my own seventeenth-century cottage, as different from a Manhattan apartment as anything could be, kept me going for half an hour or so. I felt safe for the first time in a year.

Finally I climbed the narrow, boxed-in staircase again, carrying my baggage. I was too weary even to bathe. I got my flannel nightgown out and put it on, found the mystery I'd started on the plane, and slipped into bed under the one thin blanket.

I read for a while, finishing the book. When I clicked the bed lamp off, the dark was profound with no street lights outside, and the silence I had so looked forward to was actually a little scary. Now I didn't feel so safe. I was used to the night sounds of screeching brakes, voices in the street, the rumble of the subway under the sidewalk. This was like being the last person left on the planet. Except, of course, for George Crocker, but somehow knowing he was nearby wasn't all that reassuring.

"What are you going to be scared of next?" I demanded into the darkness. "Maybe you'd better get a can of paint tomorrow, and make a line around the floor to keep the witches out!"

A minute later, I was asleep.

CHAPTER TWO

I opened my eyes to the glitter of sunlight through wavy old glass in the casement at the foot of my bed. For the past year my first thought on waking had been that Quin was gone, my first chore of the day to bully myself out of the resulting depression. But this morning it wasn't like that. I remembered with a rush of joy that I was in my own house on the other side of the ocean from all that misery. Who could say what new places and people were waiting for me outside? Whatever they were, I knew they would be so fascinating, I would forget him and the old days in no time.

I tried out my shower, got into a pair of comfortable old slacks, and layered a polo shirt and cardigan. Before I laced my cross-trainers I picked up the phone and dialed my daughter's number.

"Mom!" she exclaimed with unmistakable delight. "You're really here! When did you get in?" When I told her, she demanded, "Why didn't you call right away?"

"I was really tired, darling. I thought I'd come over and see you this afternoon, if it's not inconvenient?"

"Inconvenient! I can't wait. But we're coming out there. No, no, we want to. We have to see your house, don't we? We're going to take you to dinner at the Longbow to celebrate. Expect us about two, after Archie's nap. Oh, Mom, I'm so glad you decided to come!"

After that, of course, last night's worries weren't even a memory.

I didn't bother to lock the door when I went out to explore my new world. Why should I, in this peaceful countryside? I knew character was a product of environment, and as those who grow up in ugly slums are likely to become criminals, so people nurtured in the innocent beauty of a place like this would be virtuous.

George Crocker's place looked even more decrepit in daylight. There was no sign of life inside, but he must have been up because the black cat was out, sitting on the overgrown front path, glaring sullenly at me. I made a face at it as I turned left from my gate, figuring I'd take a look at the open country beyond my house and explore the village later.

My side of the road stretched out in a grassy meadow just starting to green. On George's side it was all deep woods, a tangle of great, gnarled oaks and beeches that must have been old before America was discovered.

St. Etheldreda's Church was the only building in sight. It stood on a rise, maybe a quarter of a mile beyond Rowan Cottage. I could see it from the road, almost fortress-like, the squat tower and small round-topped windows, and the leafless trees and stone grave-markers in the churchyard around it.

I turned down Church Lane between steep hedgerow banks, drinking in the clean, fragrant air like a cordial. Bumblebees droned as they burrowed into the barely opened primrose flowers under bushes that still held their blossoms inside tight brown buds. Birds were darting among them with dry grasses dangling from their beaks, and I stopped to watch them. A little grey bird with a white breast eyed me speculatively, and then actually ran into a hole in the ground! I'd never seen a bird do that. And another, a big brown one, rose into the air and hovered over the meadow, warbling. A skylark, I was somehow sure, and Browning's words came back to me:

> The lark's on the wing,
> The snail's on the thorn,
> God's in His heaven—
> All's right with the world.

Quin and I had looked around St. Etheldreda's and taken one of the pamphlets left out for visitors, so I knew it was built in the twelfth century by order of the Norman lord who had got this area as his share of the Conquest. This gentleman, a Monsieur d'Ameurle, had it built right down the lane from his manor house, so the family wouldn't have far to walk on Sundays. I could see the big house at the end of Church Lane, where according to the pamphlet his descendant still lived. Now it was a mixture of architectural styles, torn down and built onto by every generation of the family, whose name had long since been anglicized to Damerel. There was very little left of it a Norman lord would recognize.

As I got closer to the church I began to hear a heavy, metallic banging. It drowned out the bumblebees, even the skylark. I opened the lych-gate under its arbor, built to shelter coffins and pallbearers waiting for the priest to escort them into the church. Now I was among enormous trees, some of them as big and old as those in the woods around George's cottage. Most of the tombstones that filled the yard were very old, weather-beaten, and colonized by mosses and lichen. The few newer ones I noticed were farthest from the church, beside the low stone wall.

I had meant to go inside and poke around, but it was impossible to ignore that noise, a heavy clanking like the chains of Marley's ghost, like the ghosts of the whole Marley family. A few moments of silence, then more clanking. It was coming from the other side of the church. I hurried past the front entrance, a stone arch carved in the fang-like zigzags beloved of Norman architects. I was getting increasingly indignant at whoever was disturbing the peace of this beautiful place—*my* peace.

I came around the corner and stopped in amazement. My eyes were caught by an object that definitely didn't fit into the scene, a piece of heavy machinery, a glass box on huge tires with a yellow engine compartment in front, and behind a deep, toothed bucket which was in the process of tearing out a thick square of the churchyard's turf. Two yellow lights blinked incessantly on top, and inside the glass box a stocky, grey-haired man manipulated long levers and moved his legs up and down, pushing pedals. I didn't know much about such mechanical monsters, but I was pretty sure it was called a backhoe.

In great contrast, at the edge of that opened square of ground a stone cross rose from a low pedestal. Small, exquisitely detailed figures were carved from top to bottom and across the two arms, centering at the axis on a crucified Christ whose agony leaped out at me despite the effects of centuries of weather that had blurred the contorted features of his face.

I looked on in horror as the backhoe started up with a growl, shuddered forward, and dropped its bucket again. Grass and wildflowers hung over the side. It swung into the air on a jointed, yellow arm and dumped out another big chunk of the churchyard. One whole side of the cross was exposed now, almost to its foundation three or four feet below ground level.

Then I caught sight of a young man standing close to the church, only a few yards from the digging. He wore his dark, curly hair to his shoulders, loose and unkempt, and he was dressed in frayed jeans, dirty-white running shoes, and a grey jersey with the word "Manchester" across his broad chest. He stood with folded arms, watching the desecration of the cross with a satisfied smile.

"Hey!" I yelled at him, straining to be heard over the din as the backhoe jolted forward a few feet, beeping a raucous warning. The man inside pushed and pulled and the bucket sank into the soft spring earth again with a hungry clank.

The fellow by the church looked over in surprise as I charged toward him. Close up, I could see that his nose was flattened like a boxer's, and a silver stud gleamed in one earlobe.

"What do you think you're doing?" I demanded. "What right do you have to come here and vandalize this village's antiquities? That cross must have stood there for centuries!"

"Seven, actually," he answered in a matching shout. "High time it made way for the needs of today's world!"

"Who are you to decide that?" I yelled. I looked around desperately and spotted a two-storey stone house on the other side of the wall, without doubt the vicarage. "I'm going to tell the vicar!"

As I started away he called out, *"I* am the vicar."

I turned back and stared. He held out a beefy hand, threw me a rather nasty grin, and shouted, "Ian Larribee, incumbent of St. Etheldreda's parish. In no way required to take orders from Yank tourists."

"I am not a tourist! And I don't believe for one minute you're—"

Suddenly I realized I was shouting into a silence violated only by the comparatively low hum of the backhoe's engine, idling. It was standing still, bucket suspended, beside the cross which seemed to teeter at the edge of that hole in the earth. The man inside was talking on a cell phone, glancing over at us.

The Manchester man strode over and rapped on one of the windows. The operator slid it open, still holding the phone against his cheek.

"What's wrong? Why have you stopped?"

The man muttered a few more words into his phone, then folded it up and looked out at Ian Larribee, quite unintimidated by his bluster.

"Job's done," he said. "Cost me my license to go on now."

"Done? You've only dug out one side! The whole object has to be dug out and moved to the far end of the churchyard, you were told that."

The backhoe man pointed calmly to the trench he had made.

"Human remains," he said. "I just been on to my gaffer, and he's contacting the coppers at Oxford. Can't be no more digging here till that's been investigated proper."

He started up his machine again, reversed, and backed away from the cross.

Ian Larribee was staring into the excavation with an expression of mingled disgust and disbelief. I went over and peered down, and for the first time I knew what Hamlet had meant when he saw the skull of Yorick— "My gorge rises." My gorge had to be the creature writhing up through my chest and into my throat, stopping my breath, gagging me as it made its way into my gullet. I tried to turn and run away but I couldn't tear my gaze from the thing in the trench.

It had once been a man or woman, but now all its flesh had been consumed and its bones had separated. Some of them were still partly submerged in the clay subsoil, but I could see an arm, broken at the elbow, both legs bent in the fetal position, parts of a spine still covered in tattered strips of rotten cloth. They clung to the delicate flanges of the ribcage, too, whose ends were soft and dark with the beginnings of decay.

Just beyond, the skull rested on one side, eye cavities caked with dirt, teeth, like pebbles, scattered near the un-hinged jaw.

Larribee spoke to me in a bewildered voice, as if we had not been in a fight moments before.

"This isn't part of the cemetery. There are no graves just here—certainly none right up against the cross like that."

The backhoe man had joined us. "There's a funny hole in that skull," he said in his unflappable way. "See, just behind where the ear went."

I saw it, one neat, round circle.

"Odd, that," he went on. "*And* the way the bones is just laying there loose, not in a coffin like they ought to be. What I'd say is, that poor chap was shot in the head and dumped here so nobody'd find him."

"Shot!" Ian Larribee boomed, as if he was being accused.

"No, that couldn't be," I choked out, "not *here!*"

The backhoe man shrugged. "Coppers'll be coming directly, they'll sort it out. Any road, it needn't bother you. Happened years ago, from the state of them re-mains—long before your time, vicar."

I backed away, unable any longer to resist that creature climbing up my throat. They didn't even notice me stum-bling toward the gate. Before I reached it I had to stop and grab hold of one of the big trees for support. I doubled over and let the creature have its way, escaping seemingly with everything I had eaten for the past couple of days.

Then I could breathe again, though I felt shaky. I had seen my parents dead, but they had been laid out with care, posed as if sleeping in satin-lined caskets, surrounded by wreaths from friends and family—death as we want to think of it. A human being thrown into the ground without shelter or marker, rotting away in secret, that was the cold reality of death.

In this haven of peace I had dreamed of for so long, everything was not right with the world after all.

I didn't raise my eyes from the ground as I made my unsteady way down Church Lane and then the town road toward my house. The idea of exploring my surroundings was as dead as that poor soul huddled by the cross. I just wanted to get inside and sit down.

But as I came near Rowan Cottage I glanced down the road and saw a little group of people standing in front of one of the cottages, looking in my direction. Before I could get through the gate one of them came trotting toward me, a woman about my age, a little plump, with grey hair braided and wrapped around her head. When she reached me I saw clear blue eyes and a smile that held nothing back.

"How do you do?" she said, putting out her hand. "I'm Fiona Bennett. We all want to welcome—Oh, my dear, are you all right?"

Her smile changed to a concerned expression, and I realized how stricken I must look.

"I don't know. I just saw something—horrible. In the churchyard."

Her lips set in an angry line. "Right, the churchyard! I don't wonder you're upset, especially if you're a believer, or even just a lover of art. That cross is one of the few in the country to escape Cromwell, and now it's fallen to another rampaging clergyman! Did he actually get it moved into some back corner? He didn't—break it, did he?"

"No, it's not that," I said. "There's a dead body in the ground beside it!"

The other four members of the group had now gathered around us, and one of them, a thin, silver-haired woman in a lacy old-fashioned dress and hat, said, "A dead body in the churchyard? But that's where the dead belong, isn't it?"

"P'raps it's done different in America," said a big, lumpy woman, looking at me with a suspicious scowl.

"No, it wasn't in the cemetery part," I explained impatiently. "It was right beside the old cross, where they were digging to move it. It hadn't been buried in a coffin. And it had been murdered."

There was a general murmur of consternation.

"Who could that be, then?" said the lumpy one, squinting at me. "I've never heard of nobody in Far Wychwood getting themself murdered, and I've lived here all me life."

"Let me introduce you round," said Fiona Bennett. "We can discuss it all better if we know each other's names. This is Enid Cobb, our shopkeeper and postmistress."

The last speaker gave me a grudging nod, her small

eyes traveling over me appraisingly. A short bald man stood beside her, smiling serenely.

"And Henry Cobb, of course."

The silver-haired lady, introduced as Alice White, shook my hand shyly.

"Alice was our schoolmistress when that abandoned building next to your cottage was the village school. Then the juvenile population went too low to justify it, so now they bus the little blighters off to the big consolidated at Oxford."

"Yes, indeed," Alice agreed with a sigh.

"And this is Louisa Barry. Her husband is our local G.P."

She, too, offered her hand, and then I told them my name.

Enid continued where she'd left off. "Where'd you get this idea of a murdered body in our churchyard, then? Happen vicar made it up. I'd not put nothing past that one."

Louisa started to agree, when the up-and-down song of a siren broke into the stillness and a moment later a black-and-white police car came careening through the village past us, down Church Lane, and screeched to a stop by the lych-gate.

Everyone turned and stared at me in amazement.

Before they could speak, a highly polished black BMW followed in the police car's tracks, only a little more slowly. It pulled onto the shoulder beside us. The driver's window glided down and a woman's large, horsey face showed in the opening.

"What on earth is happening?" she said in a high-pitched affected voice with an exaggerated Oxbridge accent. "That Panda car passed me on the Oxford road and stayed ahead of me all the way here, and now I see it has stopped at St. Etheldreda's, of all places." She looked out at us with the air of one who never doubted she would be answered promptly and satisfactorily.

Alice White said timidly, "Apparently a murderer has buried his victim right up against our churchyard cross."

"How very odd," said the woman in the car. The corners of her mouth turned down in disapproval. "I've never heard of a *murder* in Far Wychwood."

"This body must have been there for years," I told them. "There's nothing left but the bones and some scraps of cloth."

She stared at me, and Fiona said, "This is the American lady who bought Rowan Cottage. Catherine Penny, Philippa Damerel."

"Damerel?" I said. "Then you must be from the family at the manor house?"

The horsey face broke into a smile. She got out of her car and offered me her hand with the attitude of one conferring a great privilege.

"How very well-informed you are, Mrs. Penny!"

"Just Catherine, please. Well, I read the brochure—"

"My husband's people," she went on as if I hadn't spoken, "go back to Roger d'Aumeurle, who came over with the Conqueror—"

"And pinched all this land from Enid's poor old Saxon ancestors," Fiona said. "Yes, Philippa, she did say she'd read the brochure."

Philippa threw her an offended glance.

"We were all very glad to hear that Rowan Cottage was to be occupied full time again," the doctor's wife said. "The previous owners, you know, were Londoners who kept it as a holiday cottage, and came down less and less often in recent years. Of course, this end of the village is awfully isolated. I hope you won't be lonely."

"Well, I've already met my only neighbor," I said, "the old man across the road. He's not the greatest company— but I do think it's a shame the way his family neglects him."

"Do you mean George Crocker?" Louisa said, wide-eyed.

They all stared over at his cottage, then back at me as if amazed.

After a moment, Fiona said, "Well, of course, she's not to know about George Crocker! That's purely a local scandal."

They glanced covertly at Philippa, who looked as if she were trying to swallow a large slice of lemon.

"I would recommend you to keep away from that man," she said to me. "Not only is he filthy and evil-tempered, he has in fact a *criminal* past."

"Criminal?" Now I was the one amazed.

"There was some unpleasantness a few years back," Fiona told me, "and George Crocker, as a result, is sort of the village pariah. He's not at all a nice old man. Even his son seems to have given up on him."

"Doesn't he have a daughter, too?"

"Oh, well, Annie, she's not been heard of for over forty years. She left Far Wychwood when she was just a girl."

"The Crockers are another family that were here to greet the Normans," Louisa said, "but when George dies, there'll be no more of them in the village, as Arthur's lived in Oxford since he's been grown. And, of course, George is quite an age."

"Ninety-three," said Enid Cobb decidedly.

"Yes, the Cobbs are by way of being related to George," Fiona said.

"Just by marriage," Enid retorted. "George's wife, Emma, was Henry's cousin."

"Don't you ever go to see him?" I asked.

"Who, us, hang about with that old bugger? No, thank you, I don't pass my time with thieves, and no more does Henry. Old George has a standing order for his provisions and I just send the boy over with them when it's time."

"I'm sure you needn't concern yourself with such people, Catherine," Philippa broke in. "There are plenty of nice people for you to know. We must introduce you to some of them—and show you that our village is not, for heaven's sake, a hotbed of violent crime! Would you care to pop over to the Manor tomorrow evening for drinks? You are all invited, and your husbands, of course. I'll ring up a few suitable people for her to meet."

I agreed to go, with a shiver of excitement at seeing the inside of that house. There were murmurs of assent from all the others, except the Cobbs.

Enid said, "Well, I'll say good day, and very pleased to meet you, I'm sure. I'll expect to be seeing you at the shop regular," she added pointedly.

She jerked her head at Henry and he followed her, still smiling, as she stomped off down the road.

Philippa said in a stage whisper, "Good heavens, you don't suppose she took my invitation to include *them?*"

"Not to worry," Fiona answered wryly, "she knows they'd never be asked to the Manor along with the suitable people."

"Shall we say fiveish, then?" Philippa proposed as she climbed back into her car. We all agreed to be there. "I wonder if the police would give me any information about this incident in the churchyard, if I stopped by on my way down the lane?"

"I'd guarantee they won't," Fiona replied. "They have standing orders not to reveal anything to the public. And at this point they won't know any more than Catherine does. The homicide squad will be sent out next, so I'll try to find out something from John tonight and pass it on to everyone." She turned to me. "My husband is a sergeant in the homicide division at Oxford, so he's very likely to know what's happened."

As Philippa drove away, Louisa mused, "In a way, this skeleton turning up could be providential. The authorities certainly won't let the vicar proceed with his plans for a while. It may give us enough time to talk the bishop round."

"*Why* is he attacking that beautiful cross?" I asked.

"Ian Larribee has decided this village needs a youth hall," Louisa answered, tight-lipped, "and that it must be built onto the side of the church. We've seen his plans, it's just an ugly cinder-block box. He won't listen to any of us, although even the young people for whom it's intended tell him they don't like his ideas. The old cross is in his way, so he's determined to move it to an obscure corner of the churchyard."

"He practically ordered the whole village to turn out today to watch it done," Alice said indignantly, "quite like some sort of fete. Everyone agreed not to go near it. Show him how the parish feels."

Louisa added sadly, "Most of us don't even go to Sunday services any more. My husband says he will not enter the church again while that dreadful man is there."

"Yes," Fiona put in, "Dr. Barry is the leader of the opposition to Larribee's schemes. But we've kept you standing here far too long. If you'd care to come home with me, I'll be happy to give you some luncheon. A bit of nourishment is what you want now, and I've been making biscuits this morning."

"No, thank you," I said quickly. "I just want to clean up and rest for a while. My daughter and her family are coming out this afternoon—oh, dear, in just a couple of hours," I exclaimed after looking at my wristwatch. "It's been lovely meeting all of you, though."

They left me with expressions of regret that my first day in their village had started so traumatically.

I went inside, closed the door, and sank down on the sofa. Now that I was over the original shock, I was able to look at things more calmly. Whatever had happened, it had been long ago. The people I had met were certainly normal and civilized. An old tragedy could not affect my new life in Far Wychwood where, as everyone agreed, murders did not happen.

After about ten minutes I heard a knock at the door. A little irritated, because I thought I'd made it clear I wanted to be alone for a while, I opened the door. A paper shopping bag sat on the doorstep. I looked down the road and saw Fiona's sturdy figure walking away.

I brought the bag in and opened it. There was a fat brown teapot, a box of loose tea, a half-pint glass bottle of table cream, and a bag of homemade ginger cookies. A note was pinned to the shopping bag, written in a big, slapdash hand: "Don't mean to disturb you, but you'll want to give your family tea, and I'm sure the cottage isn't provisioned yet. Fiona."

I had time to take a leisurely bath and change my clothes before my company arrived, right on time. Emily looked thinner than I remembered, and there were dark circles under her eyes, but she still had the endearingly prim features and flowing blonde hair I knew and loved, with the new addition of horn-rim glasses. They failed to give her the mature and scholarly appearance I knew she was aiming for.

Her husband, Peter, was a quiet young man with a dry sense of humor, good-looking in an angular sort of way. Only in his twenties, he was already a recognized authority on the minor Elizabethan poets.

Archie, of course, was no longer a babe in arms, but an unstoppable toddler, curly and rosy, and obviously in better shape than his mother.

"It's so hard," she said as we drank Fiona's tea and watched him empty out the cabinet under the sink. "I have an adolescent group Tuesday morning, emotionally abused women the same afternoon, then on Thursdays my recovering alcoholics, and still the hospital wants me to take on more groups! Then Wednesday evenings I have two private patients. That's when Peter and Archie do their bonding." She smiled at them fondly. "But this child still won't sleep through the night. I can't let him cry, of course, I know too much about the effects of parental rejection in early childhood—so I'm pretty much a wreck."

"Isn't 'rejection' a bit strong for letting him cry it out once or twice so he learns to put himself back to sleep?" I asked.

Peter caught my eye and made a grimace that obviously meant "dangerous waters."

Sure enough, the Look solidified on her face. "There is a whole school of psychoanalytic study that traces adult neuroses back to trauma like that. You'll just have to accept that I know more than you about this sort of thing, Mother, even if I am your child."

"Of course, darling, of course. Only—" I hesitated, then plunged recklessly on, "it worked with you, and I'm sure I didn't give you any 'adult neuroses.'"

"Come along, let's look over the property," Peter said quickly, standing up. "I don't think the son and heir can get much more out of that cabinet, and personally I'm ready to explore the gardens, aren't you, darling?"

Emily threw him a rather rueful smile, and we followed him and Archie outside to discover the twin rowan trees in the backyard that must have inspired the house's name, the budding cowslips, the shelves full of perlite and peat in the stone potting shed by the front wall. Emily and I forgot our little disagreement as we exchanged ideas for decorating the cottage, although I had a feeling it would just be a process of random accumulation, like in New York. She insisted on arranging a shopping expedition in Oxford the next day for the several dozen things I needed most urgently.

We set out at twilight down the village road to its only eating establishment, the Longbow. The old inn is recommended in several food guides for its kitchen and its carefully cultivated Georgian atmosphere, so people come from as far as London to eat there.

I was all right until we were past the Cobbs' little shop, when the inn was close enough for me to pick out the stone profile of a woman set in a medallion over the entrance. Quin had said she looked like Fergie.

Without warning, I was caught up in the memory of the first time I had seen the place, from the window of our rental car. It had been almost four years before, and the cottages had glowed just the same way in the lowering sunlight. We had gazed in astonishment at this living illustration from one of Emily's fairy-tale books. I had been to London after college and again a year or two before our marriage, but I'd never ventured into the countryside, and Quin—

Suddenly I smelled the combination of pipe tobacco and Old Spice that had been part of his identity, saw in my mind's eye his stocky, muscular body in the Harris tweed jacket he'd bought in London the day before, his face with its cocky grin and square jaw, and his salt-and-pepper hair, a little shiny from the oil he used to keep the curl in check, regardless of the natural look the rest of the world had adopted.

Emily and Peter were chatting and didn't notice me fighting with myself, unsuccessfully, to cast away his image and the memory of that night. We had laughed, while we looked through the vast building for our room, about Quin's first right turn from the left lane, which had momentarily stopped all traffic on Lambeth Road. He had bet I'd do even worse if I drove back into London, and I took the bet and lost it.

We'd had drinks and dinner, and walked beside the river in the dark. We'd made love and lain in the afterglow listening to car doors slamming below our window, people calling goodnights and driving away as the bar closed, leaving us in the silence, falling asleep together.

"I love this old place," I heard Emily saying. We were coming into the forecourt of the inn. I managed a stiff smile.

"Yes, I'm glad they haven't modernized it," I said brightly.

I had said something very like that when Quin and I came back fourteen months ago. He had changed, but I didn't admit it to myself. When I'd made a joke about those previous driving fiascos, he'd said he could get us there in one piece, even if I didn't believe it. He'd spoken little on the way, and I'd told myself it must be business problems. He was an attorney with a high-pressure Manhattan firm and it was easy to lay his tension to that.

Tears stung my eyes as I followed Emily into the bustling lobby. How could I get through an evening here? I wanted to turn and run from the memories that waited to drift out of every corner.

He had fallen asleep without touching me that night, as he had for weeks. And though we could have stayed for more than five days, he wouldn't consider it. Once I found him talking furtively on the phone in the lobby, his face furrowed with anguish. Business must be really dicey, I had told myself.

Emily's lips brushed my cheek. I saw her blue eyes fixed on me, full of concern.

"I'm okay!" I said fiercely.

"I know you are."

We went in under the dining room's low, timbered ceiling. Red-shaded lamps on the tables bathed the rough-plastered walls and windows of wavy old glass in soft light. Big bowls of tulips and daffodils made splashes of yellow and orange above a dark Jacobean sideboard and a hunt table. A liveried waiter showed us to our table beside an enormous fireplace filled with leaping flames. There couldn't have been a more comforting room, but I was still so distraught that when I went to hang my purse on the back of the chair, my shaky hands dropped it. Since I hadn't snapped it shut, my keys, comb, pen, and lipstick rattled out onto the oak floorboards.

Peter started around the table to pick everything up, but a man dining alone at the next table got there first.

He crouched down and scooped my belongings back into the bag, his silver hair gleaming in the firelight.

"One more little thing to make this day just perfect!" I said bitterly.

He stood up, holding the purse. He was around my age but as lean as a man in his thirties, tall and straight, with the striking combination of silver hair and deep brown eyes that were looking into mine with a galling sympathy.

"Yes, I know," he said in an American accent. "My luck hasn't been so good today, either."

I felt an irrational resentment toward the man, knowing all the time I was really angry at myself. Brave, adventurous Catherine, indeed, her defenses crashing down at the first feint from the armies of memory! Turned such an emotional mess that any stranger could see it. What right did he have to offer me his sympathy?

He smiled as he hung my bag on the chair.

"Ohio, right?" he said.

The unexpected question startled me. "Oh—yes," I answered reluctantly, "Cincinnati."

"I grew up in Chillicothe," he went on. "You never lose that midwest twang, do you?"

I had no answer, my mind on the wrong track for idle conversation.

Peter must have felt someone should be polite to the man. "Are you staying awhile in our village?" he asked him.

"No, I planned to when I came down this afternoon, but things didn't work out. So I'm going back to London tonight."

He smiled at me again as I sat down. "Nice to hear that accent so far from home."

The waiter came to take our orders and when he left the man had gone. I wondered why he had made a special trip to this obscure place, only to leave again after a few hours. But my attention was quickly refocused on Emily, putting her hand over mine and saying, "We shouldn't have come. I should have known you'd have issues with this place."

"Oh, please, don't you feel sorry for me too! I'm ashamed of myself."

"No, Mom, it's much healthier to express your negative—"

"Whatever the books say, *wallowing* is a distasteful practice that tends to make one a total pain in the neck."

I could tell she was offended by my rejection of her expertise, but it was important to me to deal with it by myself. I had never had much faith in psychiatric treatment, and unfortunately she knew it.

After a few moments of uncomfortable silence, I asked, unwillingly, "Do you hear from him?"

"Oh, sure, he sends presents and everything." A few more seconds, and she asked hesitantly, "Would you mind very much if he paid us a visit?"

"Of course not! I've told you, there's no reason for you to go fatherless or Archie grandfatherless because of what he did to me."

She looked relieved. "He has kind of suggested he might come sometime. I've made it clear that while he's welcome, the Barbie doll is *not.*"

Although neither of us had ever seen her, Emily and I had pictured Quin's new live-in love and nicknamed her accordingly.

Archie, who had sat silent while the grown-ups performed, grabbed his mother's sleeve and began babbling incoherently, waving at the fire.

"What is it, darling?" she asked eagerly. "Try to say it. Is it about the fire?" She pointed to it. "Fire. Fire. Fire."

"Um wum," Archie replied happily. "Da doob."

"Oh, dear," Emily sighed. "Why doesn't he show any interest in language acquisition? He's sixteen months old and he hasn't said his first word yet!"

"Runs in the family," I told her. "Your Uncle Billy didn't talk until he was two and a half. Mother used to tell people he was just waiting until he had something worth saying. And once he started, we couldn't shut him up."

Things went more smoothly after that, helped along by a wonderful dinner: Scottish salmon with roasted potatoes, a green salad and, in honor of the occasion, a trifle topped by a big mound of whipped cream.

Archie was sleepy and cranky by the time we finished, so when we got back to my house they went right to their car. I was opening my gate when I noticed that the light wasn't on across the road. I felt a pang of guilt at having forgotten the old man's supper. Too busy feeling sorry for myself, I grumbled inwardly. I had to see if he was all right, and fix him a little something.

He didn't respond to my knock, but the door was unlocked as it always seemed to be. He was there, in the same chair, leaning forward with his head on the table, and I could hear him snoring. The cat's eyes floated near him, two disembodied spots of green light. After a few minutes I made out its shape in the darkness, curving up from the table where it had posed itself like an Egyptian statue.

I started to leave, but he must have heard me. He raised his grizzled head slowly, blinking in confusion.

"Annie?" he said.

CHAPTER THREE

"No, I'm still not Annie," I said softly, shutting the door behind me. "Remember last night, George? I've come to fix your dinner."

He only stared at me, returning slowly to consciousness. I lit the heavy brass lamp from a souvenir matchbook I'd picked up at the inn, and got some eggs off a shelf of the hutch, stepping warily past the cat. I noticed for the first time that it was missing half an ear, and several patches of bare skin showed through its fur, probably where it had been mixing it up with the other tomcats. It looked like a cat that would fight dirty.

As I started chopping chunks off the log-like side of bacon, I heard the old man speak.

"Cathern?" he said uncertainly.

"That's right!" So his short-term memory wasn't completely gone.

"You'll be a pal of Jimmy's, then?"

"Jimmy?" How many irresponsible children did he have? I thought Fiona Bennett had said there was only one son and a daughter. "No, I don't know Jimmy. Where is he? Why doesn't he come over and help you?"

He gave a sudden cackling laugh that made me jump. When I looked around, he was eyeing me with his grizzled head on one side and an unsettling grin stretching his sunken lips.

"Think I'd tell ye where Jimmy bides, when I never told nobody yet? Aye, they all tried to get it out of me, but I wouldn't tell 'em, would I? What good would that do me?"

"That's right," I said, completely at sea. I went back to chopping up bacon. "How about some fried potatoes?"

"Nor the money, neither. Ye'll not get it out of me, where the money is, no, nor them papers neither. It's all put away safe and sure, aye, where none but I'll ever know. Not unless they're needed."

I looked at him again, and he looked back with the same toothless, self-satisfied grin. Maybe he was talking about the "bit of unpleasantness" Fiona had mentioned that morning. But I didn't see much hope of getting anything sensible out of that addled mind.

"Do you want a potato, George?"

He didn't answer, just sat chuckling to himself. He held out one shaky hand toward Muzzle, who crossed the table and curled into his lap. George stroked its shabby fur, and the cat kneaded his leg with its paws.

I lit the stove, got the bacon sizzling, and had started slicing up a soft old potato from a burlap bag, when he spoke again.

"That's right. Annie allus put a potato in along of egg and bacon."

"Annie sounds nice," I said, over my shoulder. "She'd be my age now, would she? I guess that's why you keep thinking I'm her."

"She never meant no harm," he muttered. "It weren't her fault. She made it right in the end."

I turned the bacon. The dim room, redolent of years of bacon smoke, cat urine, and rotting vegetables, became for a few beats very peaceful. The past he lived in of lost children and half-remembered secrets enfolded the two of us and the black cat in a moment out of real time.

"Was she pretty, Annie?" I asked idly. "Do you have a picture of her?"

When he didn't answer, I looked around. Now he was gazing up at me with a calculating expression, chewing on his toothless gums. He raised a shaking finger and pointed at me.

"Who sent ye?" he demanded.

"Nobody. I live across the road, remember?"

"Nay," he said, shaking his head, "ye'll not fox me that way, woman. Asking after the picture—aye, ye were sent to get it out of me where Jimmy is, and they papers, that's what!"

I turned back to the stove and let him rant on, slipping two eggs in beside the potatoes.

"I keep me word. Crockers keeps their word, ask anybody!"

"I know you do. I was just curious because you were talking about Annie and Arthur before."

"Arthur, aye. He'll never want, won't Arthur."

"Nice for him," I muttered. "And how about Annie?"

"Ahh, lasses bain't worth the trouble. A lad, a son, that's what a man wants. A lass is good enough for the cooking and the cleaning. A man can talk to a son, but not a silly lass."

"Is that how you made Annie feel?" I said angrily. "No wonder she left you and didn't come back!"

Suddenly the old man lurched to his feet and pounded on the table, shouting with all his paltry force, "Where's me supper, woman? I've had naught but bread and dripping all the day, there bain't a match in the house, they witches has been and took all the matches! I'll bide no more of yer bloody questions, they'll none of 'em be answered. I'll have me supper!"

When he rose so abruptly, the cat made a flying leap from his knees. It almost hit the wall, overcompensated, and landed on a big covered garbage pail standing beside the back door. The pail toppled over, the lid came off, and the contents spilled out on the floor. It had been a very long time since that pail had been emptied. The stench was so strong, my dinner started to rise into my throat.

Muzzle pounced on the malodorous mess and sank his fangs into a hunk of unidentifiable meat covered in grey-green mold. I swatted him away. He slunk under a chair with his prize and began nibbling at the edge, where the mold was not so thick. It occurred to me, fleetingly, that it must have been quite a while since he'd had any cat food, or indeed any kind of decent meal.

"This is too much!" I exclaimed. "Where's the garbage can?"

George had lapsed into his usual confused state and only stared from me to the garbage and back again, working his jaws soundlessly. So I grabbed the stubby remnant of a broom and swept the mess back into the pail as best I could. I certainly wasn't going to touch it.

I jammed the lid back on and carried the pail out the back door. Although it was dark out, I could tell the back garden was at least as overgrown as the front. Weeds almost as tall as I was waved gently in the breeze, and it was hard to walk over the broken bricks that had once been a path. I set the pail down and parted the vegetation with my hands on either side, like an explorer in some jungle movie, peering about for a gleam of metal. Even George Crocker had to have a garbage can!

My foot hit something sticking up out of the ground. I tripped and fell to my knees beside a hydrangea bush covered with last year's dried bunches of flowers. Now I started swearing seriously.

"What the bloody hell ye doing?" the old man yelled at me from the doorway.

"Trying to find the garbage can!"

"What? What?"

"The dustbin," I suddenly remembered. "Where do you keep the damn dustbin?"

He lurched out the door. When he saw me kneeling there, his face turned a startling shade of purple. He came over and grabbed me by the arm and I scrambled up, bewildered.

"What ye doing there?" he demanded in a shaking voice. "Why ye digging there?"

"Digging? I wasn't digging, for heaven's sake. I fell! George, hey, George, it's Catherine. Remember?"

I couldn't pry his bony fingers from my arm. His face alarmed me. Besides the color, it was twisted to one side, the eyes wild back in their deep sockets. Spittle was running from the corner of his mouth and dripping on my arm.

"Prying, questioning," he gasped out. "Ye've come to steal the papers, that's what! And I know who's sent ye, right enough. I knowed somebody'd be coming one day to steal it all away."

"No, George, you're wrong," I said, forcing myself to speak calmly, soothingly. "Nobody sent me. I just fell over something, that's all. Listen, George, your supper's ready. Egg and bacon, George."

He still shook with fury, but he had spent his strength. He kept holding onto me, but for support now. I put my other hand on his shoulder as he staggered. His eyes were fixed on the spot where I had fallen.

Now I could see what I had tripped over. It was a square of wood sticking out of the ground like a sort of marker, carved with letters I couldn't read. A couple of big rocks had been sunk a few inches into the earth in front of it. Above it, the dried hydrangea flowers drooped like a floral tribute, rustling in the breeze.

"See, that's what I fell over. What is it?"

I leaned over to peer at the piece of wood. The crudely cut letters read, "Malkin."

"Who's Malkin?" I asked nervously.

He fixed his eyes on me, for some reason fully alert again.

"Me cat," he muttered. "Me cat before Muzzle, that's all. That's all it is."

"Well, for goodness' sake! Did you think I was going to dig up your dead cat?" I let go of him and started toward the door. "Come along and eat, George."

He labored after me and grabbed the door frame while I started dishing up his food.

"I hope it's the way you like it this time," I prattled, still a little nervous after that strange scene. "But you really shouldn't be living on eggs and potatoes and that old hard bacon. I'm going to get you some nice vegetables and fresh fruit, and you'll see what a good dinner I can fix with nutritious food. Do you like fish? Everybody should eat fish once a week, at least."

"Get out of me house," he growled.

I set down the frying pan and looked at him earnestly.

"Look, George, I'm sorry if—"

"Get out. You're naught but a bloody spy! Did ye think I could be foxed so easy? I'll tell ye nothing about the things that happened back then, nothing. And ye can tell them that sent ye, too."

I hesitated, unwilling to leave him alone when he could barely stand.

"I promise you, George, I didn't come over here to find out any of your secrets. I just got here from America. What could I know about your past, and why should I want to get anything out of you that you don't want to tell me?"

"I don't credit a word of it," he answered. "I didn't ask

ye for help or cooking. I can bide on me own and I will. It ain't safe to have folk about. Go on and let me be!"

There seemed to be nothing for it but to go. Obviously the poor old man was not only senile, but paranoid as well. Witches, hidden papers and money—it was sad. Something had to be done.

When I got back to my cottage I got out the Oxford telephone book and turned to the C's, hot with indignation at that son he was so concerned about.

A pleasant female voice answered the phone, saying, "Dr. Crocker's residence."

So he was a doctor. That meant he must be pretty affluent, in my experience. It made me all the angrier to think of that squalid cottage, the uncollected garbage, the suppers of bacon and eggs.

"I'm a neighbor of Dr. Crocker's father in Far Wychwood. I'd like to speak with him about some problems out here."

I heard her say, off the phone, "There's a woman calling for you, Arthur."

A moment later a man's voice came on the line, low and tense. "Yes?" he almost whispered.

"Hello, Dr. Crocker," I began, more politely than I wanted to. "My name is Catherine Penny. I just moved in across the road from your father in Far Wychwood, and I thought I should talk to you about his condition, in case you weren't aware of it."

"My father?" he said in a normal voice, with an undertone, I thought, of relief.

"George Crocker is your father, isn't he?"

"He is."

"Well, I noticed smoke coming out of his door last night, and when I went to investigate, I found he had the place on fire, trying to cook his own supper, which, by the way, was nothing but bacon and eggs, not very nourishing for an old person, as a doctor I'm sure you'd agree."

"I am an optometrist."

"Oh. Well, anybody could see he isn't fit to be lighting any matches, so I cooked his bacon and eggs for him last night, and tonight as well, but of course that's only an emergency solution. He needs to have somebody with him. You know, his hands shake so badly he can hardly hold a fork. Also, he's not clean. In fact he smells." I waited, but there was no response. "And so does his house. The garbage pail hadn't been emptied for, I don't know, weeks. It was full of rotted stuff. I just had to let you know, and now that you do, I'm sure you'll want to find a home for old people where he'd be properly cared for. Or don't the welfare agencies over here have something called a home help, I'm sure I've heard of that, people who go out and help old people in their homes?"

I stopped for breath. Again, there was no answer.

"If you don't want to take the responsibility," I went on, more caustically, "maybe you could give me your brother Jimmy's number. He might be more concerned about his father than you seem to be."

"Brother? I have no brother." There was a definite edge to his voice, as if it came from between clenched teeth. "I take it you are American?"

"I am, if it makes any difference."

"Yes. Well, in this country we do not thrust ourselves unasked into other people's affairs. I believe privacy is almost nonexistent in your country. So let me tell you, whatever your name is, my father's mode of living does not concern you, and I will—"

"A helpless old man living under such conditions would concern anyone with an ounce of humanity!" I almost shouted into the phone. "If something isn't done soon, Dr. Crocker, your father is going to die!"

"My father is never going to die," he replied stonily. "He is going to go on living, merely to spite me, until long after *I* am dead, unless someone does me a favor and murders him."

"That's the cruelest thing I've ever heard," I gasped.

"Continue to wait on him if you wish, but I warn you to make no more calls to me. It is none of your damned business."

George Crocker and his son between them had left me so shaken, I was sure I couldn't sleep. My proven remedy for emotional battery was a little Bach, maybe a Brandenburg concerto or three or four replays of "Sheep May Safely Graze." But I couldn't resort to that because my CDs hadn't yet arrived. I substituted a hot bath in my deep, clawfooted bathtub, with the lights turned down low.

When I got under the covers I couldn't shut out the image of George holding onto the door frame and accusing me of trying to steal his secrets. But I fell asleep surprisingly quickly, to find myself frying another egg. Its yellow eye seemed to glare up at me accusingly.

It was important to get it cooked as quickly as possible, but shadowy forms were crowding around, plucking at me with their bony fingers so I couldn't concentrate on my work. From among them I heard a shaky, aged voice complaining: "Where've you been all this time? I've been waiting for you to come. You have to take me home, Cathy!"

"I'll have your egg done in a second," I pleaded. "I'm doing the best I can!"

"But you have to take me home," the old man insisted, in the singsong plaint of an exhausted child. "Why did you leave me here? Nobody listens to me here."

"But it wasn't just me," I argued desperately, turning the egg. "The boys all thought you would be better there, and you know, we all have our jobs, our families. Their wives didn't want you, and neither did Quin—"

The thought of him brought him to stand beside me, looking down at a narrow bed, only wide enough to hold the old man's cruelly shrunken body. My brothers, Billy, Gary, and Joe Jr. stood at the other side, their wives a step or two behind them, looking down with hands folded and faces set in a decent solemnity. Our father had passed beyond complaining, beyond expecting our help.

But why was Quin beside me? Why was he putting his arm around my shoulders? I couldn't remember why I hated his touch, but involuntarily I tried to push him away. He held me even tighter. I knew I was not going to be able to loose myself. Helplessly, I subsided into the warmth of his side, murmuring, "We did do our best, didn't we? There was no way we could bring him home, was there?"

His deep voice murmured in my ear, gravelly as it always became when he was forced to deal with emotion.

"Sure, we did our best. Things happen, Kit. We had a right to our own life. Don't get all hysterical on me, now. It's over."

In an instant I was gazing at the slanted ceiling of my cottage bedroom, wide awake and furious.

"What the hell was *that* about?" I said into the darkness.

I sat up, wiped the sweat off my forehead with the sheet, and concentrated on answering the question. All right, it was obvious that my sleeping mind was telling me I was still full of regret about my dad. George's neglected state and uncaring son had stirred up the sharp cinders of guilt after all these years of successfully damping them down. One of his children should have been able to take him in when he was old and helpless. Instead we had pooled our resources to maintain him in a "home" we knew treated him with cold efficiency, not love. We had stood at his deathbed pretending that the end of our mutual problem brought us only grief, not release from a burden.

I had been made to feel that I was the right one to take him in, being the only girl in the family, but I had never bought that. I couldn't remember Dad showing much interest in me as I grew up. He and his sons had played catch, gone to Reds games, laughed together about mysterious male things Mother and I were not supposed to understand.

I'd had her, of course, sweet, submissive Mother, until the day I'd come home from junior high to find Billy, my youngest brother, kneeling beside her on the kitchen floor. I was the one who called Dad and who sat holding him while he sobbed in a chain-smoker's hacking gasps as the ambulance people tried to revive her and finally took her away to the funeral home. She'd had a massive stroke and died there on the floor, alone, a month before her thirty-third birthday.

Dad had hired a woman to help me with the housework, and I'd applied myself to becoming a good cook with the kinds of food he wanted, like meat loaf, lemon pie, and home fries, and the scrapple, unique to Cincinnati, that we called "goetta." His approval filled me with the same sort of relief Annie must have felt when she put a potato in along of egg and bacon.

But Dad still had his special relationship with the boys, something I could never be part of. More and more as I grew up, I believed that men didn't find girls like me interesting, and turned my attention to the things I could excel at and enjoy. When I got to New York I discovered that lots of people enjoyed those things and didn't expect me to be a conventional housebody. I assumed I'd go on contentedly to the end without husband or children, until the day I met Quin Freeman at the big Vietnam War peace demonstration in Washington.

We were a pair of idealists, lovers of books and Ingmar

Bergman's films and off-off-Broadway, and finally, to my amazement, of each other—

I realized where this was going and climbed out of bed, reining in my imagination by force.

"You're not doing this, Catherine!" I said aloud, tramping around the room, turning on the lights, straightening the hangers in the clothes press, anything to drag my thoughts away from those things I'd never expected to have, and now had lost.

I put on my bathrobe and slippers and went downstairs. The old house was peaceful and still, moonlight streaming through the casements and turning the wood floors the color of stone. I wandered from kitchen to dining room to sitting room, touching the furniture that had belonged to strangers and didn't yet seem to be mine. Memories rose up of the shabby, comfortable sofas and chairs we had lived with in New York and the few good antique pieces we had allowed ourselves, a graceful oak hall tree we'd hung our coats on for thirty years, his mother's Tiffany lamp, the little writing desk we'd splurged on to celebrate the positive pregnancy test.

I couldn't forget. The ghosts of my past lives lurked everywhere, unwilling to let me go. The old man across the road brought back my father, my father brought back Quin, and I had no way of knowing what would come next to stir my memory. I couldn't protect myself.

Was it possible that I still loved him, in spite of what he had done to me? I couldn't let myself admit that possibility. I had loved the man I'd known all those years but, I told myself, he wasn't that man any more. He had become capable of cruelty, and the man I had loved had been compassionate, unable to see a stray dog suffer, devoted to a little girl, a rock of support at times like my father's funeral.

I went out into the dark front garden. The chilly night breeze made me shiver, but I walked around the perimeter, following the low stone wall, hoping to make myself too tired to dream any more. Back in the woods I heard a faint trill of bird-song, and I wondered if it could be a nightingale, the wonderful singer I only knew from Keats and Shelley, and had always hoped to hear someday. But it must have been clear at the other side of the woods, and I wasn't about to go in there at night.

Up the road, the bare branches of the churchyard trees were moving in the breeze, sheltering that secret grave beside the cross, the bones of the murder victim. Were they still lying there, or had the police taken them away to be probed and tested, stored in a cold metal cabinet until they were through with them? What a dismal end to a life that must have begun with some sort of hope.

I turned up the path toward my front door, and before I went inside I cast a glance at George's cottage. The light was out. I imagined the old man in there, lying on unwashed sheets, dreaming of the children who had forgotten him. Although my brothers and I had let our father down, at least we had not abandoned him to fend for himself like that. There are degrees of guilt—but they all leave scars.

CHAPTER FOUR

When I woke the next morning it was pouring rain. But Emily and I had agreed to meet at her flat at ten for the big shopping trip, and I knew the English don't cancel their plans for rain. I fortified myself with what was left of Fiona's tea and cookies, but the first item on my shopping list was a box of steel-cut oatmeal, the only way to start the day in the British climate.

Making lists had become a habit in the past few years, as I finally admitted my lifelong absent-mindedness was getting worse with age. Today's list was longer than usual, because I needed just about everything. I got so absorbed in it that when I glanced at my watch I was shocked to see it was after ten.

I found my purse in record time, and drove nervously above the speed limit on what still felt like the wrong side of the road, to find Emily waiting under an umbrella in her parking lot, her lips pressed tightly together over what she wanted to say.

She had relaxed by the time we started through Debenham's Departmental Store, piling parcels around

Archie in his stroller. I bought an Eiderdown quilt, along with towels, dishes, and utensils, and a new CD player I could use on the English electrical current. I gave into impulse, too, and splurged on a hand-hooked floral rug that I knew would look great in front of my fireplace. After a pub lunch I opened a bank account, and then we were off to Blackwell's for books and a big supermarket for groceries.

From childhood, Emily had been a well-organized person, not a bit like me. If I had been alone I would have dawdled in Blackwell's for hours, instead of the forty-five minutes she allowed me, and never made it back in time for Philippa Damerel's gathering.

But with her in charge we came out of our last stop, the Central Library, at exactly four o'clock. I was carrying a new library card, which the nice librarian referred to as a "reader's ticket," and the latest mystery by my favorite author, not yet available in the States. It was comforting to find that English libraries are just counterparts of those in America, right down to the good old Dewey Decimal System.

"I'm in awe of you, darling," I said to Emily as we kissed goodbye, huddling under our umbrellas outside her apartment building. "We got everything done except buying a car! I can't wait to eat that lovely steak tonight off one of my pretty new plates."

"We can get the car later in the week. Of course, I do have my groups, and I have to take Archie for his checkup tomorrow, and I really must make time to go to the eye doctor, these glasses are just not doing the job any more."

"Don't worry, best beloved. I know how busy you are. I'm perfectly capable of shopping for a car all by myself." Inwardly I determined to do it on a day when I wouldn't have to cut into her free time.

"Well, I'll go with you if I possibly can. Oh, and one more thing—I've taken on a new patient. Tomorrow is her first session, so you won't mind staying until seven with Archie, will you? Peter will be late, too, I'm afraid, but I'll leave a pizza or something in the freezer for dinner."

"Of course I don't mind. It will be our first time alone together, and we're going to have all sorts of fun, aren't we, Archie? And you don't have to leave anything for dinner, either. I'll cook a nice big meal for all of us."

She shook her head emphatically. "Mom, you have no idea what a whole day with your grandson is going to be like. I will definitely leave something that only needs warming up, and I don't want to hear any argument about it. You'll see, you're going to thank me tomorrow evening."

It took a little while to put my purchases away, so I was running late when I got out of the shower and put on my one nice dress, a red silk shirtwaist kind of thing. I had debated with myself whether to bring it, feeling sure I wouldn't need anything so dressy, but now I was glad to have it. It was a little wrinkled, and there was no time to accessorize it, but I was sure Philippa and her friends were not going to be overcome by my elegance, no matter what I did.

Although The Manor was no distance, I drove the

rental car there to spare my low-heeled but dressy pumps. Making the left turn into narrow Church Lane from the left side didn't seem such a challenge anymore. Things were definitely getting better, I thought. I wasn't going to be sitting around alone, or with only the old man across the road for company, as I had feared. I was on my way to a party at a stately home, on only the third evening after I'd arrived in England! Nothing like this had ever happened to me in New York.

At least a dozen cars were parked at the Manor when I drove around its circular driveway. Most of them were Bentleys and Jaguars. The few well-worn Fords and Austins had to belong to my fellow villagers.

I was trying to fit my car between two of these when a young man in livery ran up, holding a large black umbrella over his head. He tapped on my window and when I rolled it down he said, "Just move it up by the door, Madame. I'll put it away for you."

I pulled over to the front entrance. The Manor was not Blenheim Palace, but it was certainly roomy enough for a big family and all its in-laws. At least twenty windows marched across a façade of Cotswold stone that glowed through the rain like fire behind a waterfall. Half a dozen chimneys rose above the roof slates. Alan and Philippa couldn't possibly use it all for living in. Much of it must be some sort of museum.

A heavy-set butler in a cutaway held the door open when I left the shelter of the umbrella. He bowed as I came in, and I smiled and nodded, uncertain how I was expected to respond.

He led me across the marble-floored, oak-panelled entrance hall and past a long staircase lined all the way up with portraits of people in historical costumes. He bowed again as he left me at the door of a room with a ceiling covered in flowers and vines that looked as if they had been carved out of whipped cream. Half a dozen well-dressed people turned their heads to look at me coolly.

It was a long, narrow, mostly green room. The walls, the sofas, and the chairs were covered in a silky green damask material. The outside wall featured a row of floor-to-ceiling windows overlooking walled fields as far as I could see. Two horses were grazing in the one nearest the house.

Philippa emerged from the group of staring people, baring her large teeth.

"Here you are at last!" she sang out in a piercing, high-pitched voice. "How very odd to be late when one is the guest of honor. But then, I've never claimed to understand the behavior of foreigners." She gave a phony, tinkling laugh.

I heard Fiona Bennett say drily, "After all, Philippa, the host hasn't shown up yet, either."

She was sitting on one of the green sofas, with Alice White and Louisa Barry. They all beamed at me encouragingly. A couple of men I hadn't seen before stood to one side of the sofa.

Small side tables were scattered around, so that it was impossible to walk straight from one end of the room to the other. Fragile porcelain figurines perched on the tables, giving me pause when Philippa beckoned, for fear a momentary stumble might put me in debt for the rest of my life.

"Ah, you've noticed Julian's little collection of Chelsea ware," she informed me. "Just one of the dear man's expensive, and fortunately brief, passions. Now you must come along and meet some of my very closest friends."

Who's Julian? I was thinking as I navigated my way carefully through the obstacle course of fragile statuary. I was beginning to feel overwhelmed by the number of names I was hearing.

The six or eight men and women standing by the fireplace had evidently watched me long enough to decide I was worth just the slightest twitch of the lips and inclination of the head.

"First, you must meet Honour and Robert Verity. Honour was one of the Sussex Wynne-Smythes, you know. We are terribly close friends."

Honour shot her a glance that seemed to belie that claim, as she offered me her limp fingers. The others were equally unenthusiastic about meeting me, so it was a great relief to finally be led over to the three village women I already knew, and the husbands who had accompanied two of them.

Fiona's husband, John Bennett, was tall and thin, with a naturally solemn face and an air of quiet strength.

Dr. Barry, in contrast, was short, round, and white-haired, with a rubicund complexion that looked to me like high blood-pressure. He greeted me courteously and then went back to glaring at the Reverend Ian Larribee.

The vicar was dressed in the same style as the day before, jeans and a bright yellow turtleneck. When he saw me he looked startled, and began to talk rapidly to a man standing near him, gesturing toward me rudely. I was sure he was telling him about our previous encounter.

I sank down beside Fiona on the sofa as Philippa hurried back to her upper-class friends.

"There," said Fiona, "now you'll be safe with us. They've seen you're a regular person, not their sort, so they'll leave you alone, and a good thing, too."

After a few minutes the master of the house joined us. Alan Damerel was a quiet, self-possessed man in, I estimated, his mid-thirties. With his entrance there was a general relaxation. The irritable tension his wife had created faded away as he went around greeting his guests. The servants, who had smirked watching her performance, came to attention.

He was dark-haired, of medium height, very well-groomed, but there was nothing extraordinary about his looks. He was simply that old-fashioned figure, a gentleman. While his wife worked constantly at making sure she was the center of attention, he possessed the natural charisma that attracts all eyes without trying. And he spoke with that perfect enunciation that makes us Anglophiles melt.

"Afternoon, everyone," he said. "Sorry to be late. Haines," he made a slight gesture toward the butler, who immediately started to the door, "will bring the drinks."

"I'm going to show them round the house first," Philippa complained. "I don't want the drinks brought yet!"

"Sorry," he said quietly. "Didn't know there was a schedule."

"Come along, then, everyone," she commanded. "What fun!"

"I'll entertain the fellows here," he said firmly. "They've all been round before, and that sort of thing is usually more interesting to women, anyway."

"Actually, I've been round, too," Honour Verity tried to say, but of course Philippa ran right over her.

She herded us out the door with an offended glare at the men as they settled back in obvious relief.

We followed her like baby ducks across the entrance hall again and into another sumptuous room, this one in Victorian style, with red sofas, draperies, and carpets, a baby grand piano as centerpiece and, dominating one wall, a full-length portrait of a woman in a scarlet gown that must have inspired the color scheme.

"This was the music room," Philippa announced, "not actually used now, as none of us is skilled in that line. But Cordelia, my mother-in-law," she gestured toward the portrait, "was a talented pianist, as well as a celebrated hostess whose parties were the highlight of county society." She gave a dramatic sigh and shook her head sadly. "We were very close," she explained for my benefit.

"Cordelia couldn't bear her," Fiona whispered gleefully to me, as we moved on. "Used to refer to her as Frightful Phil."

"So Cordelia was Alan's mother?" I whispered back.

"That's right. Very beautiful she was, very elegant. She

was one of the Gloucestershire Farradays," she went on, in such a perfect imitation of Philippa's affected tone that I had to giggle in spite of myself. "But not very happy, I always thought. Her marriage was pretty much a failure, but of course there was no question of divorce in their position in society, at that time. So she threw herself into her music and an endless round of parties. A brilliant hostess, everybody said, though of course I can't speak for that as Cordelia never knew I existed. All in all, I think people felt rather sorry for her. Still, I suppose being filthy rich was some consolation."

We went through a jumble of period rooms, the Jacobean dining room, the Georgian morning room, the Regency ballroom and, in contrast, Alan's small, austere stone study, the only room left from the original Norman house. Philippa didn't waste any time on it.

Finally, we climbed the portrait-lined staircase I had noticed when I'd first come in. The wall was a family album of the Damerels, from medieval Rupert, clasping his hands and rolling up his eyes to demonstrate his piety, through foxy seventeenth-century James in curls and laces, to the current master and mistress. Alan had been painted wearing tweeds, resting one hand on the head of a collie, while Philippa glittered in red satin and rubies.

There was another portrait of Cordelia, too, just as lovely in blue as in red. I studied her face for the sadness Fiona had talked about, but evidently the artist had not been perceptive enough to reveal it. All I saw was a rather off-putting imperiousness.

Next to that portrait were two empty spaces, two rectangles paler than the rest of the wall.

"What's become of Julian and Eugenia, then?" one of the ladies inquired.

"They've gone off to be cleaned," Philippa said. "It's been one of my little projects to have all these portraits professionally cleaned. When I first came to live here, I noticed how dark and obscure some of them had become, quite depressing to look at. So I suggested the cleaning to Julian and he quite liked the idea, at first. We had medieval Rupert done and then Julian lost interest. You remember how he was, I did find it most annoying. He took up boating and wouldn't spend another penny on the portraits. So when we inherited I began again, one or two at a time. Now they've all been done except for Julian and Eugenia, and they're due back later this week. It has been rather expensive, but I would never begrudge the Manor anything it needs, simply because of money. My next project is to restore the statuary in the gardens."

"All right, Julian was Alan's father, right?" I whispered to Fiona as we climbed the stairs. She nodded. "There's two of them I've got straight! So who was Eugenia?"

"Julian's mother, Alan's grandmother, and a right old dragon. Julian and Cordelia were scared to death of her and of his father, old Alan. He was always threatening to cut off their allowance because they were so extravagant, Cordelia with her parties and Julian with his endless new hobbies.

"If Julian wanted something, he didn't care what he had to spend or do to get it. Then once he had it, he'd soon lose interest and simply have to have something else. Regular Mr. Toad he was. He wouldn't rest until he'd got Cordelia to marry him, then he ran true to form and broke her heart with all sorts of women. A self-centered bastard is basically what he was. The current son and heir, young Rupert, is very much like him, only without the charm that made Julian such an expert at getting himself forgiven."

"Yet Alan Damerel doesn't seem to be like that at all," I said. "Quite the opposite, in fact."

"Oh, absolutely. I doubt he's even been unfaithful to Philippa, and anyone can see he can't stand her. It's odd how these traits seem to skip generations. Alan's like his grandpa, too—old Alan. Not that he's a dictator, of course, like the old man, but he has the same sense of family duty, in his own quiet way. He should go round wearing a ribbon saying 'Noblesse oblige.' Julian and Cordelia were always too busy with their own interests to pay attention to him, but he got a gruff kind of approval from old Alan for being conscious of his obligations, and I imagine that's what made him the kind of man he is."

I would have liked to linger over the portraits. They were vibrant after their cleaning, and some of them had real artistic merit. Besides, the idea of living so intimately with your ancestors appealed to me. We Americans are descendants of people who broke with their ancestry, voluntarily or involuntarily, and started all over from scratch. I had hardly known my grandparents. One set lived in Kentucky and the other in Iowa, and our vacation every summer was a week with one or the other of them, we kids moping around, bored and longing to get back to our friends. Further back than grandparents I had never imagined. It was as if we had sprung up like native plants from the soil of America. I was the latest in a long line of varied and interesting people, just as Alan Damerel was. The difference was that I didn't know who they had been, and I envied these people who did know.

But Philippa kept us trotting along, into a corridor lined with closed doors.

"These bedrooms aren't in use, now there are just the three of us. Only one is kept with its original furnishings, because it was occupied by Elizabeth I when she visited the Manor in 1569." She threw open one of the doors. "You simply must see the bed, Catherine. It will leave you speechless!"

The bed-curtains were certainly magnificent, a heavy gold brocade, but since they were closed I couldn't judge the bed.

"Who's closed those curtains?" Philippa exclaimed. "One of those stupid little housemaids is going to lose her—"

She pulled the tasselled rope and the curtain swept back to reveal the historic bed. As she had predicted, it left me speechless, but not because of its beauty. Because it was occupied.

CHAPTER FIVE

Four teenagers in various stages of undress looked at us, then at each other, and collapsed in laughter. The two boys were down to their underpants, and so was one of the girls, but nobody was yet completely naked. A sweet smoky smell hung in the air, and the whites of their eyes were quite rosy.

"Rupert!" Philippa screeched. "What are you doing?"

Smoking pot and having it off was obviously the correct answer. But Rupert, a skinny kid with an unruly shock of blond hair, giggled, "Entertaining my friends, Mummy," and they were all off in another fit of hysteria.

"Get up this instant! Put your clothes on! Go to your room!"

Rupert did none of those things. He lay there staring at her insolently, although the others began to look nervous and to get into their clothes.

"Who *are* you?" Philippa demanded, jumping back as a pretty red-headed girl climbed out of the bed, dressed only in bikinis.

"Patty Jenkins," she giggled, cocking her head pertly,

as she retrieved her jeans from a fantastically carved Elizabethan chair.

"Patty's my bird," Rupert announced. "Aren't you going to say, 'Pleased to meet you,' then? Where are those manners you're always on at me about?"

"I've seen you in the village, my girl, your father drives the milk float!" Philippa cried. "How dare you come into *my* house and lead *my* son into this low behavior?"

Rupert fell back on the pillows and started singing "Rule Britannia" at the top of his voice. After a few seconds' hesitation, his friends joined in, drowning her out.

Then she seemed for the first time to remember we were watching. She turned red, briefly. She came back out in the hall and slammed the door, and stood looking around for something to say that would salvage the situation. There was, of course, nothing.

So she just led us off again, down the corridor, pointing out this antique and that painting along the way, as if the outrageous scene had never happened. Fiona and I exchanged disbelieving glances. I noticed Philippa's very best friends were doing their best not to laugh in her face.

When we got back to the drawing room she spoke to her husband in a low but agitated voice. He sighed; then, without answering her, he rang for Haines. I heard him tell the butler to go to the Elizabethan bedroom and inform Master Rupert he wanted to see him.

Then he turned to me and asked, with perfect composure, "Do you like our house?"

"It's magnificent. But I can't imagine what it must be

like to live in such close connection with your ancestors. I haven't any idea who my great-grandfather was!"

"A bit like living in a museum," he said with a smile. Just what I'd thought, but it was surprising to hear him say it. "If it weren't for family duty and all that, one might prefer a nice flat in town and some useful work to do."

"Don't be absurd, Alan!" Philippa snapped.

He gave a little shrug, smiling at me.

The butler and maid were going around with glasses of sherry on silver trays. I took one, and it was delicious.

"I hope you'll not be bored in Far Wychwood," Alan said. "There's not a great deal of diversion in these country places."

"Something that needs seeing to if the village is to survive," the vicar boomed.

I looked around, and saw all the villagers listening to Alan and me, while the gentry had gathered a little apart and were talking to each other, ignoring the rest of us.

"Do you ride?" Alan went on. "There's a fairly good hunt hereabouts."

"I've never even been on a horse. But I'm going to be helping my daughter. She's having a hard time running her practice and caring for a small child. Tomorrow, for example, I'll be in Oxford until after seven in the evening, chasing a toddler around, so I don't think I'll be bored."

"Catherine does seem to enjoy caring for people," Alice White piped up. "She's even taken on George Crocker, isn't that extraordinary?"

Why did that look of amazement come over people's faces every time my interest in George was mentioned?

"It's just that I happened to catch him setting his house on fire, the first night I was here," I explained defensively. "So to prevent it happening again, I fixed him some dinner. He's really an interesting old fellow. I could hardly believe it when he started talking about witches!"

"Ah, well, Wychwood, you know—witch wood," Dr. Barry said. "That's the wood adjoining Crocker's cottage. Covens did meet there, years ago. In point of fact, it's only been in the past sixty years that such practices have finally died out, and many of the very old folk still give them credence."

"Dr. Barry is our local antiquarian," Fiona told me.

"But not even antiquarian interest would get me to pass any time with old Crocker," he said gruffly. "He is not liked in this village, Mrs. Penny."

"But why?"

"George Crocker was involved in a burglary of this very house," Louisa answered. "It was one of the most scandalous things that ever happened in Far Wychwood."

"Well, it was ten years ago, ancient history now," Alan Damerel said, smiling as if the subject amused him. "And my family were never as scandalized as the rest of the village. Although it was rather sad to find that an old retainer like Crocker would betray our confidence in that way."

"George worked for you?" I asked.

"George Crocker was a gardener on this estate," Alice White answered eagerly, "as his father had been. In fact, the Crockers had been servants at the Manor for generations, and so were all George's family. Emma, his wife, had been a kitchen maid before she married, their daughter, Annie, was a parlormaid, and Arthur, though he always had his sights set higher, used to help George in the summers for pocket money."

"George planned this burglary with an accomplice, you see," Louisa said, "a man no one in the village had ever seen!"

I had the impression that involving an outsider made George's crime all the worse.

"The man came," she went on, "and stayed with George one night, never coming out or speaking to anybody. The next day, he and George were seen going furtively into the Manor's grounds, and later in the day the robbery was discovered and the man was gone!"

"Did they catch him?"

"Got clean away," John Bennett answered. "We questioned George Crocker extensively, of course, but like most of these old countrymen, he knew how to keep his mouth shut."

"You know," I said slowly, "I think he was talking about that last night. He was saying he'd never told anyone where 'Jimmy' had gone, and talking about some sort of papers, and he mentioned money, too. Is that what they took?"

"Yes," Alan said, and went on ruefully, "I was to blame. It was payday for all the estate workers, many more than we employ now. A lot of the property and workers had to go when my father died. Death duties take a tremendous bite out of inherited property over here, you see. It happened during Father's last illness, actually about a week before his death. The workers had always been paid with cash, so I had it all, nearly 20,000 pounds, in my desk. That was the way we did it then, never thinking that one of our own people could be less than trustworthy."

"But wait a minute," I put in. "Why would George need some guy from London to help him steal that money?"

"Professional," Louisa said cannily. "Knew the way to go about it."

"And how would George know a professional thief from the city?" I demanded, feeling more and more skeptical.

"Well, the man was here," Alice said defensively, "and then the money was gone, and so was he. One can't explain *everything*."

"The police asked the same questions," John said. "And as there was no solid evidence against George, and the Damerels declined to press charges, we had to drop it."

"Everybody has always thought," Alice hurried on, quite pink with excitement, "that George still has his share of the *swag* hidden somewhere in that dreadful cottage of his."

"But surely," I protested, "if he had, he wouldn't live in such squalor."

"Fellow's a bit cracked," Dr. Barry said. "But when young Arthur wanted to go off and be an optometrist, we all noticed how the money was available, though old George never made more than laborer's wages."

"We think he has it hidden in his cottage," Louisa

said. "Then he can hold it over Arthur's head, so he doesn't desert him completely."

Suddenly we became aware of Rupert and his friends. Clothed now, they were standing in the doorway, and Rupert, at least, had been listening for several minutes with rapt attention.

Seeing we'd noticed him, he threw his arm around Patty Jenkins' shoulders and favored us with a nasty grin.

"Hello, everyone. Don't let us interrupt your little knees-up. Sherry the drug of choice, I see? Better than none."

He snatched a crystal glass from the maid's tray and swallowed the contents in one gulp. Giggling, his friends moved in on the tray.

"That will do, thank you, Mary," his father said. The maid gave him a grateful look and scurried out.

"You may wait in the study for me, Rupert," Alan said gravely. "These other people had better leave. They've been told they're not welcome."

"Common little creatures," Philippa shrilled, "can't you see how unsuitable they are——"

"I need money," Rupert said, turning sullen. "Ten pounds will rid you of me for another day."

"Please go to the study, Rupert," Alan repeated quietly.

"I've got to have some money! If you won't give it me, I'll be forced to go and get it some other way—a way you won't like."

"How can you expect us to give you money," Philippa said, "when we know the use you'll make of it?"

"Just a moment," the vicar's chronically loud voice

rang out. "Not to worry, kids, I'm not going to lecture you. I know you're only looking for a comfortable place to get together and some interesting things to do. Games, films, the occasional mystery tour, am I right?" Getting no answer except incredulous stares, he hurried on, "I'm going to build you such a place, right here in the village! There's been a temporary delay, but it's nothing serious, we'll be back on track in no time."

"Right, Vicar," Rupert drawled, "you build it, and we'll put on our playsuits and be over for some jolly fun."

Their raucous laughter floated back to us as he and his gang crossed the entrance hall to the front door.

"I apologize, Vicar," Alan said.

"Not at all," he answered heartily. "He's not a bad kid. You mustn't let that youthful bravado discourage you. That was a perfect example of this village's crying need for a facility where—"

"So, you'll be back on track in no time?" Dr. Barry burst out, springing to his feet. "Well, John Bennett's been telling us it could be weeks!"

"I really can't commit myself," John said with some embarrassment. "It's impossible to predict the course of a homicide investigation, particularly with an unidentified victim and a lot of time intervening."

"Homicide?" Honour exclaimed. She and her friends were suddenly giving us their undivided attention.

"This may just be the fatal delay for your schemes," the doctor stormed on. "It will give us time to petition the authorities, and the press. If the council's been taken in with that blather about saving our young folk, we'll see you don't put it over the bishop the same way! You've got no respect for the history, the traditions—"

"That's the trouble with the church in this country," Ian broke in, "only bloody history and tradition, no room for today's needs!"

"You need to be working in some city slum, not in a country village," the doctor shouted. "Six months you've been here, and you're set to uproot a great work of art from the spot where it's stood for seven hundred bloody—"

"I'm afraid we really *must* be toddling," Honour Verity said with steely graciousness. "*Such* a lovely time, Philippa. Do ring me up soon."

She moved quickly to the door, followed by her husband. The maid appeared with their coats as if by magic.

"Lovely meeting you," she tossed over her shoulder at me as they beat their retreat.

A general exodus ensued, while the doctor and the vicar went on shouting, Philippa looked ready to scream, and Alan grimly rang for the butler to see people out.

I felt terrible for Philippa, but it did help when she said, as I tried to thank her for inviting me, "Yes, well, I knew it would be a thrill for you to have a glimpse of our home and lifestyle, so different from anything you would have experienced before."

Alan grimaced at that, and bade me goodbye with a sad smile. I decided I felt sorrier for him than for her.

Fiona and John had waited for me outside. The rain was over for the moment, and the evening air smelled clean and faintly fragrant.

As we waited for our cars to be brought around, Dr. Barry erupted from the house, calling to us.

"Now we've been given this reprieve," he said breathlessly, "I mean to go to work immediately getting on to the press, even petitioning the bishop, though from what I've heard his thinking is right in line with the vicar's. Will you help me if I call on you?"

Fiona agreed, although John said in his position he couldn't get involved. The doctor bustled off in search of more recruits.

"He's right, of course," Fiona said, "but I do wish he'd be a bit more temperate. I mean to say, behaving like that at a party—"

She dissolved into laughter while John and I stared.

"I'm sorry," she gasped, "but I suddenly remembered the expression on Philippa's face during that rumpus. You must admit, pomposity can be funny, especially when all the air goes out of it."

"You're a disgrace, Fiona," John said, smiling down at her fondly.

"I know," she said, patting her hair in an attempt to regain her dignity. "Well, we can only hope Donald is right, that your investigation will help our side in the war of the cross."

"It may," he admitted. "But as a check of records showed there hasn't been an unexplained disappearance in these parts for more than thirty years, it seems clear the fellow was an outsider, and that makes matters more difficult."

"The murder wasn't as long ago as that?" I asked.

"No more than a decade ago, they say. We've determined that the victim was a male, neither adolescent nor elderly, and that's about all. They'll be getting the DNA, of course, and checking it against missing-persons files at Scotland Yard. Sooner or later we'll find out who he was—but who put that bullet in his head and buried him, we may never know."

"All very odd, as Philippa would say," Fiona put in.

"She is a pain," I agreed, "but I feel kind of sorry for her. Nobody deserves a kid like that Rupert."

"You're quite right," she said. "I'm afraid Rupert is turning from a mere brat to something close to a sociopath. It's too bad for his parents, although I think they're at least partly to blame. They can't help being the kind of people they are, but I don't think they ever gave him what a child needs. I can remember him, years ago, toddling round after Alan, doing silly things to try to get his attention, but while Alan of course was impeccably polite to the child, he'd never had displays of affection from Julian or Cordelia and so he never thought of giving them to his son. Even his grandfather, who was kinder to him than his parents, would have given him to understand that such things were in frightfully poor taste. After all, Alan provided young Rupert with an excellent set of genes and admittance to the best schools. To our upper classes, that's considered good parenting."

"And then, of course, Philippa's not exactly the picture of motherly warmth and understanding." I shook my head sadly. "It's no wonder he's messed up."

"Yes," Fiona said. "I doubt the poor kid has ever felt loved by anybody."

"Whatever the cause," John said, "all my experience tells me that boy is going to finish up in some sort of major trouble."

I put a potato into the oven when I got home, and broiled myself a steak. While I ate it I had George's potato baking. I sliced up a tomato for him, too, broiled a nice patty of ground sirloin, and arranged it all on one of my new plates, speckled beige with a dark blue rim.

I could see the brass lamp flickering in the window as I crossed the road and picked my way through the weeds to the doorstep.

Something was lying there. It was a dark, overcast night with no moon, so I couldn't identify the thing, except to see that it was small, flat, and circular. I stepped over it to knock.

In a few seconds the door was jerked back and the old man peered out warily. He was wearing the same filthy shirt and pants I had seen him in the last two nights. His feet were bare. I thought it quite likely that he'd lost his shoes.

"It's Catherine, George," I said brightly. "You remember me. I've made you a really good dinner."

He stood there for a minute, swaying a little, trying to bring his mind to bear on the question of where he had seen me before. At least he seemed to have forgotten he'd been mad at me.

"Cathern, eh?" he finally said. He nodded as if he'd

placed me, took the plate from my hands, and squinted at it suspiciously.

Then his eyes lighted on the doorstep. The look that came over his face sent a cold ripple down my backbone. For some reason, the old man was seized with terror.

I glanced behind me and in the lamplight I could see the thing I'd stepped over. It was a circle of twigs from a yew tree, so dark green the leaves almost looked black. Someone had twisted it around and tied the top and bottom of the branch with cord.

George stepped back, away from it, away from me. I went into the cottage after him, feeling a stitch of the same fear I'd known when he'd grabbed my arm and shouted at me the other night, out by Malkin's grave.

"What's the matter with you, George? It's just a bunch of twigs, some kids probably—"

He kept backing away until he was against the far wall. His filmy eyes stared at me in sheer panic, as if at some terrible apparition invading his sanctuary.

I was obtuse enough to try to soothe him with words. "Come along, George," I said briskly, "sit down and let me help you cut your potato. Then afterwards, you can tell me about Annie and Arthur while I do some cleaning up."

He threw the plate at me. It fell short and smashed to pieces against the floor. The food went flying and the black cat darted out from under a chair and went for the meat.

"Go away," George whispered hoarsely. "Don't ye never come back. I'll not tell. I'll never tell!"

"You've got no business breaking my new plate, George Crocker!" I retorted furiously.

Then he came at me. His face was contorted and off-color, the way it had been the other night. When it was so close to mine that I could smell his sour breath along with the many other odors that hung around him, I started to back away. His shaking fingers closed on my shoulders. I had no trouble breaking loose, and I left at a run.

Plunging across the road in the dark, I heard him still yelling, "Don't ye never come back!"

"All right, that's it," I gasped as I closed my own door behind me. I was shaking so, I went straight into the sitting room and collapsed onto the sofa. I had done as much as I could for that ungrateful old burglar. It was time to notify the social-services people and get out of their way. He was crazier than I'd realized. He was probably dangerous.

A hot bath calmed me, and I settled under my lovely fat quilt and relaxed into the delicious sensation of opening a new mystery by an author I trusted to do it right. I was finally able to push away that guilt I had transferred from my dad to George, the old fear that I should have done more. This time, I had done as much as anybody could. Or would have, as soon as I reported him to people qualified to deal with such cases. George Crocker would get along without me all right for another day or two. Without matches, what danger could he be in?

CHAPTER SIX

Not a great day for car shopping, I had to admit as I ate my steel-cut oats the next morning. That unforgettable day, destined to end in such horror, began with a wild March wind.

I sat at the table in the little dining room at the rear of my house and watched the two rowan trees bowing together from side to side. In less than a month I could actually be setting out plants of my own choosing in the back garden. All those years in city apartments, I'd devoted myself to my houseplants, never imagining I would someday have a yard to fill with flowers.

I'd had shelves under all the windows on West Eighty-third, massed with plants. Quin had called it "Kit's jungle." He and Emily had kidded me about being on safari when I worked among my plants, crowding the kitchen sink and drainboard. One birthday they had presented me with a pith helmet and a plastic machete.

But another time, when I was getting over the flu, they had come home with an enormous clivia in full bloom and a card reading, "It's almost as big and almost as pretty as you." I had kept that plant going for over six years, a long life for a clivia. All my friends got offsets from its roots. It succumbed to some kind of disgusting rot just before Emily left us for England. She and I actually cried over the silly thing, and Quin took us out to a funny movie. Maybe it wasn't just the plant we were crying about. He'd wanted to buy me another one, but the time of the clivia had been the last few years with my blue-eyed girl, and I knew that time was over.

When we got home from the airport after seeing her off, I found a big potbound fern waiting for me.

"I knew why you didn't want another of those what-you-callums," he said when I put my arms around him to thank him. "I got you one you never had before. It's time to start over."

I jumped when the phone gave its twin rings, and picked it up to hear Emily's voice.

"Just wanted to make sure you're on your way," she said. "It's after eight, and I know how you can lose track of time. I have to be at the hospital at quarter past nine."

"Of course I'm on the way!" I was furious with myself, once again letting pointless memories invade my new life. "I'm practically out the door."

I ran upstairs and threw on a pair of slacks and a sweater. My hair, being short and curly, took only a few seconds to brush into place, and I hadn't worn makeup since my marriage ended, so I was back downstairs in less than fifteen minutes.

Searching for my purse and keys, however, took another fifteen, and so it was nearly eight-forty when I drove away.

Emily and Peter had a pricey flat right by Folley Bridge. They had never expressed any interest in buying a house, and it was not hard to see why. The view of the river from their windows was endlessly fascinating, and the sunsets were memorable.

Emily was obviously a bit irritated when she let me in. I heard the electric clock in the sitting room chiming nine.

"Sorry, love," I said as she led me silently to Archie's room. "I really did hurry. But you can make it, can't you?"

She started to speak, then pressed her lips together and smiled with the bottom of her face. She looked very businesslike today in a navy blue pantsuit and white silk blouse, with the flowing hair firmly twisted behind her head.

Archie's room was filled from wall to wall with educational toys. He sat in the midst of them, banging at a four-legged pegboard with a little hammer.

"Oh, it's okay," Emily said, "only I'd hoped to have a few minutes to tell you how we do things with him."

"Don't worry, I have done this before."

"It's important that we keep his environment predictable, with excitement at a minimum. An extroverted child like Archie can easily get overstimulated. *No* TV, of course. You wouldn't believe the trouble I've had with babysitters about that!"

"Well, I never stuck you in front of it to keep you quiet, and I won't him either." As she started to go on, I said quickly, "Better hurry or you'll be late. Have a good day, and don't worry about us."

When she was gone Archie stopped pounding for a moment, looked me up and down, and then returned to work.

I found another toy hammer, sat down opposite him on the floor, and joined in the pounding. He regarded me solemnly before giving a delighted squeal. When we had all the pegs through I turned the board over and we pounded them back again.

He made it clear when he'd had enough of that by picking up the pegboard and throwing it against the wall. Babbling excitedly, he toddled around the room selecting his favorite possessions and bringing them for me to admire. I felt I had been accepted.

At quarter to ten I went through the kitchen cabinets until I found those little boxes of Cheerios mothers stock, and a baby-size box of apple juice. These I tucked into my tote along with a couple of disposable diapers from the changing table. I got Archie into his coat and knitted hat, tucked him into his state-of-the-art stroller, and headed out for Debenham's.

It was a bit of a walk to the end of Cornmarket, along the narrow sidewalks full of shoppers and tourists and students in their billowing black robes that looked like graduation gowns to me, although they seemed to be everyday wear at Oxford.

Archie raised his face to the wind and laughed when it hit him extra hard. When he was older, I mused, I'd read "Who Has Seen the Wind" to him. I could hardly wait to get his reactions to Stevenson, and to Milne and Carroll and all the other incomparable authors I had discovered with Emily. It was wonderful to think of all the great books waiting for Archie and me, and all the windy days.

I spent a little over an hour buying an infant car seat at Debenham's. Of course, it wouldn't have taken nearly as long if we hadn't passed a display of really serious hand tools for gardeners, the kind that are only made in England, with solid oak handles and unbreakable points. I bought a set of them, and then we came to the footwear department and the one absolute essential for an English gardener, real Wellington boots.

We had almost made it out of the store when a display of Beatrix Potter characters loomed before us, and Archie's wide eyes as I introduced him to them made it impossible to leave without, at least, Peter Rabbit.

As we walked back down Cornmarket, the stroller and bag were both packed to capacity. The bell at Carfax was clanging noon when I noticed a sign on a shop window reading, "Eleanor Coleman, Estate Agent."

I had never met the woman who had found Rowan Cottage for me. A colleague at the University had recommended her to Peter when I'd first spoken to Emily about coming over, so I had written to her. I'd vaguely said I was looking for a cottage near Oxford, if possible in Far Wychwood. I had expected to wait months, even years, but I got a letter from her almost immediately with pictures of the cottage. It had looked exactly like my dream, and I'd bought it by transatlantic mail.

I had been meaning to look her up and thank her for

everything she'd done. Now seemed a good time, so I crossed the street and entered the office backwards, bumping the stroller over the doorsill with some difficulty.

When I turned around I saw a slim, attractive woman, probably in her late thirties, with black hair sleeked into a chignon. She was sitting behind her desk, watching my efforts with a quizzical expression.

"May I help you?" she asked in a cool, rather deep voice.

"I'm Catherine Penny," I said, holding out my hand. She rose, looking puzzled, and accepted it in beautifully manicured fingers. "You know, Rowan Cottage? You handled everything so efficiently, I've come to thank you."

Her face cleared, and she shook my hand graciously.

"Rowan Cottage, of course! I'm so glad finally to meet you. You've settled in, then? Everything is satisfactory?"

"Oh, yes. I'm in town until sometime this evening, caring for my grandson here, and we just happened to pass your sign."

"That's right, your daughter lives here, doesn't she? Do sit down. You appear to have been doing a little shopping."

There was a slightly sardonic tone to the last remark that made me wonder how glad she really was to have a windblown old woman with a toddler and a crowded stroller in her tastefully decorated place of business.

She gave me a cup of tea from an electrical gadget behind the desk, and I sat down in the chair facing her. She smoothed her pleated skirt carefully and seated herself again behind her desk.

"I must tell you, what impressed me most was your finding a perfect cottage, in the very village I wanted, so quickly," I told her. "I expected to have to wait a long time."

She threw me a rather smug, even superior smile. The lady was definitely intimidating, with her perfectly coifed hair, perfectly shaped red fingernails, and perfect, fashion-magazine clothing. Her suit was made of some silky material in an understated grey-green shade, the businesslike jacket offset by the femininity of the pleated skirt and the lace collar of a matching blouse. Her only jewelry was a pair of small circles on her ears, without doubt solid gold, and a delicate golden chain bracelet from which a heart-shaped charm dangled. She made me feel like a cowgirl.

"Now that you're the owner," she finally said, "I'll tell you the truth about Rowan Cottage. I was afraid I would never sell that property. Every time I showed it, the prospect would take one look at that eyesore over the road and immediately lose interest. I had almost given up hope of ever getting rid of it when your letter arrived."

That smile was becoming more and more irritating. What she was telling me, I realized, was that she had taken advantage of my willingness to buy sight unseen.

Archie had begun to squirm and grumble. He threw Peter Rabbit to the floor to notify me that we had been sitting still long enough. Eleanor Coleman looked at him with distaste. I knew she wouldn't appreciate my breaking out the Cheerios.

"I suppose I really should apologize for a certain lack of candor. But, in fairness, Ms. Penny, I felt sure the old man in that hovel wouldn't be around much longer."

"What do you mean?"

She was toying with the charm on her bracelet.

"Well, he *is* very old, isn't he?"

"With proper care, he might live for years yet." Really, this general callousness toward poor old George was getting irritating.

She gave me a patronizing look and went on, "I doubt that will happen. And I have reason to expect that when he's gone, I shall have the disposal of that property for his heir. I assure you I shall only sell it to people who plan to put up a substantial house. Property in nice villages like Far Wychwood is valuable, and becoming more and more scarce. So we can both look forward to an improvement there in the near future."

Archie had progressed from restlessness to desperation. He was twisting himself around, trying to find a way to slip through his seat belt. I retrieved his rabbit and got ready to beat a retreat, to Eleanor Coleman's evident relief.

"Delightful to meet you," she said, raising her voice over Archie's howling. She hurried to hold the door open. "If there is ever any problem with the cottage, do let me know. I can recommend the best repair services in the area."

Who no doubt give you a nice kickback, I thought, as

we made our conspicuous way down Cornmarket, Archie screaming lustily. I decided I didn't like her much after all. Her greedy anticipation of George's demise was just as unpleasant as Arthur Crocker's indifference. And, although I did love my cottage, the way she'd unloaded it on me left a slightly bad taste.

Archie screamed when I strapped him into his new car seat and kept on screaming until I got the car onto Banbury Road, where Peter had told me I would find car dealers. When we picked up some speed he gradually sank into a trance, the way babies always do in moving vehicles.

Bringing him had been a major mistake, I realized as I signed a check for more than the little blue Cortina was worth, at the first dealership I tried. He had come out of the trance as soon as we were stationary, shrieking and struggling while I tried to inspect cars, and the salesman had cheerfully assured me he couldn't take a penny less than the sticker price. He wouldn't have been worth his salary if he hadn't recognized that he was dealing with a desperate woman. At least he was nice enough to accompany us to the rental-car company, driving my new car for me.

Back at the flat, I fed Archie and put him down for a nap. He had worn himself out and fell asleep right away. But in barely an hour he was up again, ready to spend the afternoon running and climbing and falling and banging. After a while, I began to cast longing glances at the television set.

It wasn't yet four o'clock, and I was stretched out on

the bed, watching him dismantle his father's sock drawer, when I heard the door open and Emily's voice call nervously, "Mother?"

Archie ran to her and she picked him up for a kiss as I came out of the bedroom.

The expression on her face told me how exhausted I must look.

"I'm fine," I declared quickly. "We had a great time."

"Why isn't your car in the parking lot?" she asked me as we followed Archie's meandering path toward the kitchen.

I told her about our day, and she frowned.

"You took him to all those crowded places? But I told you—"

"For goodness' sake, he needs some stimulation! He soaks up new experiences like a sponge. You should have seen how he enjoyed the wind."

"And that's another thing, that cold wind—"

"I thought you'd be out until seven," I jumped in.

"The patient cancelled. They often do the first time, they lose their nerve, but I think she'll be back. And now you're here, I agreed to take another group. You won't mind watching him one more day, will you?"

Of course I agreed, but while I drove home every muscle in my body was arguing with me.

When my cottage came in view I felt a homecoming warmth. It was actually a good thing Eleanor hadn't warned me about George's place. I might have lost interest and never known Rowan Cottage, the only place I'd ever felt I could make a home just for myself. *Would* make a home, I corrected quickly. The only thing I had to work on was evicting Quin. His ghost was not going to move in here with me. If I let that happen, I would have no place left to run.

Parking by the hedgerow, I heard the sharp slam of a door. I glanced across the road and caught a flash of movement behind George's place. Then I made out what it was—a person, or at any rate a dark, bulky form was running from the cottage into the woods.

I got out of the car. The figure was gone now, disappeared among the big trees. It occurred to me that I should go over and make sure George was all right. But I quailed at the idea of being attacked again.

Only then did I remember I'd meant to ask Emily for the phone number that would send Social Services out to deal with the Crocker problem. I'd forgotten all about it. I was annoyed with myself, but much too tired to put up with George right then. He had made it clear he didn't want me, and I hadn't come clear across the ocean, I grumbled, to spend my time fussing over somebody who repaid me with attempted assault and battery. I'd ask Emily in the morning—

With paralyzing suddenness, the interior of George's cottage became as bright as the sun at midday. I heard a rushing noise, and the door burst open. Smoke poured out, far faster and thicker than it had before, curling around the weeds in the front garden.

I didn't stop to think. I ran to the door. The smoke blinded me and threw me into a spasm of coughing. I saw flames, not rising from the stove this time, but from a spot on the floor between me and the table. Then I caught sight of the old man. He lay sprawled on his stomach by the back door.

As I got inside the flames shot under the table, following a straight line toward that still figure.

The heat kept knocking me back. I turned sideways, threw my whole body against it, and finally reached him. When I stooped to take hold of him, my hand hit against something lying on the floor beside him, a searing piece of metal. I jerked my hand back, and saw dark blood all over my fingers. I squinted through the smoke. It was the brass lamp. Blood covered it, smoking hot.

I slipped my hands under his shoulders. He didn't move when I screamed into his ear. I never considered whether I could move him, I had the strength because I had to have it. I started dragging his dead weight out the back door, but before I made it out a tongue of fire, sharp as an arrowhead, slashed my right arm.

I went on, backwards, kicking the door open, pulling on him until I didn't feel the heat any more. We were in clean air, under trees. I dragged him as far from the cottage as I could, and when I couldn't go any farther I dropped him in the weeds.

Then, for the first time, I saw his head. The back of it was a mess of blood and broken bone. Nausea swept over me.

"Oh, God, George," I gasped, "I'm so sorry, I'm so sorry!"

His left hand made a sudden spasmodic movement, and I thought I heard him moan.

"It's Catherine." I sank down beside him. "Can you hear me?"

I turned him over, and cradled his gory head in my lap, forgetting about being sick. I hadn't thought he could be alive with such a head wound, but he was. Faintly, somewhere behind the roar of the fire, I began to hear shouting and footsteps.

"It's going to be all right," I told him. "People are coming to help us. Just hold on!"

His eyes were closed. I laid my finger against his neck. There was nothing, then a pulse, thready, irregular. I thought it was gone, but in a few seconds it fluttered again. And I realized that he was trying to speak. I held my ear just above his mouth.

"What, George? What is it?"

His breath barely stirred my hair as he whispered, "Jimmy—Jimmy—"

"What about him?"

"Jimmy—church—"

He rubbed his head back and forth in agitation. After a minute, his eyes flashed open and focused on my face. Shocked, I gasped and pulled away involuntarily. He wanted desperately to tell me something, and I couldn't understand. I bent over him again and caught one more word.

"Malkin—"

"Malkin's gone, George," I said gently. "You mean Muzzle, don't you?"

I glanced back toward the inferno, the fire-wind eating the bushes by the back wall now, blowing the stones off Malkin's grave. If the black cat had been trapped inside the house—

"Muzzle's all right, George." I realized I was sobbing.

His eyes closed again, and this time when I felt for a pulse, I didn't find one.

Old though he had been, George Crocker had died before his appointed time.

CHAPTER SEVEN

I still don't remember what happened between the moment when I knew George was dead and the moment I looked around and saw my own sitting room, the table lamp softly glowing, a small, unthreatening fire dancing in the fireplace, and Fiona Bennett sitting opposite me, looking worried.

I was on the flowered sofa with my feet up, wearing my flannel nightgown, my bathrobe, and slippers. Fiona was in the wing chair, on the other side of a low table that had been up in the bedroom the last time I'd seen it. When my eyes focused on her face it broke into a smile, and she got up and bustled out of the room.

Something was hurting me, rather badly. It was my right arm, I realized as my powers of concentration slowly returned. I looked down and saw an irregular area of raw, oozing skin just above my wrist, with three or four bubbly blisters on its surface.

I cried out involuntarily. Fiona was back in a second, setting down a tray that held the fat brown teapot she'd left on my doorstep, along with a pitcher of cream, a sugar bowl, and two cups.

"Yes, it is rather a nasty burn," she said, "but not to worry, Dr. Barry's on his way. I know it hurts, only I don't like to give you aspirins or anything until he's been." She patted my cheek. "I've been so concerned since we found you, because you were so unresponsive until now. You can't know what a relief it is to see you taking notice."

Then memory flooded over me. I gasped, and put my hand to my mouth. The skin around it stung, although not nearly as badly as my arm.

I had been burned, then, in the fire at George's cottage. And he was dead. In a flash, I saw his gaunt face staring up from my lap, the terrible intensity in his eyes the last second before they finally closed. I put my hands over my face.

"It's all over now, dear," Fiona murmured. She had come to sit beside me and put her arm around my shoulders. "I want you to have a cup of this tea, strong and hot, with two spoons of sugar, that's the best thing for shock. I brewed it up, so it's properly made, none of those tea bags."

She added some cream to the cup and handed it to me. It was the color of terracotta, and it was delicious, if sweeter than I would have made it. Before it was all down, I did feel steadier.

"George—" I began. And stopped, knowing what she would say.

"They took him to Oxford. Poor old George, after such a long life he should have died in his sleep, shouldn't he? Still, nobody could say he didn't have a good innings."

"Somebody killed him, Fiona."

She looked startled.

"We assumed he fell in the dark and hit his head."

"No. He was lying on his stomach, and the whole back of his head had been knocked in. There was a big brass lamp on the floor beside him, and it was covered with blood." I started shivering as the images came back into my mind.

"Don't think about it. It will all be sorted out. Have another cup of tea."

"I should have done something! I should have got the people from the social services there sooner, but I kept forgetting to call them. He was afraid of something, I could see that, and I didn't take him seriously. If only I had, this wouldn't have happened."

"You're not to talk like that," she scolded gently. "You did far more for that old fellow than anyone in the village was willing to do, even those of us who'd known him all our lives. Come along, drink that tea, and let's hear no more nonsense."

As I sipped slowly at a second cup of tea, I became conscious of a lot of noise outside; a roaring sound, people shouting, and vehicles coming and going. I could see flashing lights through the drawn curtains at the front window.

"Is the fire out?" I asked.

"Yes, finally. But the cottage was destroyed. Just parts of the walls left standing. It was an awful eyesore, but I suppose a new owner could have made it over into something livable. You can hear the hoses, they're still watering it. I think the whole village is out there watching."

"And you brought me home and—" I waved a hand at my night-clothes. "Thank you, Fiona."

"You don't remember? Enid and Henry helped me to get you over here. You couldn't walk very well. She and I cleaned off the worst of the soot and helped you to undress, just down to your smalls, and get into those things. We put the clothes you were wearing into a polythene sack for the dustman, they were all soaking with— Well, and then Enid left me to it and went back to watch the fire brigade."

I winced and closed my eyes again. The pain in my burned arm was getting worse, making it hard to concentrate on what she was saying.

"How can these things be happening?" I said. "Two men have been *murdered* in this village, Fiona."

"My dear, what a thing to say! I'm afraid you're rather going off at half cock. The fellow in the churchyard was certainly not one of our people. We all agree he must have been killed in one of those crime-ridden cities and just brought here to be dumped. Where could a villain find a better place to conceal a corpse? And as to George—well, your memory's not going to be at its best just now."

"You don't believe me!"

"Let's not talk about it any more. How about a biscuit?"

I shook my head, irrationally angry with her for not accepting my word without question.

There was a knock at the door, and she let in the plump

little doctor. He gave me a reassuring smile and then looked me over shrewdly while he made conversation.

"I hear you are a very brave lady," he said, bending down to peer intently into my eyes. "Three-quarters of the world's population would just have run for the telephone to ring up the fire brigade. Although I can't say I approve of risking one's life so recklessly. And, sadly, to no purpose." He clicked his tongue. "Ah, well. The shock appears to have passed off, and there's no sign of head trauma. How long has it been since you were last inoculated against tetanus?"

"I had that updated right before I left the States."

"Then we'll not have that to bother about. Now, this burn on the arm is second-degree, but it's not extensive. The couple of small first-degrees on the face will heal on their own. Much better to leave them alone. I'll just apply some sulfadiazine and dress the arm, but first—" He took a pill bottle out of his bag and shook two white tablets into his palm. "Take these for the pain."

I swallowed them with some more tea.

He set the bottle on the table. "Two every four hours. They'll make you a bit drowsy, but that's all to the good. You should get as much rest as possible."

Then he started working on my arm. Every touch hurt horribly, but I pressed my lips together and stood it. Choleric as he had been quarrelling with the Reverend Ian, in his professional mode Dr. Barry was gentle, his fingers moving with practiced skill over my wound.

"I just feel so terrible that I couldn't save George," I muttered through gritted teeth.

"Don't start that again," Fiona said sternly. "Nobody could have saved him in the end. Just be thankful you weren't taken along with him."

"I know, you're right, it's pointless to dwell on regrets. But at least, I can still do something for him, because I got there in time to see what really killed him. I can make sure whoever did it won't get away with it."

Dr. Barry paused in dabbing ointment on my arm.

"Just fell," he said slowly, "stumbling about in all that smoke—that's what everyone is saying."

"No. Somebody bashed him with a lamp."

He went back to work. After a few minutes he said, "My dear lady, it's almost inevitable that patients will display some post-traumatic stress as a result of an experience like yours. After all, you barely escaped the cottage before the fire reached you. I have known many people who have been through less terrifying events, who gave quite impossible accounts of what had happened. I mean to say, you may very well think you saw this or that, but your memory of that period of time will not be very reliable."

"I am perfectly all right now, and I know what I saw!"

It was infuriating. They were treating me like a fool, just because the idea of murder in their village was preposterous to them. I didn't want to believe it either, I wanted Far Wychwood still to be the haven I had chosen for a peaceful old age. But I was not going to deny the evidence of my own eyes.

"Very well, very well," he said quickly, "we'll say no more about it. I must say, I am delighted how well you've come through this. You shouldn't have any permanent scarring. Perhaps a few slight striations on the arm, no more."

"Oh, well." I leaned back and closed my eyes, suddenly overcome by exhaustion. "Vanity isn't one of my problems."

"Of course, it would be a good idea to visit the hospital in town for a more complete evaluation," he went on. "You might think about that, but if you would rather not go, I think you'll recover nicely without a lot of tests and treatments. It depends on whether you are willing to trust my opinion, and I would not presume to influence you there."

"Donald has been in practice here since I was a child," Fiona said. "You couldn't ask for a more experienced or caring doctor."

"Thank you," he said gravely. "Now, for tonight I prescribe a hot bath to remove the rest of that soot, and a tuck-up in bed. Just keep the burned areas out of the water. Come by my surgery in a couple of days and I'll change the dressing."

Someone else was knocking at the door. Fiona admitted her husband, John, the tall, solemn Detective Sergeant I'd met at Philippa's party.

He came over to me, smiled without losing his serious expression, and said, "Good evening, Mrs. Penny. How are you feeling?"

"Actually," I replied crabbily, "I am not now and never have been 'Mrs. Penny!' Catherine Penny is the name I was born with, and I really wish everybody would start just calling me Catherine. I used to be married to a man named Freeman, and that's what he is now. A free man."

"I see." Still smiling, he sat down in the wing chair. "I didn't know any of that, of course. Well, are you feeling well enough to talk to me for a few minutes, Catherine?"

"Of course I am," I said, "but you'll probably just tell me to forget about it, the way everybody else keeps doing! Oh, hell—I'm sorry to keep snapping at you nice people, but I feel as if my nerves got burned right along with my arm."

"She is suffering some post-traumatic stress," the doctor put in, "which accounts for some of the things she claims to have seen, in my opinion. It's quite common in such cases. No doubt you've seen it as well in your police work."

"It happens sometimes," John said noncommittally.

"More often than not," the doctor insisted. I was getting more and more annoyed, he seemed so determined to convince everyone, including me, that I couldn't possibly know what I was talking about.

"Perhaps I should stay while you speak with her," he went on.

"Thank you, Donald," John Bennett said, turning his smile on him, "but I think it would go better if I spoke to her on my own. Our usual procedure, I'm sure you understand."

Fiona saw the doctor out while John turned back to me. I liked his face. Besides intelligence, it revealed a kindness and concern that made one inclined to trust him. No doubt many interviewees had regretted that later.

"Now then," he said, laying his arm across the back of the chair in a relaxed way. "I understand that if it hadn't been for you, all this might have happened three days ago."

"Not this. The house burning down, yes. But tonight it was murder."

He didn't look amazed like Fiona and the doctor, just interested.

"What makes you say that?"

"Didn't you see the back of his head? He couldn't have done that to himself, just bumping it against something!"

"It's possible, if he hit a sharp edge as he fell to the floor."

"He did not fall on the back of his head," I said. "I found him lying on his stomach."

"Ah." He sat up, increasingly interested. "Can you describe just what you saw when you went in? I'm sure the smoke was fairly thick."

"Not so thick I couldn't see. I'm sure the fire had just started—yes, that's right, I *saw* it start!" The memory of that flash of light made me jump. "I got out of my car, and I was looking at the cottage, and it was pretty dark— Oh, John, I saw somebody running into the woods behind the cottage, just before this enormous light burst inside the place, and then the smoke started pouring out."

"You actually saw someone running from the house?"

"Yes! Whoever it was must have been setting the fire, not knowing I was there."

My memory was galloping now. I forgot the pain in trying to get the words out fast enough as the images went past.

"The fire was coming from a spot by the table, not from the stove like last time, and it started racing across the floor in a straight line, right toward George."

"It followed a path?" he said, sounding surprised for the first time. "A straight line from the point of origin?"

"Yes, yes," I said, impatient with interruptions now the memories were rushing in, "and George was lying there behind the table, and that brass lamp was beside him, and there was blood all over it and all over his—"

I faltered, seeing that shattered head again.

"Slow down just a bit, Catherine," he said quietly, putting his hand on mine. "I want to be sure I understand you. The fire was confined to a straight pathway, and a heavy object covered in blood lay beside Crocker—is that what you mean to say?"

"Yes." The momentum of recollection had died as suddenly as it had begun. I was overwhelmed by exhaustion and leaned back with a sigh. The painkiller was starting to do its work.

He stood up. "I think you've done enough for tonight."

"Did you find the cat?" I asked.

"I haven't heard anything about a cat. But I'll find out."

"He was worrying about it, just before he died. Only he got it mixed up with the one he'd had before."

Once again, someone was knocking at the door. This time it was a young police constable, who saluted John smartly.

"Sorry to interrupt, sir," he said, "but I thought you'd

want to know the victim's son is outside, wanting to see you."

"Here? I thought he'd been told to go straight to the morgue to identify the body."

"Yes, sir, but what he's saying is, there couldn't be anything left of his late father but a pile of ashes, and it's crazy to talk about identifying a pile of ashes. He says he's more interested in seeing the extent of damage to the property."

John shook his head, then started to button his overcoat.

"All right," he said, "I'll be out in a minute."

"He can come in here," I said. "You don't need to stand out in the cold."

"Are you sure?" I nodded. "That's very good of you. I'll see it doesn't take more than a few minutes."

He signed to the constable to bring Arthur Crocker in.

He was not a tall man like his father. He was a little below average height, and one could tell that his luxurious black cashmere coat hid the flabbiness of sedentary middle age. He had probably been rather good-looking when he was young, but now his dark hair was thinning, probably tinted to that too-intense black, and his face was going a little slack. Few men, even in England, wear mustaches any more, I mused as I looked up at the luxuriant specimen on his upper lip. It made him look as if he belonged in a movie from the thirties. He exuded self-importance, and when he spoke I recognized the cold voice I had heard on the phone.

"I'm told you are involved in investigating my father's death?" he said to John, as if reprimanding a servant. "I should have thought the police had better things to do with their time than rush out to investigate every time a man of ninety-three finally gives up the ghost!"

"By law," John said equably, "every unnatural death must be investigated, Mr. Crocker."

"Unnatural? Ah, meaning by fire? Well, this shouldn't occupy you for long, then. My father was senile. I had a telephone call only two days ago from this woman. At least, I assume it was this woman, as she said she lived over the road from him."

"That's right," I said.

"Very well, you can ask her. She told me he had almost burned himself to death the night before. Obviously he finally succeeded, and there's an end to it."

"That is not true," I couldn't help saying, although John glanced over at me with a frown. "Your father could not have set that fire, because I happen to know he had run out of matches."

"Mr. Crocker," John intervened, "I must tell you that there are suspicious circumstances surrounding both the fire and the manner of your father's death. This witness's description of the scene strongly indicates arson. She arrived just as the fire started, and did her best to save him. I'm sure you'll want to express your gratitude to her."

Arthur Crocker only stared in amazement.

"What she saw sounds like a petrol fire, deliberately set. Thanks entirely to her, we will be able to have a postmortem performed on the body to determine the exact cause of death."

"The *body?* Do you mean to say the fire didn't destroy it?"

"No, it didn't, Mr. Crocker, although it was evidently intended to do so. This lady, at great personal risk, dragged your father out. Indications are that he had been struck on the back of the head with a heavy object. If these indications prove accurate, you can see that there will have to be a much more wide-ranging investigation than a simple death by fire would have required. I know you'll want to cooperate with us in finding out the truth."

Arthur Crocker's eyes had gone wider and wider, and his face redder and redder, as John had explained all this in his quiet voice.

"This is insufferable!" he burst out. "So I am to be delayed in selling that property, simply because this *foreigner* could not mind her own business! It is—it is—"

Apparently unable to think of a word that would adequately express what it was, he turned and strode to the door. There he met the young constable, looking over at his superior for orders.

"P. C. Bricker will escort you to the morgue, Mr. Crocker," John said affably. "We're still going to require that identification."

When they had gone, he smiled down at me and said, "You've been kept from your rest for too long, Catherine. I do thank you for allowing me to speak to that gentleman in your home. Strange chap, isn't he? Not at all relieved to be able to bury his father properly, as most people would be."

"Let's not talk about all this any more," Fiona said briskly. "I don't suppose I'll be seeing you until the small hours, love, so I'll leave a plate in the fridge."

"Are you going to interrogate him tonight?" I asked John, as she was helping me to the stairs.

"Early days to think about that. It sounds as if you're a devotee of those very involving American police dramas. Things go a bit more slowly here. Some of our people will be set to looking through the ruins for traces of petrol, or anything else suspicious. That's as much as we'll get to tonight. I may speak to Mr. Crocker again one day, if they find any hard evidence of a crime. Goodnight, Catherine. Sleep well."

Fiona ran a bath for me, and then I sent her home. Kind though she had been, I wanted to be alone now. I was getting more and more sleepy, and I hoped the painkiller would bring me quick oblivion. I didn't want to think about death any more.

I didn't want to dream, either, because this time I knew any dream could only be a nightmare in which I would see a shadowy figure bring the brass lamp down on George Crocker's head, drop a match, and run for the woods.

CHAPTER EIGHT

I woke to the phone's double rings and the beat of a rain that meant business. When I got my eyes open I could see it, slanting across the bedroom window. My watch said eight o'clock.

I curled up tighter for a few minutes but, being constitutionally unable to ignore a ringing phone, I finally got up, put on my slippers, and shuffled down the stairs, stiff and sore.

"Mom," Emily said when I picked up the phone, "are you all right? It's on the morning news, about that house across from yours burning down last night."

"I'm fine," I said. "Nothing to worry about. My house wasn't touched."

"Thank goodness! It startled me so when that house came on the screen, after I'd seen it the other day. The poor man, burning to death!"

"He didn't burn to death, I got him—" I stopped quickly, but it was too late.

"You? There was nothing on the news about you!"

I cursed my drowsy wits, but blessed John Bennett for keeping me out of the media's clutches.

"Oh, well, I just sort of pulled the old man out of the fire," I said lamely.

"Mom, you could have been killed!"

"No, no, I wasn't in any danger," I lied. "The fire was just starting when I happened along, and we were out of the house before it got really bad. It barely got near me."

The burn on my arm had started to throb again.

"I don't believe this. One night I don't call, and you get yourself into a life-threatening situation! You said you were having an early night, so we went to visit some friends who have a boy Archie's age. I certainly never imagined—"

"Listen, dear, you don't have to brood over me like a mother hen. I'm glad to know you care, but do try to have a little confidence in me. I'm not going to get myself killed because you leave me alone for an evening! I'll tell you the whole story when I come over tomorrow to watch Archie."

"Are you sure you'll be up to it, after what you've been through?"

"I'm up to anything. In fact, it will be good for me to get out and do something fun instead of lying around here feeling all sad and regretful. How is the little guy?"

"He's great. We're going over to the pediatrician in a while for his check-up, just to make it official. Right now he's taking the kitchen drawers apart. I guess that's educational. At least I hope so, it's such a job putting it all back. Look, you certainly don't have to come tomorrow if you don't feel well."

"I feel fine," I reiterated, squeezing my arm above the wound in a futile attempt to dull the pain. "But I'm going to take it easy today. I think I will lie down for a while. But I'll be there tomorrow, at eight-thirty this time, I swear."

I took two painkillers and went back to bed. The next thing I knew, a hammering noise was breaking into my lovely oblivion. I gradually realized it was someone knocking at the door. This time the clock said 11:50, and I was able to wake up more quickly.

Fiona stood on the doorstep with a thermal pitcher and a wicker basket covered by a napkin.

"I'd begun to wonder if you were all right," she said as she came in. "I've been knocking for at least five minutes. I thought, as it's almost noon, you might be rested enough to have a bite with me before I go on to the shop."

"What shop?"

We settled at the kitchen table and the smells of coffee and baked goods filled the room, making me instantly ravenous. Fiona poured coffee from the thermos into mugs, fetched milk, butter, and strawberry preserves from the refrigerator, and uncovered the basket to reveal half a dozen golden-brown scones.

"Just baked," she said. "Not the usual thing for your breakfast, of course, nor yet for my lunch, but I thought they would be nice with the coffee."

She spread butter and preserves on a scone and handed it to me. It was wonderful, soft and flaky and comforting.

"I have to thank you yet again," I said. "You are a such a good person!"

"Nonsense. *I* haven't the courage to pull somebody out of a burning building. Oh, maybe John, or somebody else who meant a lot to me, but not a stranger, as George Crocker was to you. I must say, you look most amazingly well. How's the arm?"

"It's okay just now. When it's mentioned, though, it makes its presence felt, so we'd better talk about something else. Tell me about this shop you're going to."

"Right, I own a little antiques shop over at Broadway, the day-trippers' mecca. It's quite fun. I go to the auctions and estate sales, just buying things that appeal to me, then I sit like a spider and wait for the trippers to fall into my web. Which they do, in droves."

"What a good idea! It must be the same thrill a collector gets, when you find a really good piece, but then you make money from it as well. A practically perfect occupation."

"Yes, I like it. You must come and see the shop when you're feeling better. The village itself is quite a spectacle, and I know you'd appreciate my nice old things. I handle only the best quality."

"Is John interested in antiques, too?"

"Not particularly. He's more interested in the doings of the criminal classes during the week, and his rose bushes on the weekends. By the way, I got the distinct impression that he's of your way of thinking about George's death. I could tell by the way he looked as he listened to you, and since then he's been doodling a lot, which he always does when he's on the trail of a crime. And if he's convinced, I'm afraid I must be, too."

When she left about half an hour later, I was feeling myself again.

"Now, you're to come have dinner with me this evening," she insisted, as she stood in the doorway raising her umbrella. "I'll be all on my own unless John has an early night, which would be a miracle. Spend the day resting, and come at sixish. If you'd rather not walk, I'll nip over and get you."

"A walk would be the best thing for me," I answered. "Goodness, look at that rain!"

As she ran through the downpour to her car, I saw for the first time the sad ruins of George's cottage. Nothing remained except the stone walls, and even parts of them had collapsed. The room where I had passed those two evenings with him was now just empty space, except for the rubble that littered it. Three unfortunate constables in plastic rain capes were poking around behind the yellow crime-scene tape, occasionally dropping some small object into a plastic bag.

When I looked in the mirror to comb my hair, I grimaced at the two red patches near my mouth, the first-degree burns. They didn't hurt unless they were touched, but they certainly didn't improve my appearance.

I cleaned up the dishes and put the food away. There was very little milk left from the pint I'd bought in Oxford, so I decided to visit the Cobbs' little shop. A short walk would keep me from stiffening up, and I could see how much I could count on buying there regularly.

I opened my umbrella and plodded down the road past the derelict school building, a patch of woods, and then Miss White's cottage, its front yard bordered with multicolored primroses. The next house was Cobbs', and instead of flowers their yard was filled with overflow from the shop next door, packing boxes, and burlap bags full of produce.

Five people looked up as I came in heralded by the bell above the door. That was a sufficient number of customers to fill the shop. The walls were covered with shelves of staple goods, and there was a refrigerated case of perishables at one side. Any remaining wall space was decorated with signs from the postal service about commemorative stamps and shipping prices and the correct way to wrap a package.

Louisa Barry gazed up at me with voracious interest.

"My dear Catherine," she said, "I did want to come by and see you last night, only Fiona said you weren't up to having visitors. How are you feeling? What was it like?"

"Was he dead when you found him?" Alice White joined in.

"Almost," I answered shortly. "And it was pretty awful."

Louisa quickly introduced me to Joe, the church sexton, and to a couple of young women in jeans, named Jilly and Audrey. Jilly's blond hair hung down in dreadlocks. Audrey, wearing a Grateful Dead t-shirt and a nose ring, was holding a baby nine or ten months old.

I said I was glad to meet everybody, trying meanwhile to edge closer to the counter where Enid stood with folded arms, scowling at us. Her little husband was beside her, smiling sweetly as always.

"Shame about old George," Audrey said.

There was a general murmur of regret, not all that convincing.

"Poor old geezer'd been a fixture ever since I can remember," Jilly chimed in. "Seemed like he'd always be around, Mrs.—"

"Catherine," I said firmly.

"Did he utter any last words?" Alice asked lugubriously.

They all waited intently for my answer, and seemed quite disappointed when I said he hadn't. I was definitely not interested in getting into a discussion of the possible meanings of "Jimmy" and "church," not just then.

"Outlasted any number of better men, did old George," said the sexton, a vigorous man who looked close to eighty himself. "They do say the wicked live longest, don't they? I'm sorry he went that way, but he were always a bloody-minded bugger."

"Now, Joe," Louisa admonished, "you mustn't speak ill of the dead."

"What's the good lying?" he went on impatiently. "George Crocker were always a bad hat. Look at the way he brought that light-fingered mate of his out from London or somewheres to steal Damerels' pay-money."

"With the best will in the world, Louisa," Alice said, "that can't be denied. I don't think one could find a soul in the village who would say George Crocker was a *nice* man."

"I can't wait to hear what vicar says at the funeral," Audrey put in with a giggle. "How's he going to think of any good to say about George?"

"The man didn't even know him," Louisa said tartly. "I'm sorry, I know it's not Christian of me, but I cannot stand that Ian Larribee! Coming in here and behaving as if he had a right to rule the place—he's been here no more than a year and there's more anger and ill will in Far Wychwood now than I can remember in my lifetime. And the bishop's as bad as he is! Though I suppose I oughtn't say it, I just don't know what the Church is coming to. Donald delivered a petition to his offices by hand two nights ago, and was told that the bishop believes the needs of youth have to take precedence over 'historical sentiment.' "

"Sucks, that," said Jilly.

"That's exactly what he called our arguments," Louisa went on, " 'historical sentiment!' Which shows that to the present Church leadership, it's quite acceptable to have a horrid ugly building where a churchyard cross has always stood, and the cross stuck off in back of the churchyard where it can't be seen without organizing a search-party."

"Thinks we've youth gangs running amuck here, I shouldn't doubt," Joe scoffed. "There's only that handful of young cockerels, that Rupert Damerel and his mates, and they're off to the city when they want to make trouble. They never bother nobody round here."

"Was you going to buy something, then?" Mrs. Cobb finally growled.

"Yes, indeed," I answered with relief, as her voice parted the little group like a scythe. "I need a quart of low-fat milk and a loaf of bread, whole wheat—you know, Hovis. And some canned soups to keep on hand, let's see, three of the oxtail and three of the vegetable."

"You mean that semi-skimmed milk?" Enid said, wrinkling her broad nose as if she smelled something offensive. "We'd not stock that muck if we *were* to sell milk—which we don't."

"Everyone has the milk delivered, you see," Alice told me. "What you must do is put in your order with Mick Jenkins, the roundsman. He'll bring it round every morning at five o'clock."

"I'll have a word with him, if you like," Enid said, "and tell him to add you to his rounds. What will you be wanting?"

"Oh, just a pint of the low—I mean, semi-skimmed, if it's going to come every day," I said happily. "How nice to have the milk brought to your door! We used to get it that way when I was a child, but it's only a memory now in the States."

They murmured in amazement at that, except for Enid, who stuck to business now she had me buying.

"What about a nice chop? I get an order fresh every morning, and there's four left now, cut extra thick."

"Oh, she's going to dine at Fiona's," Louisa said. "You'll do well there, my dear. Fiona's a first-class cook."

It was amusing to see how rapidly a person's movements became known in a village, I thought as I sloshed back up the road to heat some of the soup I'd bought, and then take another pill for the pain in my arm. I did hope I could stop dosing myself soon, because it made me so sleepy. I curled up on the sofa and slept away most of the afternoon, mercifully dreamless.

The rain was just "mizzle" when I set out for Fiona's at quarter to six. I wore slacks, feeling sure she was not a dressy person. She met me at her door in jeans, a Guernsey pullover, and bedroom slippers.

The Bennetts' cottage was not an old one like mine. It was in the style of the twenties or thirties. The front garden had a relaxed, slightly out-of-control look. It was filled from wall to wall with dormant rose bushes.

"Those are John's bit of a hobby," she said as she took my coat. "He seems to find a Sunday afternoon pottering among the roses soothing. And of course, soothing is what one wants after a week of road deaths and malicious woundings."

"Will he be here later?" I asked.

"I've no idea," she said with a laugh. "A policeman's wife's lot is not an easy one. Dinner always has to be something that will keep, and usually one eats it alone."

The sitting room was like the garden, comfortable and a bit messy. The upholstered furniture was set off by some really choice antique pieces, no doubt the pick of those auctions and estate sales she'd mentioned.

She had lit a fire and set a decanter of sherry with two cut-glass goblets on the low table in front of the sofa.

"Have you heard, the bishop is going to let Ian move the cross?" I asked her.

"Oh yes, I was there with the rest of the 'reactionaries' night before last. And there was quite a showing of villagers on our side. Donald Barry was beside himself, which I don't think the bishop appreciated. He's a modernist, though not as bad as Ian. But one could tell he was impatient with arguments from historical or aesthetic perspectives. Donald simply has to recognize that there's nothing more we can do."

"What a shame," I sighed. "Oh, well. It will make the churchyard less beautiful, but at least they're not talking about getting rid of the cross, only moving it."

She shook her head. "There are those of us who think this is only a first step. Here, let me pour you a sherry. It's not to be compared with Philippa's, but it's quite passable."

Our dinner was excellent, loin lamb chops breaded and cooked in butter, with a marvelous sauce on the side that I had never tasted before.

"It's Reform Sauce," Fiona told me, "supposed to have been invented by Queen Victoria's chef after he moved on to the Reform Club in London. Rather a nice thing, isn't it, to be remembered after more than a hundred years for a sauce?"

"I love it. Will you give me the recipe?"

"Of course I will. It has garlic, little bits of carrot and onion and ham, some red wine and meat stock, red currant jelly, and a lot of spices. I'll put it down in writing later."

The richness of the sauce called for simple accompaniments. We had a tossed green salad, little roasted potatoes, and runner beans. She had baked a loaf of bread, too, full of all kinds of nuts and grains.

"There you are," she said, "a very British kind of meal."

We sat talking afterward for about an hour before John came in. The shoulders of his macintosh were wet, and he shook out his tweed cap before laying it on an eighteenth-century pie table.

"I hope I've made it in time for pudding," he said after he returned Fiona's kiss. "What are we having?"

"Only apple tart," she answered, on her way back to the kitchen.

He sat down opposite me, smiling.

"Have you enjoyed your meal, Catherine?" he asked. "Though given Fiona's skills, I hardly need ask."

"You're right, she's a great cook. Too bad about the apple tart, though."

He looked puzzled.

"You said you were hoping for pudding."

At that, he laughed aloud for the first time since I'd met him.

"You've got that a bit wrong, I'm afraid. 'Pudding' over here means anything that comes directly after the meal. A tart, a cake, a trifle—it's all 'pudding.'"

"Familiarly known as 'pud,'" Fiona added as she came in with a set of pretty silver plates and spoons, then bustled back to the kitchen.

"Too confusing! Maybe I need a course at Berlitz if I'm going to be living here. Wasn't it Churchill who said that thing about England and America being two nations divided by a common language?"

"Shaw, I believe," John said, with the usual British air of embarrassment at correcting another's mistake.

Fiona came back with a deep-dish apple tart which she set down on the table.

"I'm so glad you got home before I left," I said to John. "Have you learned any more about the George Crocker case?"

"Not much, other than the fact that you were quite correct. He was murdered."

The tart smelled delicious, but I couldn't look at it for a minute or two. Of course I had known the police would conclude I'd been right, but hearing the official word made me queasy.

"Your account told us what to look for," he said, dishing up a serving of tart and passing it to me. "Postmortem showed the cause of death to be that blow to the back of the head. If you'd been a few minutes later, the fire would have incinerated the body along with all the other evidence, and we should never have known about the head wound. Bits of twisted brass were found in the ashes, too deformed to tell us anything, but your having seen blood on the lamp certainly indicates that it was the weapon. Most conclusive of all, there was evidence of petrol."

"I wish I'd been wrong," I said. "I wish— Oh, well, it's no use wishing to do the past over. I ought to know that!"

"You must comfort yourself, Catherine," he said quietly, "with the knowledge that you are the one who set the investigation in motion. Because of you, George Crocker will have justice."

We poured cream over our bowls of tart and ate in silence for a little while.

But I couldn't help finally blurting out, "It's obvious, isn't it, who the main suspect will be? The person who left him alone out there and told me he *wished* someone would murder him. That son he loved so much, and trusted more than anybody, the poor old fool!"

"We've not concluded anything as yet," John said. "Arthur Crocker's not a very likable fellow, I'll grant you, but he is a respected professional man with no history of violence. Although we will be speaking with him about his movements yesterday afternoon, there's at present no real reason to suspect him."

"Have you found out any more about the other murder victim—that skeleton in the churchyard?" I asked.

He shrugged. "That appears to be a dead end. He doesn't match any of the missing persons on file at the Yard. They're still processing what little DNA they could get from the bones—but the fellow seems never to have been missed by anybody, so I'm sure it won't be long before he ends in the open-case file and we move on to something more promising. Excellent pud, Fiona," he said with a smile.

Between the news about George, and the thought of a man who had died without anybody ever missing him, I was ending the evening in a state of mild depression, when John said as I got ready to leave, "Oh, by the way, our chaps searching the ruins did see a black cat lurking about. I don't know whether it was Crocker's, but when they approached, it fled into the woods, moving like a streak of lightning, one of them said."

"That sounds like Muzzle," I said happily. "He can definitely move fast when he wants to. I suppose he's surviving on mice and birds. I don't think he'll ever let himself be caught. He's an ugly, bad-tempered old thing, but I wish I could help him."

"Very much like George Crocker himself," said Fiona, and she gave me a hug.

CHAPTER NINE

When I woke the next morning, the rain had ended and the world had burst out in spring colors. The view from my bedroom window was like a watercolor, the woods touched with a delicate haze of new leaves, the fields dotted with white puffs of sheep as the blue sky was with cumulus clouds. It might be only a "sunny interval," as the English forecasters always put it, but it certainly raised my spirits.

I hurried through my oatmeal and coffee. My aches and pains were gone, and even my arm wasn't bothering me too much. I was sure I saw some spots of yellow and purple in the back garden. I longed to go out and see what kind of flowers they were, but I had to get to Emily's by eight-thirty as I had promised. In this lovely weather, I could walk there along the towpath that follows the Thames, which for some reason is called the Isis while it drifts through Oxford.

When I opened the front door I found a little glass bottle waiting on the doorstep, my first pint of milk from Mick Jenkins. I tucked it into the fridge, happy to know there would be one there every morning from now on.

I remembered the lane Quin and I had followed to the river, just opposite the village shop. The towpath, peaceful and overgrown, ran beside the water through fields and coppices, under ancient stone bridges and through wooden weirs, all the way to Oxford. It was so early that the birds were still chorusing, but the college rowing crews were already out, sharing the Isis with big white swans.

We had walked there every evening on our first visit, once or twice on the second one, when our silences didn't feel companionable any more. The one time we had really talked, it had been about Emily, remembering the school soccer game when she'd made the deciding goal, the ballet class where he had taken those charming pictures the year he'd gone in for photography, senior prom night when we'd sat up tensely playing Scrabble until she got home at four in the morning.

"You know how great it's been, Kit," he'd said in a voice full of misery that only bewildered me. "You know how much happiness you've given me all these years."

"Of course I know," I'd said. A night bird had called from a tree beside the water, and now in my mind I heard its brief music again. I'd brushed my hand over his cheek. "I've been happy, too, you know."

I was trying hard to understand what he really wanted to tell me. It seems strange, looking back, but I trusted him so completely then that the true situation never even occurred to me.

"Whatever's wrong," I'd said, "it will blow over." I longed to hold him but I could tell he didn't want me to. "We've been through a lot together. We'll get through this, just like the rest."

He'd stared down at me for a minute, then turned and strode away quickly toward the weir without looking back.

Less than two weeks later, back in New York, he told me he couldn't fight any longer against his love for another woman.

"You see," I said, when Emily opened the door to me at eight-twenty, "I can be on time."

As soon as Archie saw me he disappeared into his room and came staggering back with the peg-board and hammers. He rejected hugs and kisses, squealing urgently until I sat down to bang with him.

Emily made futile attempts to get his attention, pointing to me and repeating, "Granny, Granny!"

"Oh, I don't know about 'Granny,'" I objected. "It makes me feel about eighty-five. How about 'Nana?'"

"All right, Nana, Nana," she said. The baby paid no attention. "You know, Susan and Jeremy's boy is saying all sorts of words, and he's two months younger than Archie."

"Darling, he's just not ready yet. You've made sure there's nothing wrong with his hearing or intelligence, so just relax and wait."

She said nothing, but didn't lose her worried frown as she watched him. After a few minutes she turned it on me.

"I knew you were fibbing yesterday," she said. "You *did* get hurt. That bandage on your arm is enormous, and there are red spots on your face. Tell me what happened."

I told her about the murder as we followed Archie around the apartment, and she clicked her tongue in consternation all through. At eight-fifty she kissed us both goodbye, with one last admonition.

"I left the pushcart by the door so you can take him to the playground if you want to, but don't keep him out for more than an hour. And I'd really rather he didn't spend time in places like used-car lots. That's not exactly—educational, is it?"

"*Everything* is educational," I retorted to the door, after it had closed behind her.

Archie followed his previous method of operation, one fascinating experiment after another, from attacking the educational toys with the hammer to flushing them down the toilet, from dumping flour into the stove burners to eating it. In a very short time, we were on our way to the playground.

There he switched to eating sand, and hit another child over the head with his bucket, which led to a hot discussion between the mother and me. He screamed furiously when I crammed him back into the stroller and ended his fun.

After lunch, most of which I had to clean off him and his high chair, I tried to quiet him for a nap by looking at a picture book in the rocking chair. But since that involved sitting still, it held no interest for him.

I finally put him in the crib cold turkey and left him

weeping pitifully in a way he obviously found effective with his mother. When I looked in ten minutes later he was asleep, clutching Peter Rabbit for comfort.

I took my painkiller and dozed off on the sofa. Of course, he was up again in an hour, reenergized. Still dopey from the medicine, I went back to preventing him from falling off, swallowing, or impaling himself on anything available.

I finally gave up and got a puppet show on the television, but it turned out he was no more interested in sitting still before the set than in the rocker.

This was not what I had expected. His mother had been the sweetest, shyest, most cooperative of little girls, inquisitive about the world, but not in his aggressive style, full of ideas, but not determined to impose them on other people. Well, not until she was much older, I had to admit. With adolescence had come an about-face that had amazed me, although Quin hadn't turned a hair. I guess I had expected that sweet acquiescence to be her style for life, but seemingly overnight she knew her own mind about everything and met any disagreement or unsolicited advice with a sullen resentment that wounded me to the core. I didn't have it in me to stifle my opinions, while Quin coped by coolly supporting her in everything, so she had grown closer to him than to me, and thanks to his encouragement that dogmatic attitude had become part of her adult self.

But there were other parts of her personality that I cherished—she was an achiever, she was compassionate, and had chosen a career where she believed she could help people. She had the kind of idealism I remembered from my youth, and she loved her husband, her child, and, I knew, both Quin and me deeply.

And at least I'd had a really easy time with her for thirteen years or so, I reminded myself as I got there just in time to keep Archie from tipping over the television set.

When Peter came home at four o'clock I kissed him.

" 'For this relief much thanks,' eh?" he said drily.

"I'm just not at my best today," I answered defensively.

"It's also just possible," he said, "that you'd forgotten how hard it is to take care of a toddler."

"Really, Peter, that's ridiculous," I said, sinking down on the sofa with a groan.

Emily came in soon afterward, bringing take-out chicken and chips.

"I could have cooked something," I said.

"Oh, that's all right. We all love this stuff," she answered, holding a chip out to Archie. "We get it a couple of times a week."

"You don't do much cooking, do you?" I asked, careful to sound curious, not disapproving.

"Hardly at all," she replied cheerfully. "Neither of us likes doing it, so why bother, when the world is full of good take-out? I don't know anybody who does."

They invited me to stay and share it, but I was anxious to get home and rest. Walking back along the towpath, not nearly so briskly as I had in the morning, I reflected that cooking was one of the major lifestyle losses of recent years. All my co-workers of Emily's generation had picked up their meals at restaurants, take-outs, fast-food joints. They might make something for a special occasion, but home cooking as an everyday thing seemed to have died out among the young as completely as white gloves.

I had always thought it was important to cook supper every night for Emily and Quin, making everything from scratch even after a hard day of book-checks and reference questions. As time passed I had dropped the fatty comfort foods I'd made for my father and made sure my family got the nutrition they needed, according to the ever-changing scientific studies.

Of course we'd had pizza too, but it was custom-made, every Friday night when Quin took over the kitchen to construct his specialty. "Nothing beats-a Freeman pizza," he always said. I saw in my mind the three of us laughing together, the spicy smells filling our tiny apartment kitchen. I saw Emily turn to me as she had on one of those evenings, her face flushed with happiness, saying, "Nobody else's family has fun like we do!"

Before I could sink again into the morass of memory, I forced myself to concentrate on the big white swan on the river keeping pace with me, its webbed orange feet floating just under the surface of the water, now and then fanning slowly back and forth. It would be a good idea to get a book about swans—much more constructive to learn about the natural world I'd be seeing around me from now on, than to keep dwelling on things that were over and done with. He'd always put too much garlic in those pizzas, anyway.

Approaching Rowan Cottage in the twilight, I saw a

man and a woman standing amid the ruins of George's house. They turned when they heard my footsteps and I recognized Arthur Crocker and my realtor, Eleanor Coleman. She smiled, he scowled.

"You know," I called out, "the police aren't finished examining that ground. They'd probably prefer you didn't go in there."

His face reddened. "Do you mind very much not giving me your opinion as to what I should or shouldn't do?" he burst out.

Eleanor put a hand on his arm, but he shook it off.

"I was not giving you an opinion," I said. "The police—"

"I am very well aware the police aren't finished here," he broke in. "They bloody well told me so this afternoon. They are still planning to poke about in my father's garden! But let me tell you, Madame, I am now the owner of this property. Any time I wish to set foot on it I shall, regardless of what the police or any else may prefer for me to do!"

He drew himself up with the most ridiculous air of self-righteousness.

"Arthur is placing the property with me for sale," Eleanor put in. "We are just here to get an idea what kind of price it might fetch, once it's been cleaned up."

"Two days after he died?" I couldn't help saying. "I'm sorry, but—Well, I'm sorry, that's all. I don't want to interfere."

I started to turn away, but he stepped toward me. His voice went up a decibel or two per sentence.

"You don't want to interfere? Let me tell you, Madame, it is entirely due to your interference that the sale of this property will be delayed by all that police nonsense. If you had not interfered in my affairs, I could have it up for sale today!"

"He isn't even buried yet!" I retorted.

"Well, not actually today," Eleanor amended. "The will does have to go through probate, Arthur."

She moved her hand to his shoulder with an indulgent smile.

"George had a will?" I said. I couldn't picture the old man discussing his financial position with a lawyer.

"You seem to think I took no interest in my father," he said, his voice filled with phony indignation. "Well, I drove him over to my solicitors' offices years ago, before he went ga-ga, and had a perfectly proper will drawn up, something he wouldn't have had the wit to do on his best day."

"Leaving everything to you, I'm sure."

"Of course, since I am his only heir. If my sister is still alive, there's no way anyone could locate her, not after all these years without contact. So if it hadn't been for you, a brief wait for probate is all that would have held up my getting the money out of this place. Now, with the police involved, there's no telling how long I shall have to wait!"

He sounded like a spoiled child who has been told he can't have dessert until he eats his dinner. But Eleanor continued to look at him with that fatuous smile. There was a familiarity between them that I would never have expected. It made me wonder.

"You know, Mr. Crocker," I said, "somebody *murdered* your father. Aren't you at all interested in knowing who it was? I'd think that would be at least as important to you as how fast you can get your hands on his property."

"Yes, I know somebody bloody murdered him," he bellowed, "because I've had to spend the whole afternoon at the police station, being questioned like a common criminal! Oh, he was polite, your chum Mr. Bennett, and careful not to say there was any evidence against me, because of course there isn't. But I had to answer every sort of idiotic question, and to cancel appointments with two patients, because you couldn't let the old man burn along with his hovel!"

Eleanor winced. "Arthur, please."

"I shall say what I please, Eleanor. I've no cause to be afraid of this busybody!"

As I was sucking in enough breath to reply appropriately, a movement caught my eye, just outside the crumbling house wall. I glanced over and saw the black cat, creeping toward the empty space where the door had been. As soon as my glance lighted on him he stopped and crouched down, fixing me with his electric-green eyes. I knew it was Muzzle because of the chewed-off ear and those hairless patches on his body. I caught a glimpse, too, of a new, raw area on his left side. It was amazing how elated I felt at knowing George's cat was still alive.

"—outrage, that's what I shall tell them! Do they really think I'd kill my parent for the sake of his bit of back garden?"

Arthur broke off ranting when he noticed me looking behind him. He turned to see what was there.

"It's your father's cat," I said softly. "Don't move, or you'll scare him off."

Arthur stooped, grabbed up a big rock, and hurled it at Muzzle. It missed and hit the wall, but the cat was gone as if up in smoke.

"What did you do that for?" I yelled. "Your father loved that cat! What's the matter with you?"

Before he could get started, Eleanor took a firm hold on his arm.

"Come along, Arthur," she said. "We've better things to do than stand here arguing over a cat."

He allowed her to pull him toward the sleek black Bentley parked at the side of the road. She at least did give me a stiff smile and murmur, "Goodnight, Ms. Penny."

The familiar routines of making dinner calmed me. I opened a can of salmon, mixed up a couple of patties, and started them sautéing while I tossed a small salad and made a vinaigrette dressing. The whole time, I was wondering what John Bennett had learned from the odious Arthur. Did he have an alibi? For that matter, did Eleanor have one? I remembered her saying, the very day of the murder, that she didn't expect George to be around much longer. And I had mentioned to her that I would be in Oxford until evening, thus clearing the coast. As a surprisingly close friend of Arthur's, she could have passed that information on to him.

I kept remembering the black cat, too. He had looked so scared, poor thing, crouching there beside the ruins of his home. I had never been a cat lover; from childhood I'd had a succession of beloved dogs. I had never understood why people chose to have an independent, undemonstrative pet when they could just as easily have one that would worship them. But I couldn't help feeling sorry for that scruffy old tom.

While I crushed some brown bread into the bit of salmon I'd left in the can, I thought about Charlie, the mutt Quin and I had found on a Lower East Side street a few months after we'd married. He had come to us a starving, infested mess, but he had been our baby for the three years before Emily, and her reluctant companion until he died when she was eight.

I remembered the evenings at Dog Hill in Central Park, gossiping with other dog people while Charlie and his friends galloped up and down, sniffing and mouthing each other. We had been a tight little group. Several couples had remained our friends for years, even after the dogs had passed on. Quin, so far as I knew, still carried a picture of Charlie in his wallet, right next to Emily.

How could he have forgotten all that, I wondered as I crossed the road carrying the salmon can, when I couldn't seem to forget anything, hard as I tried.

There was no sign of Muzzle, although I stumbled around in the rubble making kissing noises for at least five minutes. I looked under the bushes, careful to watch out for Malkin's grave marker. I didn't see it until I was on top of it.

The fire had dislodged the rocks that had protected it and torn up the ground. A delicate white bone lay on the surface. Malkin, I thought.

I knelt down to push it back under with the edge of the can. When I started to sweep the dirt back with my hands, a metallic gleam caught my eye, the corner of something square and gold.

I pushed away the dirt and pulled on the thing, and it came out easily. It was a snapshot-size picture frame. One side had broken loose and the glass was cracked, dirt caked in the cracks so I couldn't see the picture. I put it in my jacket pocket to look at later.

When I got home I made a cup of tea and sat down to pull the picture out of the broken frame. It was an old snapshot, faded with age, stained with damp and mold. A blonde girl and a dark-haired young man looked out at me from a moment in the past, a moment in midsummer I thought, because the trees behind them were heavy with leaves. He held her close against him, and they were both smiling.

She was not a beauty but she had a great figure, a rounded bosom and hips and a small waist. *Zoftig,* as they say in New York. Her hair was short and tightly curled. She wore a full skirt and a white blouse with the collar turned up, the kind of clothes I'd worn at Cincinnati Central High in the fifties.

He was the really good-looking one, with a reckless grin and a luxuriant head of hair worn in a Presley pompadour.

I judged the picture had been taken around fifty years

ago, and when I turned it over that was almost all the bit of legible ink on the back revealed. I could make out the scrawled name, "Annie," the number "54," and nothing more.

So this must be George's Annie. Peering closely, I made out a sort of apprehension in her smile, as if she had been worried that day, or maybe scared.

In fact, the picture made me more uneasy the longer I studied it—but I wasn't sure why.

The boy had to be Arthur, he had the same arrogant air and sported the same mustache, more compatible with fifties clothes. I saw in the handsome young face the beginnings of the pompous ass I'd just been listening to. It was hard to believe he'd ever been so slender, or had such a great head of hair, but time, as they say, wounds all heels.

I decided it was the sense of intimacy between them that made me uncomfortable. In their smiles, eyes, body language, I saw a somehow excessive closeness, a kind of intimacy one didn't expect between a brother and sister.

I put the photo down. Just because I couldn't stand Arthur, here I was imagining something incestuous between him and his sister! It was probably nothing but my overactive imagination. The really strange thing was the way that picture had been buried in Malkin's grave. Could it have been some sort of funeral tribute, evidence of George's mental deterioration? But Annie, from all I'd heard, had been gone for decades before Malkin had lived with George, and Arthur had certainly showed himself no cat lover. Wouldn't George have buried something there that was connected in some way with his pet?

Maybe I should show it to the police. But what relevance could it possibly have to George's murder? I supposed, by rights, it belonged to Arthur, but I wasn't going to add even that to his loot. I laid it on the mantelpiece, to be puzzled over later.

"How are you keeping?" Fiona asked when I answered the phone a couple of hours later. "I've been off antiquing all day and thought I'd check on your progress."

"I think my arm's a bit better. I'm going to try to do without the pills tomorrow and then see Dr. Barry the next day."

"You do know George's funeral is tomorrow morning?"

"No, I hadn't heard. Well, I'll be there. What time?"

"Ten o'clock. Yes, I'm going, too. Shall I stop for you on the way, and we'll walk over together?"

"That would be lovely. I had kind of a run-in with his son this evening. He already had the agent out here to assess the value of the land. I just can't help thinking he's the most likely one to have done it. Has John told you whether he produced an alibi?"

"No, he hardly ever tells me about his work. Doesn't think it ethical, or something. They did question Arthur this afternoon, but I have no idea what they found out. Though they rang John up just a little while ago with some interesting news. They heard from this bank manager up at Manchester, of all places. He'd seen George's death notice in the papers and expected to be contacted, only he hadn't been, so he thought he ought to speak to them."

"What did he say?"

"It's extraordinary. Old George had actually bought a safety deposit box in this bank, ten years ago, right after the Damerel burglary, and it's simply full of money, at least eighteen thousand pounds, just sitting there all this time!"

"Eighteen— That's almost thirty thousand dollars."

"Quite possibly. His share of the proceeds from the burglary, of course, so that now there's no doubt he was involved. But of course, it can't be proven now, so Arthur gets the lot, providing he's not found guilty of the murder, and, my dear, doesn't that enhance his motive just beautifully?"

CHAPTER TEN

The day of George's funeral started out bright and sunny. A little British robin, smaller and paler than his flamboyant American cousins, sang from the top of a tombstone as Fiona and I walked down the path to St. Etheldreda's. Patches of violets bloomed in the corners of the churchyard and the buds of the horse-chestnut by the lych-gate looked big and sticky enough to burst open at any moment. The old cross held its ground at the edge of the empty, unmarked grave still surrounded by yellow scene-of-crime tape.

Fiona and I agreed it was a blessing, not having rain. It always makes a funeral seem sadder.

Not that there was going to be a lot of weeping over George. I had tucked a packet of tissues in my bag just in case, but none of the villagers appeared in danger of breaking down. Nor did Arthur. He came with an attractive blonde woman, I assumed Mrs. Arthur.

It brought back memories of Dad's funeral, although really it couldn't have been more different. The minister, at least, had been just as bored and preoccupied as Ian

Larribee was today. Dad had never been religious, so Joe Jr., my eldest brother, had called the only clergyman he knew, the pastor of the Episcopal Church of Our Savior, where Mother had taken us when we were children. The boys had dropped out as they had reached the uncooperative years. I'd kept going until I was sixteen, in memory of Mother, and I'd never lost a flickering ember of my childhood faith, deep inside. Quin had always been scornful of "organized religion." I remembered his funny remarks about the minister's mannerisms after Dad's funeral, making me laugh in spite of myself. He had always defused emotion with humor.

But my father had been buried in a crowded city cemetery, as great a contrast as could be from the quiet country graveyard where George would be from now on. As different as the two old men themselves, factory worker and gardener, alike only in dismissing me as a nuisance, I thought with a touch of bitterness.

After the cheap pine coffin had been lowered into the grave in the family plot, surrounded by Crockers going back to the sixteenth century, I walked back down the churchyard with Fiona and Alice White, well behind the chief mourner and his wife. They had barely waited for the coffin to hit the bottom of the hole before they were headed for the Bentley.

"I doubt he'll ever put up a proper gravestone for his dad," Fiona said as we passed the robin, still singing his little heart out.

"Yes, very mean, Arthur Crocker is," Alice agreed. "Always was, even as a boy."

"That's right, you were the schoolteacher, weren't you, Alice?" I exclaimed. "You must have taught the Crocker kids."

"Oh, yes," she said, "I saw them both grow up. Very good scholars both, although in every other way very different. It was hard for them, losing their mother so young, especially for Annie. Their father preferred the boy, and indulged him far too much, I always thought. I felt for Annie, she was a lonely girl. One could see she craved for love. But I admired her, too, because unlike so many neglected girls, she wouldn't let the boys do as they wished with her in exchange for a bit of counterfeited affection."

"Yes, very down on sex, Annie was," Fiona said.

Alice's cheeks turned pink at such frankness.

"The girl had her pride, and a very good thing that is. She was rather pretty, and so a few of the boys tried it on with her, but she'd have none of them. Do you remember, Fiona, the day Mick Jenkins actually pulled her behind the storage shed? I was on my way to intervene when he came away with a great red welt on his cheek, and Annie striding along behind him looking ready to deal with any village lad in the county. I thought, good show, my girl!"

She and Fiona laughed at the memory.

"Mick always did think himself God's gift," Fiona explained to me. "He finally succeeded in getting Jeannie Taylor in trouble, and they've proceeded to produce six more or less delinquent offspring. As for Annie, I always thought her a born old maid, for all she devoured those Cinderella-story romance novelettes. She acted as if real boys disgusted her."

"I think none of the local lads measured up to the heroes in her books," Alice said, "and she had too much self-respect to compromise for the sake of—physical things."

She was almost crimson with embarrassment now, as the conversation took this risqué turn.

"No, and she was bloody hard on any girl who did!" Fiona said. "A prig, that's what I'd call Annie Crocker."

Alice sighed. "She was what we used to call a 'good girl'—a phrase that seems to have disappeared from the language. But she was also the kind of young person who needs more than a country village has to offer, and I for one have always hoped she found what she was looking for, somewhere."

"She never came back for a visit?" I asked. "Never even wrote to anybody?"

"No, she never came back," Alice answered, "but, of course, one can't say whether her father had letters from her. He wouldn't speak of her after she left him, and since the burglary he was very much alone."

We watched the Bentley shoot away, scattering gravel.

"It's true, George's kids were nothing alike," Fiona mused. "While nobody was good enough for Annie, Arthur treated girls the way I treat chocolates—this one's tasty, but I must try that one, it may be better!"

"He was a good-looking boy," Alice said wistfully, "but I see he's let himself go rather."

I remembered the photograph I had found yesterday. It had made me uneasy the way Arthur, the Elvis-haired village lothario, was holding his sister close against him.

Could that have been the reason she'd scorned the local boys, and finally run away from home? Could the unspeakable Arthur have taken his girl-tasting that far? Maybe George had known. That would explain his hiding that revealing picture where no one would see it. But why would he hide it rather than just destroy it?

Suddenly I was anxious to show the picture to Alice and Fiona and get their opinions about it.

"Would the two of you come over to dinner tomorrow?" I said. "And John, too, if he can make it."

Alice begged off but Fiona said she'd love to come, although she couldn't speak for John. We started toward the road, and then another thought came to me.

"Since I've got you thinking about the old days," I said, "maybe you can remember something else. Was there anybody named Jimmy involved with the Crockers back then?"

"What makes you ask that?" Fiona said.

"It's something that's puzzled me since George died. He only had two last words, you know, and one of them was that name—'Jimmy.'"

They thought for a few moments and then Alice said, "Well, when Annie and Arthur were growing up, I recall three villagers called Jimmy, or Jim. The first would be George Crocker's own father-in-law, Emma's father. A very sweet old man he was, quite different from George. He was devoted to Emma's children, especially after his wife passed away and left him alone. I remember him sitting on his cottage doorstep while little Annie read to him from a book of children's stories. Old Jim couldn't read very well himself, you see. Such a charming picture they made."

"He's been dead a good fifty years," Fiona put in. "I can't imagine why George would think about him in his last moments. They never got on all that well."

"And there was Jim Atkins," Alice went on, "a troublesome fellow. Drank, you know. He and George did have a famous up-and-downer one night at a pub. But he fell off a truck and was killed—what was it, Fiona, sixteen or eighteen years ago?"

"At least that. And don't forget little Jimmy Watson!"

"Yes, he was the other one. Such a very strange boy. Always talking about spirits and the like. He was actually in Annie's class, but none of the children would play with him. Such a pity. The poor boy was an orphan, and had a clubfoot, and children can be so cruel. He used to claim he had occult powers and could cast spells, just to make himself important, of course. I'd see him many times hobbling down the road to the doctor's house to have his brace adjusted or something. Dear Dr. Barry took a great interest in him."

"Very weird, Jimmy Watson," Fiona agreed. "I've forgotten what became of him."

"He left the village, oh, near the time Annie did. Enid said he told her he'd make the people here sorry for the way they'd treated him. And one day he was just gone. His uncle, who had cared for him, had recently died, so I suppose he felt free to find a better life for himself. Like Annie, I've always hoped he did."

"What did George say about this Jimmy person?" Fiona asked me.

"Nothing. He just said the name, and then 'church,' and then he died."

"What connection could there be, I wonder?"

"None of the three was very religious," Alice mused. "Jimmy Watson, in fact, refused to go to church. The other two *are* buried here in the churchyard, of course."

"Is there anything inside the church relating to any of them?" I asked.

"Not that I've ever noticed," Fiona said, while Alice shook her head. "But then, I never was looking."

"Perhaps something is hidden in the church," Alice said, getting excited, "and George—and Jimmy—" Unable to put it together, she stopped with a puzzled frown.

"Let's take a look," said Fiona.

"Yes!" Alice exclaimed. "Yes, let's! My dear, this is so intriguing!"

We hurried back up the path, into the cool dimness of St. Etheldreda's, where we stood looking around with no idea where to begin. All that stone was daunting. If something had been concealed in its vast solidity, how could it be found, I wondered, without large-scale machinery and the callous destruction of an architectural treasure? Three ladies of a certain age, with not so much as a pocket-knife among them, obviously stood no chance.

But Fiona was not intimidated. "All right," she whispered, "the best possibility is something stuck up under a pew. I'll take the left side, Alice the right, and Catherine the choir-stalls. And don't forget to turn up the kneelers, too."

I'd never thought the undersides of choir-stalls could be so entertaining. A whole world of funny little medieval people were carved there, scowling as they held up the seats with their hands, sticking out their tongues at me, or sharing hidden kisses.

"Fiona," I called softly, "you must come and see the little people under the seats!"

She raised her head from behind a pew back. "Oh, yes, the misericords," she called back, "I know them well. When we were in the choir as schoolchildren, we had a name for each of them. Have you found anything else?"

"Nothing but chewing gum."

"No more have I," she said. "Alice—"

"Have you ladies lost something?"

The vicar's booming voice echoed off the stones and the three of us jumped up looking, no doubt, rather embarrassed. Ian Larribee stood in front of the altar in jeans and a University of Liverpool sweatshirt, smiling in a tentative way.

"Not exactly," Fiona answered. "Only we have reason to think something may have been concealed here, and so we—"

"Concealed? Here?" He raised his thick eyebrows.

"Yes, you see, George Crocker—" Alice began, but again he interrupted.

"Crocker? That old duffer I just buried? Look here, what is this, another of your quaint oldy village traditions?"

"Oh, dear," Alice quailed. "You must ask Catherine—"

"I was there when he died," I said. " 'Church' was one

of his last words. I think it must have something to do with his murder, so we thought we'd see if we could—well, find anything," I finished lamely.

The eyebrows were now drawn together over his flat, footballer's nose.

"He was undoubtedly out of his head. I'll tell you flat, you're not going to find any *clues* in my church," he said derisively. "I knew nothing whatever about George Crocker until I was asked to bury him."

"Who said you did?" I asked in surprise.

His face flushed. "Look, I'm having no scandals, no mysteries about this place, especially not now. To avoid such, maybe it's better that the church should be locked from now on, except during services."

Alice gasped. "Locked—our church? But it's never been locked!"

"I've never found villagers poking among the pews before."

"There wouldn't be something in here you don't want found, Reverend Larribee?" I asked sharply.

"Certainly not! And even if there were, it would be none of your affair. *I'm* vicar here, though no one in this godforsaken place seems willing to accept that."

"That's a strange word for a priest to use about any place," Fiona remarked.

"Not so strange, if you knew as much as I do about what goes on here after dark," he said smugly.

"Whatever do you mean by that?" Alice quavered.

He waved a hand dismissively. "Never mind. Just take my word for it that the young people here badly need help. Most of all, they need to be liberated from the obsession with the dead past that pervades this whole country, and especially holes like this."

He gestured toward the church walls, lined with stone squares commemorating those buried under the floor long ago.

"Of what use to Patty Jenkins or Jilly Carter or Rupert Damerel is a church built by a fellow who dressed in tights and chain mail, or an acre of useful ground taken up by the graves of some coves who lighted their lives with betty-lamps and had to duck out in the rain to take a leak?"

Alice sat down abruptly, her face frozen in shock at his language.

"My final aim," he went on, enjoying the captive audience, "is to take down this monument to the superstitious rituals of times past, and replace it with a new, stripped-down worship center fit for the needs of a modern, humanistic church."

He must have taken our incredulous stares for fascinated attention, because he ranted on with increased fervor.

"What's more, if all these old cottages were knocked down, the couple of hundred people taking up all this space could be replaced by a thousand at least, living in efficient, modern high-rise flats. And with the space gained we could widen the road through town into a proper motorway—then you'd see Far Wychwood join the twenty-first century!" he said with relish. "One day, ladies, one day."

I opened my mouth to protest—but what was the point? It's no good debating with a zealot, and Ian Larribee, I now realized, was just that.

Here in his church, at any rate, he held the power. With the finish of his sermon he escorted us firmly to the door, and we heard the rusty latch turning as we stood on the path.

Alice burst out crying.

"Oh, do stop that!" Fiona said miserably. "He'll never do it. He can't just wipe everything out by fiat."

She glanced at me for help, patting Alice's narrow shoulders.

"Of course he can't," I said. "He couldn't, even if he got the bishop's permission."

But I broke off, startled by the realization that the old church, at least, was pretty much at the mercy of the bishop, or of some congregation of bishops.

"Even if the government would agree to take down our cottages," I went on doggedly, "we could make such a protest they'd never get away with it. Public opinion would stop them."

But Fiona and I looked at each other with the shared knowledge that it had been done, despite protests—in Cincinnati when I was a child, in New York when I'd lived there, in London and even in Oxford. If they wanted to be rid of old things they could be, if necessary slowly, over the years, as people more and more forgot that there had ever been a time other than right now.

Easily swayed, Alice was looking more hopeful, and we smiled to reassure her. Fiona gave her a tissue, she blew her nose discreetly, and said, "How could he say such wicked things?"

Maybe because the end was closer than the beginning for me, I hated Ian's idea with an intensity that actually brought a bitter taste to my mouth. It seemed to me that wanton destruction of what lingered from the past sprang from the same mindset as murder—a belief that only the perceived needs of the destroyer have a right to prevail. It was, in both cases, the ultimate act of self-worship, the sin of Lucifer.

I felt certain somehow that just as each of us has a right to live out the years allotted to us by God, or fate, or our genes, those who lived before us have a right to be remembered, if for most of them only by the houses and churches and gravestones they left behind. And that we are obligated to protect that right. One reason I had always loved England was that so many people there understood that. But were there enough of us? Something told me that Ian and those who agreed with him, like curds in spoiled milk, were slowly rising to the top.

"How could he want to disturb this churchyard?" Alice was grumbling, mopping her cheeks as we started toward the gate. "He seems to have no respect at all for the fore-fathers of our village."

As I looked around at the mossy stones, her words re-called a poem I had studied in college, pondered for a while, and forgotten, something about "the rude forefathers of the hamlet" and "the short and simple annals of the poor." Without my shipload of books I couldn't bring back the rest of it, but I was sure I knew just about where in the *Oxford Anthology* to find it.

"Right over here," Alice went on, "are all my folk, down to Mother and Father. I'll be laid among them one day, if that awful man doesn't put some *worship center* on top of their graves." Her voice was beginning to tremble again.

"Don't worry, dear," Fiona said grimly, "it won't happen in your lifetime, nor yet in mine. These things take time."

Alice stopped and pointed to a circle of maybe twenty old markers all together under a big old tree, a little distance from her family plot.

"Those are the Davies, Catherine," she said, "a family that lived for generations in Rowan Cottage. There are none of them left here now. I have an eighteenth-century sampler given me by old Binnie, the last of them, before she died at almost one hundred. She lies over there at the far side, and near hers is the grave of a Davie girl who died, by her inscription, in 1804, only seventeen years old. Of course I don't know anything more about her, but I've always thought she must have been a sensitive girl, her epitaph is so unique and so lovely. And someone must have loved her dearly, to spend the money for the carving. It's very hard to believe there are people who would destroy such things!"

She raised the tissue to her nose again.

"Come along," Fiona said. "What you need is a nice cup of tea and a lie-down."

I lingered when they set out for home. I stepped across

the deep green turf to read the names of the people who used to live in my house. Most of them were illegible now, on some just a few letters or a date were carved deeply enough to still be read. Binnie's was quite clear, because it was the newest.

A little faded, but legible, despite the moss that had made its home among the letters, I found the stone of the Davie girl who had died young, and read her message to the future.

> Elizabeth Davie is my name
> and England is my nation
> Far Wychwood is my dwelling place
> in Christ is my salvation
> when I am dead and in my grave
> and e'en my bones are rotten
> if this you see remember me
> when I am quite forgotten

It reminded me of the man found by the cross, his name and dwelling-place still unknown, a few days' sensation who would soon, even to the police, again be quite forgotten.

CHAPTER ELEVEN

I sat down the next morning to make my shopping list for that evening's dinner. The weather was grey and chilly, so I was thinking of something substantial, like those extra-thick pork chops Enid was pushing. I wanted to serve Fiona something traditionally American, too, and scalloped potatoes came to mind as a good accompaniment for the pork. Some fresh peas and a green salad would finish off the main course, if the village shop carried such things, and I'd leave enough time to make some Parkerhouse rolls. It would have to be a simple meal, because I didn't feel up to the drive into Oxford.

Just after lunch I set off for Dr. Barry's house, following his orders to have my arm checked out.

The doctor lived in a sturdy brick house at the other end of the village, set in a large, neglected garden. Louisa let me in and took me to the doctor's office, chatting politely about the weather and how I was settling in.

It was a comfortable room, furnished in mellow old wood except for the examining table and sink which were bright steel. A massive oak desk with an armchair behind and before it stood in front of a bay window, and glass-fronted cabinets covered the upper part of the walls.

When I sat down in front of the desk a sleek, well-fed black cat slunk over to me. It rubbed its seemingly boneless body across my legs and proceeded out the door.

I waited several minutes before Dr. Barry came bustling in, clutching a bunch of papers.

"I've been drafting another petition to the county council," he said breathlessly, mopping his face with a large handkerchief. "Although the bishop has given his permission for the desecration to take place, it may be possible to prevail on them to overrule him. We can only try. I hope you will sign, dear lady, when it is finished?"

The day before yesterday I would have tried to convince him it was best to accept defeat and get on with life. But after the threats I had heard from the Reverend Ian Larribee, I couldn't say that any more. I had a feeling the cause was already lost, but maybe it was better to go down, as Dr. Barry seemed determined to do, fighting to the end for principle.

"I'll sign it," I answered. "I've come to realize moving the cross is only the first step in his plans."

"Exactly! Exactly! If only everyone could see that."

"Well, Fiona, Alice, and I do now, after the way he talked to us yesterday about turning Far Wychwood into a soulless modern suburb."

I saw too late that I was encouraging his rather alarming excitement, and tried ineptly to change the subject.

"I didn't see you at George Crocker's funeral," I began.

"I do not enter that church! Neither Louisa nor I will ever enter it again while that man is in charge!"

Seeing he had startled me, he forced a smile and lowered his voice.

"Well, well, let's see how that burn is progressing," he said.

It looked much better when he uncovered it. The flesh was a less angry shade of red and the blisters almost gone, which he said meant "the serum's resorbed." He applied a topical anesthetic and a new, less bulky dressing. Although his fingers were as skillful and gentle as the last time, I could feel the tension inside them today, like dammed water, waiting to burst out.

"Most satisfactory," he said as he taped the bandage down. "You are a lucky woman. If the flames had caught your hair instead of your arm—"

He turned abruptly to open one of the cabinets and put his supplies away.

The adjoining cabinet held rows of books behind its glass doors. Among the medical texts, I noticed a whole shelf of volumes covered in plain paper so the titles didn't show.

"What are those books?" I asked idly.

He turned with a smile. "Books about old English customs, folklore, that sort of thing. It's my hobby. Some of the subjects—Well, there are people with some rather rum ideas out here in the countryside, who might be scandalized to think of their doctor reading about such things, so I've covered them up."

"What things? Oh—you mean weird folklore, things like witchcraft?"

He nodded. "That's right—the old religion."

"It's amazing to me that some people here still believe in such things. You should have heard George Crocker. It wasn't just folklore to him."

"All that is dying out, of course, along with the old people. The folklore societies keep rushing about, interviewing them before they're all gone. I rather doubt George Crocker would have stood for having microphones pushed in his face. He'd have had the folklorists in the road on their ears." We both laughed at the image.

"You know, speaking of old superstitions, and throwing people out in the road, there's something I just remembered when you said that. The night before he died, somebody laid this circle of yew twigs on George's doorstep. When he saw it he went wild, ordered me out of the place, and said he wouldn't talk to me any more."

His smile faded. He sat down behind his desk and peered at me through his thick, round glasses.

"You saw this thing, too?"

"Oh, yes. I thought kids might have done it, you know, but he took it really seriously. I can see it means something to you, Doctor. Come on and tell me."

He waved his hand dismissively. "A common motif in witchcraft—a circle of yew left on the doorstep—is a message. If the recipient tells about something he knows, he will be killed. It's found in any number of books on the old religion."

I was struck by a new possibility. George had said there were witches around, and I had laughed at him. What if he had actually known of some crazy cult operating in Far Wychwood, maybe harming people, killing livestock, or the like? Could that have been the reason for his murder?

"What a horrified expression, dear lady!" Dr. Barry said, smiling again. "You must remember, these are the beliefs of a religious system that was stamped out long ago by the Christian priests. Although it lingered as a clandestine thing until this century, it can only be of antiquarian interest now."

"But that's not quite true, is it? I've read in the American tabloids about people practicing witchcraft, even satanism. The Nightstalker, out in California, have you heard of him?" He shook his head. "There were some kids in New York, too. I read about them in the *Daily News*. They sacrificed dogs and cats, and finally they killed one of their members and left pentagrams all around his body."

"Well, yes, the tabloids here love those stories, too. I must admit that there are people who *claim* to practice Wicca. For the most part they are a lot of publicity seekers. There was only one authentic case I can recall, a man killed in Lower Quinton, in this very county, as recently as 1945. The case was never really closed, although the renowned Fabian of Scotland Yard was brought in on it. They finally resorted to an antiquarian, who figured out that the circumstances perfectly obeyed the rites of Wicca. He had been impaled by a pitchfork through the throat, pinned to the ground so his blood would flow into the soil, to nourish it—"

His eyes were alight with the passion of the true enthusiast. It made me a little uneasy. When he noticed that, he laughed abruptly, spreading his hands wide.

"As an antiquarian myself, I find these stories fascinating," he said. "But I assure you, if any pagan rituals had been occurring in this neighborhood, or any trappings found in the witch-wood, I should have heard about it. The incident of the yew circle will have been a childish prank, just as you said. Crocker was the sort of old hermit they like to make game of, and everyone knew he was afraid of witches. The children nowadays learn about such things in their folklore classes at school, you know."

He must be right, I thought, as I walked home under an increasingly threatening sky. The whole idea was too far-out. It was like another of those tabloid stories—"The Witches' Revenge!"

I stopped at the village shop and, under Enid's unsmiling gaze, picked out chops, potatoes, and a bag of frozen peas. Obviously I was going to have to go into Oxford when I wanted fresh produce.

I bought half a dozen cans of cat food, too. Before I started making supper I opened one and went over to leave it beside the burned-out building. I didn't see George's cat, but as I was leaving I heard a rustling in the weeds that I hoped was him.

I thought my supper came out very well, and Fiona said she did, too. I breaded the chops and cooked them in olive oil, with a sprinkling of Italian herbs. The scalloped potatoes were a great success, since she had never tasted them before. I cooked up the peas with a few pearl onions left from my Oxford shopping trip, and for pud I made the chocolate mousse I'd been serving company since my earliest days in New York.

It was surprising how quickly Fiona and I had developed a comfortable friendship. Something about our attitudes toward life and senses of humor just seemed to mesh. I already felt as close to her as I had to American friends I'd known for decades.

While we ate, she told me about her childhood on a farm just outside Far Wychwood, with a sister who still lived nearby and a brother who had emigrated to Australia. The farm was a housing development now. Her parents hadn't lived to see that, and Fiona had tried to prevent it, but the money had been more than her siblings could resist.

"I can't tell you what a beautiful place it was," she said wistfully. "John and I would have lived there and kept it as it was, but we were outvoted by the others. I can't bear to go past it now. I always take a more circuitous route into town."

She hadn't been able to afford university, but she had studied on her own and acquired an impressive knowledge of antiques. They were her second passion, after John. She loved him without reservation and, after twenty-eight years of marriage, she worried every day while he was at work. I understood why when she told me stories of a couple of his narrow escapes and of the time, three years before, when he had been so seriously wounded he'd almost died.

"It's the price I pay for falling in love with a policeman," she said. "But I've run on about myself long enough. Tell me something of your background. Only what you're comfortable telling, of course," she added quickly.

What was I comfortable telling? Not much these days, I decided.

"Well, my parents are both dead, too," I said slowly. "I had a better relationship with my mother, but she died when I was pretty young. It would have been nice to have had a sister, as you did. I was the only female in the family, so I felt kind of—I don't know, alone."

"Yes, I can't imagine growing up with no women about."

"I went to New York when I grew up, looking for something, I didn't know what exactly, but I did find a good life there until—it ended. I took early retirement from the library system, not only because I wanted to get away from places that held bad memories, but because I knew I wouldn't feel at home in the totally electronic library of the future they were working toward. It took me a while to reconcile myself to the computerized catalogue. I didn't want to be around for the E-books, instead of real books with their own smells and textures and scribbles in the margins."

"Goodness, is that what they've got planned for us? I quite agree, a wall full of books of different sizes and colors is an entirely different thing from a wall of computer discs! That's one good thing about having my own business. No disc or database will ever replace the nice old things I sell."

"We don't sound very progressive, do we?" I said. "Do you think we could be getting old?" We laughed companionably.

Soon John was knocking at my door. Fiona let him in and kissed him enthusiastically. He sat down wearily in the green baize chair.

"I saw your note on the fridge," he said. "I knew I'd be too late for the main course, but I was hoping there might still be some coffee and chat going."

"Not only that, there's chocolate mousse," I told him.

I went to the refrigerator and got out pudding for all of us, and poured the coffee.

"Fiona's been telling me about your blood-curdling run-ins with the bad guys," I said. "I'd have thought Oxford would be a very safe place to be a policeman. Obviously I'd have been wrong."

"Oh, my, those old stories," he said with a smile. "Fiona shouldn't repeat them, she always makes me sound impossibly heroic, and really, one needn't be a hero to get shot or knifed. Not in these times. No, Oxford is part of the modern world. That's why we live out here. It's a great relief to come home to the quiet of a village every night. Although—" He paused and shook his head, obviously thinking of our murder.

"Have you learned any more?" I said imprudently. "What happened with Arthur Crocker yesterday? I don't suppose he actually broke down and confessed?"

John's face grew solemn again.

"I'm really not supposed to discuss all that, you know," he said. "We can't let things get about."

"Come along, darling," Fiona said, "you know we'll keep our mouths shut. Did he at least have an alibi?"

"Yes—although perhaps not a very satisfactory one," he admitted. "He said he was with a patient at the time the fire began, a woman who had broken her glasses and had to be examined, since she hadn't her prescription with her. The whole session took more than an hour, which covered all the time in question."

"And does the woman back up his story?" I asked.

"We were unable to find her. She was an American, on a solitary tour of Europe. It was her last day in England, and she's now somewhere on the Continent, where we have no way of tracing her."

"Didn't you get her name?"

"Of course, but, you see, she was not expecting to return home for another three months. The woman does exist, and was in Far Wychwood, and left the day after the fire. We've checked all that out. In fact, she had been in to see Dr. Crocker a few days before, to have the earpiece replaced on the glasses.

"At any rate, his receptionist, a Ms. Voile, supports his story. She showed us the entries in her log for both appointments. That's as far as we can go, although I'll admit it's a bit unsatisfactory."

"The word I'd use is suspicious!" I said. "Can't you go to the American Embassy and have this patient traced, or get in touch with her family to find out where she's gone?"

Now he was irritated. "*I* can't do anything, Catherine. I'm not the Chief Inspector, only a lowly Detective

Sergeant. As I understand, the woman is just traveling as the mood strikes her. She left no forwarding addresses. As we have no grounds for suspecting Dr. Crocker at the present time, we have no legal right to harass him or his patient."

"But what about the money?" I asked indignantly. "Arthur is known to like his luxuries, isn't he? Look at that car, and that cashmere coat he wears all the time! He couldn't wait—maybe literally, couldn't wait—to inherit his father's property and sell it, so wouldn't eighteen thousand pounds sitting in the bank have made his mouth water even more?"

"He denies knowing of its existence."

"Well, he would, wouldn't he? And that alibi is so full of holes! The receptionist could be in league with him, the log book could have been falsified, and did you look for a back door to his office? Even if the receptionist is honest, he could have left without her seeing him if there's another door. He could have told her he had something to work on and didn't want to be disturbed, and then asked her, or paid her, to back up his story."

"Catherine," he said firmly, setting his cup down, "all this is pure speculation. I am only concerned with evidence, and so far we haven't discovered any at all. We will keep Dr. Crocker on our suspect list, naturally, but there are other avenues to pursue. For example, there have been break-ins around the area, houses robbed in nearby villages, although no violence has been used prior to this. We're looking into the possibility of a connection there."

"But George didn't have anything worth stealing," I

scoffed. "Why would thieves be attracted to a falling-down hovel like that?"

"There *were* rumors of his having money about the place," Fiona put in, and I remembered the talk about it at Fiona's party.

"Still," I continued stubbornly, "isn't it much more likely that Arthur, who *knew* his father had money and property that he would be inheriting, would kill him, than some burglars who had only heard a vague rumor of money in the house? You must admit, John, that's a very logical conclusion."

He sighed. "Catherine, you seem to have some sort of personal reason to want to see Dr. Crocker as the killer." His face flushed with embarrassment. "Sorry, shouldn't speak to you like that. But I think we must all keep an open mind on the subject until there is solid evidence, and not let ourselves look at this emotionally. Now I think I have said more than enough about the case for one evening."

I could tell from his face that he meant it, so I reluctantly dropped the subject. Fiona chattered about some of the local sights and how we might arrange to go together and see them, and John began to relax. I had to admit the evening was pleasanter once Arthur Crocker was no longer part of it.

Fiona whispered to me as they left, "*Hates* being quizzed about his work."

What with one thing and another, I had forgotten that old snapshot I'd wanted to show her. It was several days before I thought of it again, and by then it was too late. Like the other Far Wychwoodians, I would never see Annie's face again.

Now I was worried that the police were losing interest in Arthur, despite my best efforts. They hadn't heard the things he'd said to me about his father, or seen his face when he'd said them.

I brooded about it while I washed up and prepared for bed. By the time Emily called, I had worked out a new plan.

"You know how you said the other day you needed new glasses?" I asked her. "Did you get them yet?"

"No, my eye doctor is booked up for the next two months, so I guess I'll just have to wait. Why?"

"Would you be willing to try a new optometrist? I have a reason for asking that I'll explain when I see you."

"Okay," she said, "I'll call tomorrow. What's the name?"

I hung up with a thrill of anticipation. If Arthur had killed his father, he wouldn't get away with it just because of a flimsy alibi. Not if I could help it.

CHAPTER TWELVE

"I rather wonder about this chap," Emily said. I was amused to notice the way Britishisms were creeping into her speech. "Every optometrist I know is booked up well in advance, like mine, but his receptionist had an eleven o'clock open on the very day I called."

I joined her in pursuit of Archie, then, as she stuffed him into his coat she went on, "Why did you want me to see him, anyway?"

"He's the son of that old man who was murdered. You know, I told you how he neglected his father? In fact, he told me he wished somebody would murder him. And now that the old man is dead, all he can think of is getting his hands on the property as fast as he can."

"Nasty," she agreed as she carried her struggling son to the stroller. "Here, you hold the pushcart while I strap him in. So, why do you want this character mucking with my eyes?"

"Because of his alibi. I want to know whether there's a back door to his office."

"Surgery," she corrected.

"All right, surgery. I'd go and inspect it myself, but he knows me. I just want you to notice whether there's a door he could have used to get out without his receptionist knowing."

"What are you going to do if there is?"

"Well—I don't know. I just want to find out whether his alibi can be disproved. The police seem to be accepting it without question."

"Really, Mom, what is this—'Cathy Penny, Private Eye?'"

"Don't be silly. But that old man died in my arms, and it seems more than likely that his son killed him. I can't just stand by and see him get away with it."

She shook her head, with one of her patronizing smiles.

"Let's go, then. At least I'll get a new pair of glasses out of it without having to wait a month."

"That's right, and I'm paying for them, and buying you a really good lunch afterward for your trouble."

We walked up St. Aldate's in chilly sunshine, Emily singing out the name of every object we passed for Archie's benefit, although I couldn't see that he paid any attention to her.

Arthur Crocker's surgery was on the High, in a little twentieth-century building tucked between a Victorian and a Jacobean shop.

I stopped at the corner. "I'll wait up at this end of the street. I don't want him to know you're with me."

"Mom, you're a riot."

I hated it when she put on that superior attitude, although I did have to admit that this was not what you might call a well-planned operation. But it was not as if I'd ever done such a thing before.

I walked Archie up and down for about forty minutes, dutifully announcing the name of everything we passed, while he gradually dozed off. Finally Emily came out, frowning.

"Let's have lunch while you tell me what happened," I said. "Anywhere you want."

"Oh, let's just go to that little place across the street, 'The Sandwich Shop.' Sounds straightforward, no extra 'p' and 'e' on the end. I don't want to cope with Archie in some posh place."

The Sandwich Shop seemed to have captured most of the local lunch-hour trade, always a good sign.

Archie was eager to meet all the people and sample their lunches, but he had hardly started on his circuit of the room when Emily caught him and fastened him into a high chair with a little bag of chocolate cookies, which focused his attention for the moment.

"That Crocker is a weird man," she said, frowning again, after we had ordered. "He actually tried to hit on me."

"No! Then he's unethical, too."

"You know how they put you in that chair with arms, and then stick that great heavy contraption with lenses right in your face, so you can't move? And then they keep changing the lenses and you read the charts and tell them when the letters are sharp—yes, Archie, *biscuit, biscuit!*— Well, he got me stuck in there, where I couldn't get up, and then he moved in really close, so I was breathing his minty mouthwash. Then I felt this furtive touch on my arm, and he muttered, in this low, supposed-to-be-sexy voice, " 'How's this?' "

"Heavens, how awful. What did you do?"

"I said, 'I'm afraid I can't tell, Doctor, as your breath is fogging up the lenses. And I didn't actually need my arm examined.' "

"Good for you! What did he say to that?"

"Nothing. He just sort of jumped away, and after that he was all business. But I wonder if it doesn't explain why it's so easy to get an appointment with him. He probably tries it on with any halfway presentable woman who comes in for glasses."

"Right, and womanizing is an expensive hobby, isn't it? He'd naturally be impatient to get George's money. What about the door?"

"Oh, there wasn't one. I hope your detective impulses are satisfied now." She raised her eyebrows at me.

We were eating our sandwiches—grilled vegetables for me and hot Brie for her—while Archie tore up his peanut-butter-and-jelly and smeared it on his overalls, when Emily glanced up and said, "There's the receptionist."

I looked toward the entrance. A young woman was coming in, pretty in a washed-out way, with long, straight brown hair, large brown eyes, and a trim little figure in a dark blue pantsuit. She noticed Emily and smiled shyly.

"Would you like to share our table?" I called quickly.

She hesitated. Then she saw Archie, and came right over and sat down.

"Oh, aren't you adorable!" she exclaimed. He granted her a jelly-covered grin. "Oh, look at that smile! What a dinky boy! I've got six younger brothers and sisters," she told us, "and I do so miss caring for them. Of course they're all grown up now, but it was wonderful for me when they were little, and clung onto me."

"This is Rose Voile, Mother," Emily said.

The girl expressed herself pleased to meet me, before going back to singing Archie's praises.

She wore a pale yellow blouse with a V-neck under her suit jacket. A gold chain hung around her neck, just down to the point of the V, with a pendant that was concealed under the blouse. Now, as she leaned over the baby, it swung out, a gold heart with a little diamond chip in the middle and some words carved around the edge. It looked familiar, but I didn't know why.

"What a pretty pendant," I said on impulse. "Can I look at it?"

"Oh, I don't know, I'm sure," she said nervously, glancing around as if someone might be watching. "I'm not supposed to—Well, I suppose it's all right really."

She held it out toward me with shy pride, and I leaned forward to read the inscription.

"My one and only love—Arthur."

I kept my excitement damped down. "Oh, I remember an old song with that title," I said, "from the fifties."

She was delighted. "That's right! It was a gift from someone who's a little bit older than me. He gave me a tape of that song so I can listen to it in the evenings when—when he can't be with me." She carefully tucked it back under her blouse.

The waitress came by, and while Rose ordered a ham sandwich I studied her mousy little face. A cloud had come over it as she'd said those last words. Unlike my sensible self-confident daughter, this girl had obviously been a ready victim for Arthur Crocker.

Emily slipped a hand down the back of Archie's overalls and then lifted him from his high chair.

"It's time this boy had a change and a wash," she said. "Back in a tick." She carried him off to the rest room.

I knew I had better move fast if I wanted to learn anything from Rose Voile. Emily would sit firmly on any attempt to pry. So I plunged in, with no idea where I was going.

"What a terrible thing about Dr. Crocker's father," I began.

The way she suddenly wouldn't meet my eyes showed her uneasiness with that subject. I was encouraged.

"But what a lucky thing he happened to be working on that patient at the time, and you were there to validate his alibi."

She ruffled up like a little bird defending its nest.

"Dr. Crocker doesn't need an alibi! How could the police think a man like him would ever hurt anybody, especially his old dad?"

She bent over to set her bag on the floor, and the pendant slipped out of her blouse again. Now I remembered where I had seen it before.

I leaned toward her, speaking more softly.

"I suppose I shouldn't say anything, Rose, but I am old enough to be your mother. I understand what you're going through. I wasn't always this old, you know. The evenings alone, the guilt, the misery of knowing he's with his wife— You see, I was once in love with a married man, too," I lied.

It was the first time I'd ever been grateful to Quin for trying to make me sympathize with his girlfriend by repeating her complaints.

I patted Rose's hand. "I remember how *awful* it was."

She snatched her hand away and stared at me, wide-eyed. I thought, "Oh, Lord, I've laid it on too thick. I've offended her."

Then she burst out crying. Her big brown puppy eyes filled and overflowed with tears that fell off her chin and stained her blouse. A string of gasping sobs seemed to rise from the pit of her stomach. People turned to look. I hastily found a tissue in my bag and thrust it into her hand. She buried her face in it as if trying to hide.

"Mother!" I heard Emily exclaim. "What are you *doing* to her?"

Rose's grief only intensified at the sight of the dinky boy gazing down solemnly from his mother's arms. I gave her another tissue.

"Oh, he's so sweet," she sobbed, "and I don't think I'll ever have one of my own! Three years he's been promising to leave her, but nothing ever changes."

Emily sat down. In a carefully controlled voice, she said, "Are you talking about Dr. Crocker?"

The girl nodded, trying to burrow deeper into the tissues.

"Rose, how can you?" Emily asked, leaning toward her. "Don't you mind the pain you must be causing his wife and children?"

"They don't have any children, and she doesn't know. And I know why he won't tell her. She's got lots of money, and I don't have *anything!*"

Archie was sitting perfectly still on Emily's lap, absorbed by this exhibition as he never was by television.

I pressed my advantage. "That's not the only lie he's involved you in, is it? I can see you're a good person. You didn't want to lie to the police about last Tuesday afternoon, did you?"

She sat up very straight and mopped her cheeks, trying to pull herself together. It surprised me that I felt no hostility toward her, after what had happened to me last year. But she was not like Quin's lover, who from all I had gathered had been the aggressor in their affair. Rose was clearly the victim here. She had suppressed her misgivings for so long that my sympathy had brought on a catharsis she was beginning to regret.

"That wasn't a *bad* lie," she said in a steadier voice. "A man like that, an actual pillar of the community, he has a right to spend a couple of hours shopping for a birthday gift for his one and only love, without people saying he might have killed somebody!"

"Well, of course he has," I agreed, vibrating with excitement. "And you know, if you explained it like that to the police, I'm sure they'd understand."

"Oh, no," she cried, drawing back. I saw my window of

opportunity sliding down. "I'd never tell the police. Artie would be so *angry* if I did. Please, don't you tell them either. If you do, I'll just say I never told you any such thing!"

"Rose," said Emily firmly, "you are in denial. You need professional help to understand why you're doing this to yourself. I'm a licensed psychotherapist. I conduct a women's group every Tuesday afternoon, and several of the participants are in situations like yours. Why don't you join us?"

Rose was definitely skittish now.

"No thank you, I don't need anything like that. I know Artie loves me. I was just feeling a bit down today, but I would never, ever betray his trust, so—"

"I know another woman who wears that same pendant," I cut in.

She grabbed it as if I'd tried to steal it.

"That's impossible," she gasped. "This is a one-off, Artie had it made specially for me."

"I promise you," I hurried on, "I saw that same pendant on another woman's bracelet."

"I don't believe you. Who are you, anyway? You're not from the police, are you, like those people on 'NYPD' who go round without their uniforms on to fool people?" She got to her feet.

"We only want to help you, Rose," I said desperately.

As she grabbed her bag, Emily took out one of her business cards and pushed it into her hand.

"If you ever decide you want something better out of life," she said, "call me."

But Rose was almost running for the door.

"She's not ready to make that call yet," Emily said as we came out into the High and saw her scurrying into the surgery down the street. "Something will have to push her over the edge first."

"Right," I said, my thoughts racing ahead. "Over the edge, that's exactly what she needs."

"You know, Mother," she said, putting on her superior voice again, "I don't approve of meddling in people's business like that. There's no telling what the consequences could be. You are a librarian, for heaven's sake, not a Detective Inspector. Promise me you'll leave the investigating to the police in future."

I meekly agreed. She was going home, as it was Archie's nap time. She wanted me to come and spend the rest of the day at the flat, but I begged off with the excuse of some shopping that had to be done.

Once she was around the corner, I hurried up Cornmarket. I was pretty sure I knew what would push Rose over the edge.

Eleanor Coleman was on the phone when I came into her office. When she hung up, she gave me the usual tight little smile, raising her perfectly arched eyebrows.

I had no idea how to get this woman where I wanted her. She was no Rose Voile to be reduced to tears by a few kind words.

"Yes, Ms. Penny?" she said with barely concealed impatience. "Is there some problem at the cottage?"

"Oh, no. Well, actually," I amended, as inspiration

suddenly lit up the inside of my head, "yes. In fact, I'm terribly upset. I just learned about Dr. Crocker's new plans for the property opposite mine. I was so relieved when you said you were going to consider my feelings, and only sell to people who would improve it, so when I heard his new estate agent planned to sell it to a commercial establishment, and such a very objectionable establishment at that, I—"

"New estate agent?" Her eyebrows went up.

"You didn't know? Then he's gone behind your back, as well as mine! This is really insufferable. George Crocker's cottage was bad enough, but to allow an autobody shop to move in right outside my front door—"

"Auto-body shop? What is an— Do you mean a place that repairs damaged cars? A panel-beating shop?"

"That's it! Panels being beaten across the road, day and night. I did not come clear across the—"

"Ms. Penny, there must be some mistake. Dr. Crocker would never go to another agent behind my back. That's impossible."

The same words Rose had used. Somehow, Arthur inspired an astonishing degree of trust in his women.

I plunged on recklessly. "He told me so himself, only minutes ago. We have to go over to his surgery and straighten it out, Eleanor. I'm sure he can't break a contract with you like this."

"Arthur wouldn't do that to me," she insisted. "We've been friends for too long." But I thought I detected a note of uncertainty. "Who is this other agent?" she demanded.

"Oh, I can't recall the name, but of course Arthur can tell you." I added a *soupçon* of indignation to my act. "I must say, I expected you to be more concerned. You did say you would help me with any problems that might come up, didn't you?"

She stood up, came out from behind the desk, then stopped.

"I've never been to his surgery. He prefers not—"

I'll bet he does, I thought.

"All right, if you refuse to help me I'll just have to speak to the authority that oversees professional ethics in this field, and lodge a complaint."

That got her going. As we strode in silence down Cornmarket and turned into the High, my anticipation was tempered by growing uneasiness. I had begun to wonder whether I could be wrong about that inscription. If it didn't read the same on both pendants, I was going to be terribly embarrassed.

Rose looked up in surprise when we came into the reception room. Before either of them could speak, I said, "This is the woman I told you about, Rose, the one who has the same pendant you have. See it, on her bracelet?"

For a moment, both of them just stared at me. Then Rose looked at the pendant dangling from Eleanor's wrist. Her eyes widened, she leaned forward to see it better, and her own pendant swung out, glittering brightly.

Eleanor crossed the room in two strides and took the little gold heart in her fingers. Rose grabbed the one on the bracelet. They stood there, reading each other's inscriptions, for a minute or so. Then, to my immense relief, Rose gave a little shriek and Eleanor rasped out, "*He* gave you this?"

The surgery door opened and Arthur walked out. Both women turned toward him. It took about three seconds for all the color to drain out of his face.

Eleanor gave a vicious jerk, detaching Rose's pendant from the chain and making her scream again. She held it out toward him. The look on her face scared even me.

"Two years!" she shouted. "Two perfectly good years of my life down the drain, believing I was your—" She threw the little heart to the floor. "No doubt you gave her a tape of our song, too!"

"Oh, Artie—" Rose moaned.

"How many other women are wearing these damned things?" Eleanor demanded, yanking off her bracelet and throwing it on the floor, too.

"He probably orders them by the gross," I said.

Arthur noticed me for the first time. "What are *you* doing here?" he demanded in a cracking voice.

"I'm here to take Rose to the police station," I retorted. "Now she realizes how you've lied to her all along, she's going to tell them she doesn't know where you were last Tuesday afternoon, aren't you, Rose?"

I was encouraged by the way her lips were tightening. No more weeping, I urged her silently, let's see some self-respect at last.

"Oh, Artie," she murmured again. Then her voice hardened. "You *are* a liar, aren't you? And you've made me a liar, too."

"Last Tuesday afternoon!" Eleanor burst in. The veins

in her forehead stood out under her careful makeup. "That was the day you said you were *almost* ready to tell your wife about us, wasn't it? Just before we made love, that was. But, no, I must give you another month or so, after all, we had all our lives ahead of us—that was after a couple of hours on the sheets! You probably came back here from my flat and did it all over again with this little scrubber, giving her the same bloody line!"

"Wait a minute," I interrupted uneasily. "Are you saying he was with you that afternoon?"

"Too bleeding right I am, and I was ready to compromise myself by admitting it to the police if necessary, I was so besotted. But of course that would never do, even if he had to make up that lame story about the American patient instead, and do you know why? I'll tell you bloody why! Because his wife might have learned about us. And I let him treat me like some cheap— You're taking her to the police? Well, I'm going along there, too. And after that I'll be on the phone to the precious Mrs. Crocker. She's going to find out all about her loving husband at last."

"No, Eleanor, darling, please," he choked out. He was pale as chalk, and sweat poured down his cheeks. "If she divorces me I'll lose everything, the house, the Bentley—"

"I want to talk to the police," Rose broke in tautly. "And I'll go by myself, nobody has to take me."

She opened a drawer in the desk and took out a purse, a paperback book, and a coffee mug. She pulled a key from her pocket.

"There, that's all I had here of my own. You'd better start looking for another receptionist, Artie."

She went over and hung her key on one of a row of key-hooks beside the front door, and walked out.

He didn't even seem to notice she was gone. "Please, Eleanor," he was begging, "I'll do anything, but don't tell her!"

She laughed harshly. "I can't wait to give her an earful. I have only one more thing to say to you, *Artie*. That contract on your father's property is binding, and I'll have you in court if I hear one more word about panel-beaters!"

He stared in bewilderment as she strode out, slamming the door. Then his eyes moved to me, and I started for the door pretty smartly.

"*You*—you're behind all this! You're determined to ruin me, and I don't even know why! If my wife leaves me over this, you are going to be very sorry, I promise you!"

I was out on the street by the time he'd finished, hurrying toward Carfax, feeling rather like a party balloon that's sprung a leak. Because of me, Arthur Crocker might lose his wife, his girlfriends, and his cushy lifestyle, but his alibi for the murder was stronger than ever.

CHAPTER THIRTEEN

After the violent emotions I had witnessed at Arthur Crocker's surgery—well, caused, I had to admit—I decided, the next day being Sunday, to go to church. The familiar Tudor words of the service and the hymns I remembered from childhood should take my mind off betrayal and murder for a while. I called Fiona to ask if she and John would care to come along. He preferred fertilizing his roses, but she agreed to meet me there, though she'd gotten out of the habit of going since Ian had come.

I soon saw why. The Shakespearean language was gone, replaced by modern English that fell on the ear like a lead weight. There was no singing, and Ian walked impatiently through the prescribed ritual and only seemed to come alive when he got the microphone in his hand.

"I want to be sure you all understand," he bellowed, "that despite the deplorable backwardness of this community's outlook, and the subversive activities of a few extremists, the youth hall *will* be built. The police inform me that, as there seems no likelihood of identifying those bones, the tape will be removed in a couple of days, and

I've notified the excavating firm that they can expect to start work again within the week."

There was real relish in the look he threw out over the sullen congregation of fewer than a dozen people. The only ones I knew were Alice White, and the two Damerels who sat in the front pew, doubtless the family's pew from the time the church was built. I figured Alan considered it his duty to put in an appearance on Sundays, as an example to the villagers or just to uphold tradition.

We gathered among the tombstones afterward to complain about Ian, which was apparently all we could do. Everyone seemed to have fallen into a state of glum resignation.

"You know," I said, "I'm sure a little dinner party would make us all feel better. I've been meaning to invite you all over for an American meal."

Fiona and Alice accepted happily, but Philippa said, "How too sweet of you, but I'm afraid—"

She paused, obviously trying to think up a plausible excuse. Impressing me with her grand house was one thing, spending an evening slumming in my cottage, quite another.

But Alan spoke up quickly. "Of course, we'd love to come. What shall we be having? I'm afraid the only American food I'm familiar with is the ubiquitous hamburger."

Philippa looked on with annoyance as we arranged to get together the following evening at the usual sixish. I assured them we would not be dining on hamburgers.

"But what else is there?" Fiona said as she walked me home. "I've only ever tried McDonald's once, and it wasn't actually my sort of thing."

"There are far more interesting American dishes than fast-food hamburgers," I said. "The trouble is, I probably can't get the ingredients for them over here."

"Oh, the Covered Market in Oxford has every sort of edible you could want. There's an estate sale I can't miss tomorrow, otherwise I'd go with you. Oh, that's right, there's also that fried chicken with the extraordinary hard crust, I had that at a chain in London once."

"Too fatty," I said, shaking my head. "I've never really liked— Oh! Cincinnati chili!" I stopped, struck by the idea. "It's real, downright American food, and it's delicious. Five-way Cincinnati chili, that's what we'll have!"

"I've heard of chili, of course," she said, "although I've never eaten it. I thought it was a speciality of your Far West?"

"Well, there's Texas-style chili, and then there's the kind they make in Cincinnati," I explained as we walked on. "There must be at least a hundred chili parlors in Cincinnati, some of them open twenty-four hours, and what they make is completely different from the kind everybody knows, with the jalapeños and chili powder. It will definitely be new to you, and another advantage is that it has to be made a day ahead, so the flavors blend properly. That means I can shop and cook today, and then I'll be free to visit with everybody."

"And I can go to the Market with you, if you'd like."

"Of course I would. I'll even teach you how to make it."

* * *

I called to invite the Barrys, too. She said the doctor would bring his medical bag and give my arm another treatment.

Then Fiona and I drove to Oxford and spent several hours roaming the Covered Market. I found everything I needed, as well as a number of things I didn't need, but couldn't resist.

We chopped and measured and cooked for the rest of the afternoon. Fiona could hardly believe it when she saw the expected onions, beans, beef, and tomatoes go into the pot accompanied by grated chocolate, cinnamon, cloves, cardamom, turmeric, vinegar, and just a pinch of cumin—Cincinnati chili isn't supposed to be hot.

We opened the bag of things I didn't need, ate fresh oatmeal bread with Greek honey, and drank Lapsang Souchong tea while the chili simmered.

When she tasted the finished product Fiona declared herself ready to travel to Ohio to sample all the varieties, although she still didn't get the differences among five-way, four-way, and haywagon.

"It's all in what you do or don't put in," I tried to explain. "Onions but no beans, that's four-way. Then a haywagon, that's with no beans or onions, but with spaghetti and cheese. What we're going to have is five-way, with spaghetti and cheese and *everything*. Maybe you have to have been born in Cincinnati to keep it straight."

After she went home, while I ate the nice piece of trout I had bought for my dinner, with pilaf and salad, I thought about Cincinnati, the dining room of our small frame house on one of the steep streets of Mount Adams,

Mother making us wait until Dad got home from the factory and washed off the grime before ladling out the chili, while the radio on the sideboard entertained us with the misadventures of "Fibber McGee and Molly" or "My Friend Irma." And after she passed on, my Dad and brothers talking baseball, eating my chili, while I sat lost in a book. As the years went on, Dad talking less and less, exhausted from a day tending the machines, as his emphysema got worse. That was one reason I'd had to leave—the pain of watching him fade just got too hard.

Later I took a bit of fish across the road. I hadn't seen Muzzle since the rock incident, although he had been emptying his food cans. But tonight I caught a glimpse of him, crouching under the hydrangea bush that overhung his predecessor's grave. He watched me with taut attention, ready to streak away if I made a move toward him.

As I picked my way back over the ruins, I looked around and saw him creeping cautiously toward the food, just a sinuous line of black in the gathering darkness.

It was a good thing I'd made the chili the day before, because on Monday morning I had a call from the Oxford post office to tell me that my books and CDs had arrived.

I drove right over to get them, plugged in my new CD player, and spent a lovely hour or so arranging books to the accompaniment of my favorite music. I filled the sitting-room shelves and took some upstairs to reread in bed. When they were all in their places, by subject and then by author, my librarian's soul was satisfied and I felt more at home than ever before in Rowan Cottage.

I couldn't resist dipping into a few of my old favorites, and I didn't forget to look through the *Oxford Anthology* for that poem Alice had reminded me of, the one about "the rude forefathers of the village." There it was, Robert Grey's "Elegy in a Country Churchyard." It was a perfect evocation of St. Etheldreda's churchyard and my feelings about the people buried there, except for its over-rhetorical eighteenth-century style. I had to admit that I preferred the simplicity of Elizabeth Davie's epitaph. I wondered if she had liked poetry, if she had ever read the "Elegy."

I spent what was left of the afternoon making final preparations for the dinner party. My corn sticks didn't bake up as crisp as they might have, because I'd given away the old iron corn-stick pan I'd inherited from Mother. But their blandness would contrast nicely with the spicy chili. I sliced apples and pears into a big bowl to soak up ginger and wine, and then carried the cat's dinner across the road.

John and Fiona were the first to arrive. She insisted on coming to help me set the table, while he went straight over to the shelves to examine my books.

"He'd spend the evening there," she laughed, "if I'd let him."

The Barrys came next. He examined my arm and at last left it unbandaged, saying the healing process was coming along nicely. He was still red-faced and preoccupied and, sympathetic as I was to his cause, I hoped nobody would bring up the churchyard cross.

I'd bought a couple of pricey bottles of wine, and some

beer I had left out at room temperature, the way the English like it. We left them with these while Fiona reheated the chili and boiled the spaghetti, and I grated Cheddar cheese and put a couple of chicken breasts into the oven, in case the chili was too much for any of them.

When we rejoined them Dr. Barry was exhorting everyone once more into the breach against the social hall. It was clear they were all sick of his little war. Now I understood how Philippa must have felt when he had disrupted her party.

Or maybe not. She was standing alone by the fireplace, clutching her purse as if it held something precious that might not be safe in my house. I bristled at the dirty look she threw me. Did she actually blame me for Dr. Barry's behavior? Or had something else got her back up? Well, she could just sulk if she wanted to. I was not about to try to figure that lady out.

Happy hour being less than a great success, I called them to the dining room sooner than I'd planned to.

"So, we're having some sort of American stew," Alan speculated, as I covered the plates with spaghetti and Fiona set down the chili pot. "With a pasta on the side?"

Shocked silence descended while I ladled the chili on top of the spaghetti and smothered it in Cheddar cheese.

"As Monty Python would say," I announced, "it's something completely different."

It was impossible not to smile at the gingerly way they dipped their forks and the variety of expressions that came to their faces. Most of them, after a few seconds of trauma, were willing to give it a second chance, and then a third, and finally to finish it up.

"Something like a curry, isn't it?" Alice ventured.

"No, dear," Louisa said. "The spices are *quite* different."

The experience actually silenced Dr. Barry for a while. He finished his quickly and accepted my invitation to have another serving, while his wife was still sipping uncertainly from the tip of her fork.

Philippa was definitely in a worse mood than usual. She screwed up her face after one taste, laid down her fork, and made her meal of half a corn stick and a glass of wine.

"Amazing, the sorts of things foreigners consider edible!" was her only comment.

Alan gave her his usual look of distaste.

"Philippa," he said softly, "after all these years, have you not developed even a modicum of courtesy?"

"I *beg* your pardon," she replied acidly, "I told you I didn't wish to eat outlandish foreign food, but you insisted."

"It's all right, Philippa," I said. "I knew it might not appeal to everyone. I have some plain baked chicken with salad and pilaf, if you'd prefer."

"No, thank you. I am very well as I am."

I was annoyed to see that she still had not laid down her purse. Now she was holding it on her lap with one hand.

Alan turned to me and said, "Well, *I* should appreciate another serving." I hoped it wasn't just the noblesse oblige thing.

Nobody else wanted chicken, either. I was delighted to see them finish up their little taste of Cincinnati.

While we ate I said to John, "I suppose you've heard of my adventure with Arthur Crocker and his girlfriends?"

"I have," he said gravely. "And I must say, Catherine, that that was a most foolhardy thing to do."

"This charming lady did something foolhardy?" Alan said. "What could it have been?"

John and I between us gave them a condensed version of my encounter with Arthur and the ladies.

"You Americans are most awfully cheeky, aren't you?" Louisa said, not in a condemnatory way, but as she might have said Italians have a talent for opera.

"How did it all end up?" I asked John. "Did Eleanor Coleman actually take her story to the police?"

"Not only to the police, but to Mrs. Crocker," he answered, looking at me very sternly, "and as a result, Dr. Crocker is now living at an hotel. His wife has seen a solicitor."

"Oh, dear," Alice sighed, "how very sad!"

"I don't think so at all," I said heatedly. "A woman has every right to know when things are going on behind her back, and to decide whether she's willing to go on living with a lying, cheating husband! And if it's him you're feeling sorry for, I'd say he got exactly what such a man deserves."

"That's as may be," John went on, "but it doesn't make him a murderer, you know. In point of fact, there was never much reason, apart from his attitude, to suspect Dr. Crocker of involvement in his father's death, and now there is no reason at all."

"Eleanor's story checks out?" I asked.

He sighed. "We have no need to 'check out' anything, Catherine. The woman says she was with Dr. Crocker at the time in question. It is not to her advantage to make that public, and she is at present, believe me, in no mood to lie for his benefit."

"But, John," I argued doggedly, "who else had a motive? Can you think of any reason for someone to kill an old hermit like that, except to inherit his money and property?"

"It is not my job," he said calmly, "to speculate on possible motives. Not without a suspect."

"Might old Crocker have had some sort of guilty knowledge?" Alan put in, obviously amused by our debate. "That's another common motive, I believe—at least it is in crime fiction."

"What could George have known about?" Louisa said. "Nobody was even willing to talk to him."

"No, no," I insisted, "what if Arthur wasn't alone in it? He and Eleanor were lovers, suppose they were in on it together. They had a whole plan worked out ahead of time, to cover all possible contingencies. Isn't it perfectly possible that all her anger at him is just an act, a way to provide alibis for both of them? Well, isn't it?"

"Maybe," Fiona joined in, "they planned for her to come forward with this story if he was seriously suspected, and when Catherine confronted them, it just moved the plan ahead of schedule."

John looked at both of us with exasperation.

"I have questioned a great many witnesses in my time,

and I am morally certain that this woman is telling the truth. Arthur Crocker was in a compromising position at the time of his father's murder. He could not have done it."

"Mightn't it have been the gypsies?" Alice asked. "My dear mother always warned me about them."

"I really cannot discuss this investigation any further," John said firmly. "Let us help you to clear away, Catherine. I'm told I make a rather good pot of coffee. I'll try my hand if you'd like."

"He really does," Fiona said, as she rose and started picking up dishes. "Let's set him to making some, while we dish up the fruit."

When we got back with the fruit and coffee, Dr. Barry was again working himself into breathlessness on his favorite topic, despite his wife's efforts to calm him, so it was a relief when I had to go and answer the telephone. An apologetic voice on the other end asked to speak to Sergeant Bennett.

"Sorry," he said as I handed it to him. "I gave them this number in case anything important should come up. I'm afraid it's one of the drawbacks of making friends with policemen."

After about five minutes, he came back into the dining room. I looked up from my fruit with surprise at the sadness in his face.

"I very much regret having to interrupt everyone's evening with bad news," he said.

He came over and put his hand on Alan's shoulder.

"I expect you'll both want to come into Oxford with

me. I'm afraid Rupert's been arrested over at Woodstock, along with some of his friends."

"Arrested?" Philippa shrieked.

"They were caught in the house of an old man who lived alone," John went on. "They had broken in through a window and were looting the place."

Poor Philippa began weeping noisily. Alan stood up, expressionless. One hand clenching and unclenching at his side was the only evidence of what he must be feeling.

"Was anyone hurt?" he asked quietly.

"After the old fellow called the police, he very foolishly came down and confronted them," John answered slowly, "and one of them bashed his head in."

CHAPTER FOURTEEN

The first thing Emily said to me the next morning was, "Now, what are you planning to do today? Are you taking Archie *out* somewhere?"

"Oh, I thought I might take him down the river in a punt, and try to figure out how they keep the darn things afloat."

"All right, I know that's a joke," she said, a little uncertainly. "But I would like to have *some* idea where he's going to be. You know how grateful I am to you for taking care of him, Mother, but I do wish you'd respect my wishes and keep him quietly at home."

"All right, darling, I will," I said. "I think he needs new experiences, they— But you are his mother, and I'll bow to your wishes."

As she began to elaborate on her theories of child development, a sudden thump and a yell from Archie's room sent us running. He had launched himself over the sidebar of the crib and landed on his bottom. He was so pleased with himself that he'd forgotten to cry, and just sat beaming at us.

"Oh, dear," Emily sighed, "he's learned how to get out of the cot. Well, it's a developmental milestone, though it's going to give you a problem at nap time."

She was right about that. After chasing him around the flat all morning I had to sit beside the crib and frustrate his attempts to launch himself over the side again, until he tired himself out struggling and howling, and fell asleep for an hour. Then I chased him all afternoon.

I was crazy about Archie, but I was finally ready to admit that, at my age, it might have been just a bit rash to take on a strong-willed toddler three days a week.

When Peter came home with a pizza I was so tired that I stayed to share it. He told me they never waited to eat together on the days they both worked. Whoever got home at around five o'clock brought what they called dinner, and left some for the other.

Emily came in about an hour later, and when she saw me, the Look came down.

"Mother," she said in a voice that boded no good, "would you come in the kitchen with me while I reheat a slice?"

I waited while she put the pizza in the microwave and pushed buttons. Then she said, "I didn't realize the other day that you were planning to interfere in the Crockers' lives like that. If I had, I would have told you what a mistake it would be. Do you know Dr. Crocker's wife has thrown him out and started divorce proceedings?"

"Good for her! I know exactly how she feels. That man is a—"

"Mother, calm down. You see, that's your problem, you

are too excitable, always being carried away by emotion. You've been that way as far back as I can remember, and it's time you got some help with your problem. It's painfully obvious that this thing with Crocker is some sort of revenge scenario, that you're seeing Crocker as Dad, it's just *classic*."

"Emily, do not lay that psychological claptrap on me." I heard my voice shaking with indignation, and waited for a minute until I was calmer. "I don't think there's anything wrong with emotion, I don't agree that I have a problem, and if I did, I'd handle it without leaning on some 'expert' for help."

The oven pinged but she ignored it, shaking her head in frustration.

"I know you've never respected my profession, but I do think I help people, and if you'd let me, I could lead you to find better ways of coping, so you don't get yourself in these situations by rushing off without thinking them through."

"How did you find out about all that, anyway?"

"Rose Voile called me this morning, and came to group this afternoon. She's given up her affair and her job with Crocker. She's in a very confused and unhappy state, which is actually a good thing." She gave me a meaningful look. "It means *she's* finally willing to face the fact that she has a problem."

"There you are, you said she had to be pushed over the edge and I pushed her, so why are you jumping on me?"

She sighed. "All right, Mom. We've never seen eye to

eye on this subject. Maybe we never will, but please think about changing more than just your place of residence, so bad things don't keep on happening to you."

It looked as if Muzzle had actually been waiting for me. He showed up that evening as soon as I entered George's backyard, and he was not crouched to run this time, but sitting with his tail wrapped around his feet, like the first time I'd seen him. The wind ruffled his fur and blew the dead flower heads on the bush so they rustled like paper flowers.

I sat down on one of the big rocks that had been the cottage's foundation, and we looked at each other. The burn on his side seemed to be healing, and he wasn't as bony now that he got his cat food regularly.

"If you'd come over here," I finally said to him, "I'd take you to a vet and have that burn checked out."

He didn't move, except for one slow blink.

"I'll bet you miss old George," I went on softly. "He wasn't all bad, was he? But his son, now—well, anyone who would throw a rock at an animal *is* all bad, in my book. Bad enough to have killed his own father—oh, I don't know any more! The police think Rupert Damerel and his gang are more likely suspects. But, you know, they've never burned down a house before.

"The only reason to set a fire is to destroy something, right? In this case, George. Why would those kids want to burn his body? They would have had to bring the gasoline with them, too. George didn't keep any around, I was there three times and I never saw any. And if you brought your own gasoline, you planned all along to kill him and burn his body.

"That sounds like a more personal crime, doesn't it, not just a bashing incidental to a robbery?" Muzzle blinked at me drowsily. "And who besides Arthur had a personal motive?"

I gazed down the garden to the spot where he died, remembering his face as he tried to speak, and then, what he had fought so hard to say.

"Hey, how about Jimmy?" I exclaimed.

Muzzle shifted uneasily as my voice rose louder with excitement.

"If he was the other burglar at the Damerels, and he came back after ten years to kill his old accomplice, okay, okay—why?" I searched for a reason and found none. "And, realistically, how could they find a man who only exists as a first name?"

Suddenly I sensed, rather than saw, movement among the trees behind the black cat, and then I heard a twig crack in the woods.

I peered through the maze of bare trunks but there was nothing. It hadn't been my imagination, Muzzle had heard it too. He was staring at the same place I was, his ear and a half standing straight up.

Why was I being such a coward? I knew perfectly well that all kinds of animals live in woods, and sometimes they even move around.

But I couldn't reassure myself. The woods were awfully quiet, I noticed as I slowly stood up. No birds were singing, no insects humming. Had they been scared into silence by an intruder?

Then I heard two sounds that no animal ever made: a muffled laugh, followed by a sibilant warning—"Shh!"

A few seconds later there was another formless movement among the trees, and then another, this time off to the left. More than one person was watching me.

Muzzle was long gone. I backed off, calling out, "Who's there? Is anybody there?" Nobody answered, but I felt presences, more strongly every minute.

I turned around and ran.

Fear clung to me even after I'd checked the locks three times. I tried to believe I had panicked over nothing. The woods were public land, why shouldn't people be in them? But something about the furtiveness of those movements and the sound of that laughter made my skin crawl.

After I'd turned the lights out, I stood in the sitting room and peered across the road. Things could be going on in those woods that a foreigner like me could not even imagine. For the first time since the night I arrived, I wondered how I could ever have thought I might belong here. I had wanted most of all to be near Emily and Archie, because now they were all I had. But, although I knew she loved me, I had forgotten how critical she could be, how defensive of her territory. And I had to admit that Archie was proving too much for me to handle

Far Wychwood had lived in my memories as a place of

beauty and peace, far removed from the violence and ugliness of cities, where I would be able to forget the past and live a sort of pastoral dream in my latter years. I had never anticipated the memories that waited here for me, or all the secret things the village knew, but would never share with me.

I felt, that night, as if I belonged nowhere in the world. Things were not working out here as I'd been so sure they would. New York was the past, and Cincinnati only a collection of vague images now. The young woman I had been, the girl, the child—there was nobody left in my life who remembered them. Now I was just the Yank, or Nana, or that irritating mother who still refused to learn how to cope the way a woman her age should.

A sudden impulse drove me to turn on the light, so I could search through some old notebooks I hadn't yet unpacked. After a few minutes I found the one I wanted, picked up the phone, and dialed a long number on the last page. It was a number I hadn't dialed for many years. The overseas lines took a little while to connect, and I had just begun to realize what a ridiculous thing I was doing, when the phone on the other end rang twice, and I heard my brother's voice.

"Cathy?" he exclaimed in amazement when I spoke.

"My God, it's Cathy!" he called to someone. "I never thought I'd hear from *you* again."

"I don't know why I'm calling you, Billy," I said with a nervous laugh. "I guess I was just lonesome, or something—"

"Where are you, England or someplace, right? What the hell did you go there for?"

"How's Akron?" I said, to change the subject, because he would never understand if I tried to tell him.

"Oh, Akron's Akron. I'm floor supervisor at the plant now."

"That's great, Billy. How's—" Oh, God, I had forgotten his wife's name.

But he didn't even notice. That was Billy.

"Lori? She's okay. Karen's the star of the track team, and Darryl's going out for fullback next season."

I couldn't picture any of them. Had I ever met his kids? His wife, I vaguely remembered at Dad's funeral.

"I got your Christmas card, with the note about what happened with Quin," he said uncomfortably. "It's a real shame. That's what me and Lori said when we read it, a real shame."

"Yeah. You know, for some reason I've been thinking more about the old days recently. Do you ever think about them?" How lame that sounded.

"Not much. The old days are gone, why chew 'em over?"

"Do you ever feel guilty about Dad, Billy?"

"Guilty? Why?"

"Oh, because he wanted to live with one of us, and we put him in the home instead." I knew what his answer would be, even as I said it.

"Oh, hell, Cath, that was a really long time ago. We all had our families and jobs, and he needed a lot of attention. The fact is, me and the other guys thought you'd volunteer to take the old man."

"Oh, yes? Why me? Just because I was the *girl?*" I said indignantly.

"No, because he always favored you so."

"Favored me?" I was astonished. "No, he didn't! He never even talked to me."

"Hell, he wouldn't lay a hand on you! Didn't even raise his voice to you. He didn't think twice about cussing us boys out, and he could swat us pretty good, too, if he was mad enough. You know what he always said? That you were the best of us all."

I was silent for a minute. "He never said it to me."

"He thought you were so much smarter, he didn't know *how* to talk to you. He told me he was afraid you'd think he was stupid."

"I never had any idea." Tears started into my eyes.

"When you went off to New York he went out and got drunk, which I only ever knew him to do one other time—when Mother died."

Yes, I remembered that. After they had taken her body away he had stayed out all night, and I wouldn't speak to him the next day.

"What's the matter, Cathy, you homesick? If you want to come back to the good old U.S. of A., I'll send you the fare. For a loan, you know," he added quickly, making me smile.

"Thanks, Billy. I can manage that if I need to. Maybe I was homesick for things that, as you say, are gone. I have to deal with the here and now, don't I?"

"You were always running off, doing crazy stuff. God, it's been so long, you know I can't hardly remember what you looked like. None of us ever understood why you acted like you did—but moving to some weird foreign country at your age, now that takes the cake."

Well, having memories of the younger me didn't make a person my soul mate, I thought ruefully, after we'd said goodbye. I started to laugh, sitting there alone, and I knew it wasn't just at myself, for trying to touch base with my roots, or at Billy for being who he was. It was from relief, because now I knew what I'd always needed to know to make peace with at least one of my ghosts.

When the morning broke bright and sunny, and Fiona called to invite me to go to Broadway with her, I was surprised to realize how well I'd slept and how lighthearted I felt. All those fears of the woods, all that depression, up in smoke. I had good friends here. Of course I could belong.

"I prized some more information out of John last night," she said as we drove through the sheep-dotted countryside. "They're questioning Rupert and his mates about George's murder. Though at least Rupert wasn't the assailant the other night. One of his pals has confessed to it, and this old man will be all right, thank God. Only they have admitted to that series of break-ins. The police want to detain Rupert for a while, but of course Philippa's cutting up rough and threatening them with everybody up to the Home Secretary to get the little blighter out."

She sighed. "One must be realistic, I suppose. It probably was those young tearaways who killed George—only I do hate to lose Arthur as a suspect. I've loathed him since infant school, when he'd lurk under the steps to the helter-skelter and look up girls' skirts."

Broadway is a beautiful village, as every tour company in England knows. Buses park up and down the High and tourists photograph each other all day long in front of any object even remotely quaint. Already, at ten in the morning, the place was full of them, quite a few with American accents.

"Lovely for me," Fiona said as she parked the car in an alley behind a stone building with a steeply pitched roof and a sign out front reading, "A Bit of Old England."

"The coaches let the dears off right in front of my shop. They'd buy anything, but I offer only quality. Not my nature to cheat people, though it would be as easy as kiss your hand."

Her shop was small, tightly crammed with old furniture gleaming with polish, and smaller pieces like clocks, jewelry, sewing boxes, and fragile figurines similar to those I'd seen at the Manor.

I spotted a mantel clock in a dark wood, with finials on top and a pair of cute little wooden lions on the base that reminded me of the lions outside the Forty-second Street library in New York. I knew it would cost far more than I could afford. When I looked at the sticker on the back, I set it down quickly.

"That's a very good piece," Fiona said, "late eighteenth century, the golden age of English clock-making. See there, it's signed by the makers, Quare and Horseman, a most illustrious firm."

Tourists were congregating outside the window, peering in, and finally rapping. Before she opened the door to them Fiona put the clock behind the counter, giving me a conspiratorial smile.

"I can't buy it," I told her. "Not possibly."

"We'll discuss it later," she said. "I'll be kept busy now, so you might as well go have a look round. If you'll come back at noonish we'll go to a pub for luncheon."

True to her word, when I returned at noon she mercilessly locked her customers out, and we went down the High for sandwiches and halves of best bitter.

"Broadway's very pretty," she said while we ate, "but there are lots of villages just as nice that haven't been 'discovered' with such a vengeance. If you go out the lane with the sign saying 'Cotswold Way,' you can have a lovely ramble this afternoon, and see some of the villages the coach parties can't get to."

In the States there are a few marked and maintained footpaths, all of which take you into the wilderness, where you can enjoy unspoiled nature if you are fit and strong enough to camp out and live on trail mix. One of the nicest features of the English countryside is the network of easy footpaths all over the island, passing villages with pubs and inns, meandering through countryside made not less but more beautiful by centuries of human habitation. I followed the Cotswold Way through unspoiled stone villages and green fields, the whole afternoon.

How could I have thought I didn't belong here? There was nothing sinister about this ancient countryside, where an old woman could walk for hours without fear of harm.

As the afternoon wore on, the memory of another walk came to me. I must have been eight or nine, holding Dad's big, calloused hand as we crossed Ida Street to wait for the streetcar to Eden Park. I remembered looking up to see him smiling at me shyly, the way he always had. His dark eyes lit up when I smiled back, and I remembered the sense of complete safety I had known with his hand around mine.

It hadn't been an important day. I had forgotten all about it. There must have been lots of other days like that, and somehow I was sure I would remember them, too, at odd moments, now I knew he had loved me after all.

The last customer was just hurrying to a tour bus when I got back to the shop, flushed and invigorated. Fiona took the old clock from behind the counter.

"I wish I could afford to give it you outright," she said, "but it really is very valuable. I want you to have it, because I know you'll appreciate it properly, so if you can give me twenty pounds it's yours. That's what I paid for it, and I assure you it was one of my greatest coups."

I rode back to Far Wychwood cradling the clock on my lap. The sun had reached the stage of afternoon mellowness when we pulled up in front of Rowan Cottage. I was thinking about what a very nice day it had been, and how foolish I'd been last evening, almost ready to give up on my new life, when I heard Fiona say, "It looks as if Donald Barry got his way."

I followed her gaze toward the churchyard. A white van with large black letters on the side indicating a television channel was parked in front of St. Etheldreda's. Just beyond it I recognized Ian Larribee and the doctor, both gesticulating furiously and talking very fast. A woman with a portable microphone and a man holding a camera on his shoulder were hurrying toward the hole beside the cross.

"He said he was going to enlist the media," Fiona told me, "and apparently he wasn't just making it up. Well, I think we should stay quite out of this."

"I certainly don't want my face on the television news. My daughter would have a fit."

I could hear the raised voices, faintly, as I got out of the car. I hurried inside to set my clock on the mantel. It was my first major purchase for Rowan Cottage, and it looked perfect in the middle of the bare mantel.

I wound it up and set the hands to agree with my watch. Then I sat down and waited for the chime.

Sitting there, it occurred to me that the mantel had not been bare the last time I had been near it. Something had been lying there. What had it been? I closed my eyes and concentrated on the appearance of the oak shelf the last time I had really looked at it. Right! That old photograph of George's children, the one I'd found buried in Malkin's grave, had been there.

This was extremely worrying. When had I taken that picture off the mantel, and what had I done with it? I had always thought I could enjoy life even if I ended up in a wheelchair, as long as my mind remained clear. Moments like this scared me, especially now that I had to take care of myself.

Surely I wasn't old enough yet to start worrying about *that*. I got busy searching the floor near the fireplace, kitchen cabinets, even my chest of drawers upstairs.

I never found it. Although I didn't realize it then, there was no way anybody could have found the photograph, because it no longer existed.

CHAPTER FIFTEEN

"Well, your quiet little retirement spot was on the morning news again!" Emily said as I came into her apartment the next day. "Close-up views of the hole in the ground where the skeleton was found, a quick cut of the fat little medic ranting on about the vicar's plans to move that old cross—which, I must say, deserves more respect, just as a work of art. The presenters were quite witty about the whole thing."

I sighed. "Dr. Barry thinks publicity will create public opposition to the vicar's plans, but I don't think enough people care about such things to make a difference. It's just a morning's sensation for the media, a chance to be witty, as you say. Tomorrow morning they'll have forgotten it and moved on to something else."

"Poor old skeleton," she said, winding her hair into its professional mode. "They implied that the police have given up on identifying him. Odd, isn't it, that someone could inspire enough passion to get himself murdered, without leaving any trace behind of who he is?"

Archie peered around his bedroom door and then

came staggering at me as fast as he could, chuckling delightedly.

His hugs never lasted long. We trailed along behind him as he headed for the kitchen.

"I've made an appointment for him with a speech therapist," Emily said, "a very sound woman I know at the hospital. I just don't think we can go on ignoring this problem. A child his age should be talking."

"If it will make you feel better, love, but I don't think—"

"Let's not argue about it, Mother. You don't want me to neglect my duty to him, do you, and let him fall behind other children his age?"

"Frankly, I think you could afford to neglect the little things more. He's happy, he's healthy, why don't you forget what those stupid books say he should be doing and just let him develop at his own pace? You've got too many theories rattling around in your head."

She took a deep breath. "You see, that's an example of what I was telling you. You just charge straight ahead at people, just say what's on the top of your head without thinking what effect it will have! I'm very proud of my knowledge and respectful of the advances in my field, and it offends me to hear you talk as if it's all nonsense. If you'd only learn to think before speaking, you might realize that."

"I never said it was *all* nonsense," I answered, "I just think it encourages people to indulge in self-pity and look to someone else to solve their problems, instead of standing on their own two feet and being strong."

"Mother, you don't know anything about it!" She opened the entry closet and got out her coat and brief-case, blowing out a loud, exasperated breath. "If I thought it would do any good, I could give you lots of examples of people who've been helped by psychological counseling. Rose Voile, for one, she's improving so much in self-esteem and assertiveness since she's come to group. She said Arthur Crocker called her the other night, actually wanting to take her out. And, by the way, she said he's quite distraught about losing his wife—or her money, we all think."

"My heart bleeds."

"But I mean, he's absolutely livid about you, blames you for the whole thing. Rose said he went on and on about you, and I must say—"

"Arthur Crocker's problems are entirely of his own making," I said firmly. "I don't feel even the littlest bit guilty for them. Rose surely isn't going to take him back?"

"Oh, no, that's what I meant. The group was quite proud of the way she blew him off. Talking with other women has been so good for her. She really is a sweet-heart, when you get to know her."

Archie was more than usually willful that morning. He resisted with ear-piercing screams any interference with his activities, even the most destructive ones, until I was actually on the verge of trying a swat to the bottom.

"Let's not go down that road," I said. "You've got cabin fever, Archie, and so have I. Come on, let's be naughty. Let's get you overstimulated."

It was a day of sunny intervals, and one was just ending as we started up St. Aldate's. A great black cloud took over the sky, plunging the crowded street into twilight although it wasn't quite noon.

"Cloud, Archie," I announced, and, as a chilly blast struck us, "wind, wind, wind." He put out his hands and tried to grab it.

I was heading for Debenham's to look for some cookware I'd missed when I'd made the chili dinner, and to revisit the Beatrix Potter display that had been such a hit before. Maybe we'd buy Squirrel Nutkin today. My ultimate plan was to collect all the major characters, so that when we started reading the books, we'd be reading about old friends.

I'd always wished I had done that with Emily. We'd happened upon Miss Potter's little world by accident, because I'd known nothing then about the great children's books. Comics and Little Golden Books had been my childhood reading material. Browsing idly in "J"—librarianese for the juvenile collection—she had found *Peter Rabbit* when she was six, and we had moved on, with the help of our neighborhood children's librarian, to all the other great stories about the little denizens of the English countryside.

I pushed on with head bent against the wind, toward Carfax where four main streets converge at a fourteenth-century bell tower. The bell was ringing twelve as the traffic light turned green and I stepped off the curb.

Because of the stroller, I was later entering the intersection than other pedestrians. I was only a few steps into the street when I heard a roaring sound to my left, and then several voices, one yelling, "Watch out!", another, "Stop!", and a third just screaming.

I looked toward the roar and saw a black Bentley hurtling toward us through the red light. People were screaming all around now. I froze in shock for a second, then I turned, dragging the stroller behind me, and made for the curb. But the car swerved to aim at me again.

Through the hubbub, I glanced up at it, just long enough to catch a blurred glimpse of a man's face inside, with a black mustache.

Then something, not the car, knocked me flat on the sidewalk. The stroller was torn out of my grasp. The Bentley went by, its tires scraping the curb, and picked up speed as it plunged down High Street.

I lay on my stomach trying to get my breath back and to comprehend what had just happened.

Then I heard Archie wailing. I scrambled up and ran to the stroller, sitting beside the belltower. Several people had come out and were assuring him that it was all right and he was a brave boy. Although he was crying, I could see he wasn't hurt. I unstrapped him, picked him up, and covered his face with kisses.

"I'm sorry," a man's voice said, behind me. "There wasn't time to do it more gently."

A tall, silver-haired man was standing near the stroller. He looked vaguely familiar, but my mind refused to focus on him. The terror that had possessed it a few minutes before was changing to boiling anger.

People gathered around asking me if I was all right,

asking each other if they had seen it, and whether they could believe it, and why anyone would do such a thing. A student in a graduation gown said, "Somebody call a constable. I took down the plate number. They'll find the bastard."

I couldn't speak. I could only hold Archie as tightly as possible and murmur meaningless comfort sounds to him. There was no need for me to hear any license number. I knew without a doubt what had happened. Arthur Crocker had tried to kill me.

It wasn't until we were sitting on a hard metal bench in the police station that I paid any attention to the man who had knocked us out of the car's path. All the way there in the police car, I had just sat hugging Archie, who for once didn't mind being confined in my arms. The man had sat in front with the constable and we hadn't exchanged a word.

Now we were waiting to be interviewed. Police officers passed up and down the corridor, citizens came in and out the front door or followed constables and detectives to rooms along the corridor, computer keyboards clicked, and printers hummed. I paid no attention to any of it. My thoughts were still occupied with the image of that big car bearing down on us.

Finally I glanced over at the man. He had a handsome face, good bones as my mother would have said, deep brown eyes, and silver hair.

I cleared my throat and said, "I'm sorry, I never thanked you. It's a miracle you happened to be there at that exact moment and could think so fast."

"You don't remember me, do you?" he said, revealing himself to be an American.

I had to shake my head. I wondered fleetingly if he could be someone I'd known in New York.

"We only met once," he went on. "It was about ten days ago, at the inn in Far Wychwood. In the dining room by that great fireplace. You dropped your purse."

"Oh, right! You had only come to the village for a day and you didn't like it."

"Oh no, the village was beautiful. I'd stopped by to look for a friend who told me he was moving there, years before. But nobody had ever heard of him. I even talked to some people with the same last name, and they said he'd never been there. In fact, that's why I'm here today. I was on my way to the police, to get some more information about a news story I saw that I thought could relate to him. And then as I was crossing the street, I saw you coming toward me. I was about to speak to you when that madman started up his car."

Archie had recovered now and begun to writhe and squeal.

"Come on, matie," I said to him, "you've got to be good. I can't let you run around here."

"Let me try something," the man said.

He lifted Archie to his shoulders and walked up and down in front of me while we talked. Archie twined his fingers in the thick silver hair and looked around with happy squeaks.

"You must have some experience keeping little kids under control," I said.

"I've got a couple of boys of my own. It's a long time since I've tried to keep them under control, though. They're twenty-six and twenty-nine. But I remember some of the things that used to work with them." He gave Archie a bounce that made him giggle.

"Boys are a whole different ball game, aren't they?" I said. "I raised a girl, and she was nothing like this guy."

"Depends on the kid, I'd think. I didn't have any girls, so I can't talk. Listen, do you want to call your husband while we're waiting?"

"I don't have a husband any more," I said shortly.

"Sorry. I lost my wife, too, a few years back."

"I didn't lose my husband," I said crossly. "He lost me, poor man."

"Oh, I see." He stuck out his hand. "I'm Dan Vincent."

"Catherine Penny." As we shook, John Bennett came out of a room down the hall and walked toward us, smiling in that solemn way of his.

"John," I called, "it just occurred to me—I don't want you to call my daughter about this. I don't want her to hear it from the police, it will scare her to death. Much better if I tell her myself, when it's all over and she can see we're okay."

He frowned. "Well, I'm sorry, Catherine, but she has already been notified. It's customary procedure."

"Damn! I hate to think of her being frightened, when we aren't even hurt."

John and Dan shook hands and exchanged names.

"I'm going to take you to an interview room, where we

can sort out just what happened," John said. "Very good of you to come along, Mr. Vincent. We also have the telephone numbers of several other witnesses. Remarkably stupid of the fellow to do this at probably the most congested intersection in the city, where he was sure to be seen by any number of people."

At that moment, the fellow himself came through the street door, escorted by a constable on either side. Arthur's hair was mussed and his face was scarlet.

When he saw me he stopped. It took him several minutes to get his words out.

"*You!* Everywhere I go— Why are you persecuting me, Madame? What have I ever done to you?"

"You have tried to kill me, that's what, not an hour ago, and not only me, but that innocent baby up there!"

"*Kill* you? I did nothing of the sort. I haven't seen you since last Saturday."

He turned to John. "These constables say I tried to run this harridan down. I have no clue what's given them such a bizarre idea. I was—I was in my surgery the whole morning."

"With a patient, sir?" John asked serenely. "Someone who can vouch for your whereabouts?"

"Well, you see, I have had several cancellations since this woman—since my personal life became the common gossip of the town." He raised his chin and glared at John in an unconvincing attempt at outraged innocence. "Actually, I was alone."

"I see. Then no one can back up your story this time?"

"What do you mean, 'this time'? I'm bloody well going

to sue this police department for false arrest! I'm about to line up a solicitor, anyway, because of your accusations relating to my father's death."

"You were never accused in that case, Dr. Crocker," John said, still as equably as if they had been discussing the weather. "There was never any question of it. But in this case, several witnesses are ready to swear that they saw you deliberately drive toward this lady at a high rate of speed. Now," he went on, as Arthur started to protest, "I suggest we all get out of this public place. The Chief Inspector would like to speak with you, Dr. Crocker, in interview room B, where you can give him your side of the case. Meanwhile, I shall be interviewing you, Catherine, and Mr. Vincent in room—"

He was interrupted by the street door banging back as my daughter burst in.

Her hair was straggling out of its twist, her face was drained white and set in an expression of dread I had seen on it only once before, when she was ten and somebody had called to say her lost sheltie had been hit by a car. It had all ended happily then, with Rusty back home on a splinted leg. Something told me it wasn't going to end as well this time.

She stepped up to Dan and demanded angrily, "Who are you? What are you doing with my baby?"

Dan stammered an apology and quickly lifted Archie down into her arms. She held him so tightly he squealed in protest.

"Darling," I said, "I know they've given you a terrible

shock. I didn't want you to hear about this until I could explain it, but—"

She turned on me, her eyes flashing.

"Archie is my child, Mother, not yours! You had no right to go against my wishes and take him to dangerous places and almost get him killed!"

"Now, wait a minute," I said, my temper rising. "I did not take him to 'dangerous places.'" We were just crossing the street with a green light—"

"I told you to keep him at home!"

She was on the verge of tears. I tried to lay my hand on her arm, but she jerked it away.

"They told me this homicidal optometrist tried to run you down, because of your ridiculous meddling in his personal affairs when I *told* you—"

"Pardon me," John tried to say, in his most soothing manner, "if we could all just adjourn to interview rooms B and—"

But Arthur wasn't taking an outright accusation in silence.

"'Homicidal optometrist?' Very well, my girl, there are at least ten people who heard that, a public libel that was. You'll hear from my solicitor."

She ignored him. "This is the last straw, Mother. I cannot have my baby endangered by your headstrong behavior. I'll have to find somebody else to care for him from now on."

"Emily!" I couldn't believe she'd said it.

"You know," Dan Vincent put in, "it seems to me you

might be a little bit concerned about what your mother's been through, too."

"Who *are* you?" Emily demanded again. "And why should I care how it seems to you? And I am concerned about her." The tears welled up in her eyes. "I've been worried to death about you, Mother, but I can't stop you from putting yourself in danger. The only thing I can control is Archie's safety. I can't let you risk his life like this. I was wrong to think it could work out, I knew how rash you can be, but I never thought—"

"Has it ever occurred to you that you're an overprotective mother, that you're smothering the poor child with your theories?"

She stared at me with a face full of hurt. I wanted to comfort her, even though she was hurting me, too.

She said in a shaking voice, "I'll—I'll be in touch when I can bear to talk to you, but not right now. Goodbye, Mother."

She wheeled around and left. Archie's puzzled little face gazed at me over her shoulder as they went out the door. I already missed them terribly.

"Catherine?" somebody said. I turned to see the latest additions to our gathering, all three of the Damerels. Rupert stood sullen and pale between his parents.

"What are you doing here?" Alan asked me in surprise.

"Although my superiors have seen fit to release Rupert to your custody," John said to them through tight lips, "I hope you understand that he's not to leave the area until our investigation is done."

"Yes, John, of course," Alan said apologetically. Philippa only gave a scornful laugh. She was clutching Rupert's arm tightly, as if he might try to get away from her.

"I'd rather have stayed in nick with my mates," Rupert burst out. "It wasn't my idea to go back to that bleeding museum."

"Rupert, be quiet this instant!" she commanded.

Without thinking, I blurted out, "That's right, Rupert, you might just as well be quiet. It's no use trying to tell people how you feel if they don't even care enough about you to listen!"

Philippa's eyes widened as if she had been slapped. Rupert stared at me in amazement, and then a grin slowly spread over his face.

Alan, as usual, was unflappable. "Why are you all standing about in this corridor?" he asked. "Can I do anything to help, Catherine?"

I noticed for the first time that we did pretty well fill up the corridor. Several police officers had gathered at the desk to watch the show, and people kept shuffling sideways to get past us. So it wasn't surprising that John took advantage of the pause to put his foot down.

He said quickly to Alan, "Just a contretemps, nothing to delay you," as he ushered the three of them to the street door.

Then he gestured to the constables to take Arthur down the hall.

He talked to Dan and me in the interview room for about forty minutes. I was now so miserable that I didn't even listen to the questions, so Dan did most of the talking.

How could Emily say those things to me, I kept wondering. How could she say I wasn't fit to care for Archie? They were all the family I had left, and she had as good as told me I was going to lose them, too.

When we came out of the police station Dan said, "Can I buy you some dinner? It might restore your spirits. I'll even save you the drive," he added quickly, "and take you home, if you'll let me."

"I'll be all right," I answered dully.

We walked down St. Aldate's in silence. The wind was blowing hard now, and the sky was too dark for midafternoon. It matched my mood perfectly.

"Come on and let me take you home," he said at last. "I don't want you to have any more disastrous experiences today. You're too upset to drive."

I shook my head. "I'd rather be alone. You don't even know me, and you're more concerned about me than my daughter was," I added bitterly.

"That girl didn't mean half of what she said. She'd had such a scare, she was almost beside herself. Imagine what it's like to get a call like that from the police."

We had reached Emily's apartment building, where my car was parked. Seeing the lights in their windows above, I gave up and started crying. He gave me his handkerchief. Blubbering into it, I unlocked the car door with one hand.

"Are you sure—" he started to ask again.

"Yes, yes," I snuffled. "Sorry to make such a spectacle of myself in front of a stranger. But I'll be fine. I'm used to taking care of myself now. You go on back to your hotel."

"I'm going back to the police station," he said. "That's why I'm in Oxford, I want to talk to them about that skeleton they found in your village."

"Why?" I asked in surprise, handing back the sodden handkerchief and blinking away the remaining tears. "How did you find out about that?"

"Oh, it was all over the national news, with pictures of that quarrel in the churchyard. They even interviewed the bishop, and he looked pretty embarrassed. 'Is today's church indifferent to the artistic treasures it should be protecting?' was the headline of one talk show, with a panel of art historians who seemed to think it is. Then, when they talked about that skeleton, I decided to come and spend the last few days of my trip finding out about it. It's probably a dumb idea, but I couldn't help wondering if it might be my friend, the one who was going to move to Far Wychwood, you know? They said the skeleton was buried about a decade ago, and that's when he came over."

"I hope it is," I said, then, realizing how awful that sounded, I quickly amended it to, "I mean, I hope you find out something. I'd better just stop talking for today. What I said to the Damerels was so rude, wasn't it? I'll have to apologize, the first chance I get. I was thinking about Emily when I said it, of course. She didn't even let me try to explain!"

"What you need is dinner and a rest. Then everything will look better."

I heated a can of soup and brewed some tea when I got home. The storm that had been threatening all day finally broke while I was in the tub. Even with Bach echoing therapeutically through the cottage, the thunder was impressive. When the first flash of lightning shot across the window, I finished up quickly and got out of the water. When you grow up in the American Midwest, you learn not to bathe during a lightning storm.

Rain was beating on the roof as I started to get into my nightgown. Then I remembered Muzzle. With all that had happened, I'd never thought to put out his food.

I actually had the nightgown on before my conscience made me take it off again, change into slacks and sweater, raincoat and Wellingtons, and unfurl my umbrella. I ran across the road with a can of tuna dinner in my hand, jumping every time lightning split the sky open.

He was cowering under a bush. His wet fur stuck to his body and made him look thin as a stick. When he saw me he stepped out and opened his mouth wide in an indignant complaint, drowned out by a clap of thunder.

There was no shelter in George's yard. The trees and bushes had barely begun to leaf out. I couldn't just go and leave the poor thing there in that storm. So I turned and walked back toward the road, holding the cat-food can behind me, keeping eye contact with him. He followed me at a distance.

When I went through my front gate he stopped and shrank back, realizing he was entering strange territory. I carried the can to my front door, but he stayed in the road. So I went into the little potting shed that stood by the front wall, and set the can down. From the door of the house, I watched him step warily toward the shed, his tail straight up. Then he seemed to make a decision. Mustering all the courage in his small body, he dashed inside the shed.

I woke sometime later in the night. The storm had passed over and a resplendent full moon was shining through my window. The scene with Emily came back to me immediately and drew down a curtain of depression so heavy that I got out of bed and went to look out at the night, just to distract myself. I've always felt it's better to meet my troubles standing on my feet than lying on my back, feeling as helpless as an overturned turtle.

I remembered the cat in my potting shed and leaned around trying to see into the shed, but I couldn't catch sight of him. I hoped he had ridden out the storm in there. He might have been spooked and run out into the rain and lightning again.

On impulse, I pulled my slacks on again, under my nightgown, threw a jacket over it, slipped my feet into my cross-trainers, and went out with a flashlight.

The night was fresh and cool, a light breeze whispering in the apple tree. I felt absurdly disappointed when the light told me Muzzle was not in the shed. Not even a cat would trust me, my wounded ego grumbled.

"Stupid little pest!" I said aloud.

Still, I plodded out the gate and across the road to

George's property, knowing I wouldn't get back to sleep until I was sure the cat was all right.

I found him hunched in the ruin of the fireplace, where the stones were fairly dry. He watched me closely as I came toward him, but he didn't look as if he was thinking of running.

His fur was dry, so I knew he had at least accepted my hospitality through the storm. My moment of self-centered anger had passed. I realized he probably hadn't yet gotten over hoping that if he hung around in the rubble it would all come back, the warm cottage, the old man's shaky fingers stroking his back.

Turning to cross the road again, a brightness at the corner of my eye made me look to the right. For a few seconds I saw nothing. Then a light flashed in the churchyard, close to the ground, moving from right to left. It disappeared and then it flashed again. I was almost sure it was in the vicinity of George's grave.

Without stopping to consider whether it might be something dangerous, I set off at a run toward the churchyard.

CHAPTER SIXTEEN

I didn't see the light when I stepped in, as quietly as possible, among the gravestones. Their tops gleamed white in the moonlight and for a minute I wondered if I could have mistaken that for a light. No, it had been much brighter, and it had definitely flashed on and off.

An owl hooted from the bell tower, and small, indistinct shapes swooped through the trees—bats, I concluded, as one fluttered by uncomfortably close to my face. The creatures who really owned the churchyard were asserting their rights. But what other beings might be among them? I wondered, with the shudder of fear that should have come earlier and kept me back at home.

Then something moved, over by the church. The moonlight didn't show me any details, only some bulky dark forms moving slowly toward the porch. They reminded me of the dark shape I had seen fleeing George's house.

So did I turn and run back to my cottage, the way Emily would have approved? No, I strode over to them, my rubber soles squelching loudly in the mud, and fixed them in my flashlight's beam, calling out indignantly, "What are you doing here?"

I don't think I've ever seen six more astonished people. Their faces framed by the hoods of their black sweatshirts, Joe the sexton, three young boys and two girls, none of whom I knew, stared back at me like prey animals in a hunter's spotlight.

"Joe?" I said.

"Damn it! She's broken the spell," one of the boys whined.

"What a babe ye are, Luke Jenkins!" Joe the sexton snarled. "It's not that easy to break a proper-cast spell, as a lad your size would have knowed fifty year ago." He turned to me and pushed his hood down on his shoulders, in lieu, I supposed, of removing a hat. "You'll not understand our work, missus. Best you walk on home and forget you seen this."

All of a sudden I did understand.

"*You're* the witches!" I exclaimed.

The kids shifted about uneasily.

"Nay," Joe snorted, "not this crew! In my day the young knew the old religion from their cradles. This batch know naught but rock singin' and telly stars, for all they come mewlin' to me to teach 'em the powers."

"You said we was doing real good, Joe," one of the girls protested.

"You mean you're teaching these kids witchcraft?" I said. "But you're the church sexton!"

The old man sighed, set down the big lantern he carried, and spoke to me as if I were a child.

"I'm as good a Christian as any man. But in old times that didn't have to mean forgettin' our old ways and the teachin's. We kept to both. Safer that way."

I could hardly believe what I was hearing. "Worshipping God and the devil?"

"Nay, missus, I never worshipped the devil! I leave that to them that will. Mine's only the spells everybody could cast in the old days, to get us the food or woman or man or healing we craved."

"Yeah, woman or man," one of the boys muttered, and the rest of them giggled, then quailed under Joe's wrathful eye.

"You see, missus, that's what they're out for—the love potions, and couplin' in the fields at harvest time, that's all these young brutes want!"

Their eyes shone in the dark with hope of hearing more on that subject.

"Let me try to get this straight," I said. "You, the sexton of an Episcopal church, consider yourself a warlock, and these kids your sorcerer's apprentices?"

Joe shrugged. "I don't follow all that, missus. These young folk come to me wanting to learn the old religion. I'm one of the few left hereabouts that remembers how to go about it. But I don't practice the dark rites. I don't bring on sickness or death, not me."

"What are you doing here tonight, tromping around the church like this?"

"Widdershins," one of the girls piped up.

"What?"

"You then," Joe said, "tell her what it means."

"Widdershins is against the sun," the girl answered, "west to east. If you go that way round the place a person hangs out, you put a spell on him. This tonight is a binding spell that stops somebody from doing what's in his mind to do. We're binding vicar from moving the cross."

"Well, I'm with you there," I said. "The things he has in mind to do only start with the cross. Fiona and Alice and I heard him threaten to have the church torn down to make room for some kind of center and the cottages destroyed and replaced with high-rises!"

Joe laughed. "Ah, you've only just learned about his plans? I've heard plenty about all that. Anytime he sees a set of ears within sound of that voice of his, he'll go on all the day about his big plans."

"Is Dr. Barry part of your little coven?" I asked, remembering his collection of occult books, and the way he had used that same expression, "the old religion."

Joe looked away uncomfortably. "Nay, he's not one of us. But to my mind, he may not ken what he's dealing with in them books of his."

"Are there other practitioners in the village?"

"Nay, nay," he said quickly, but I wasn't sure I believed him. "Any road, you're safer than most against dark believers, with your rowans."

"My rowans?"

"Witches hate them," Luke put in, eager to show his knowledge. "They keep away from places where they grow."

"That's right, young Luke," said Joe, obviously glad to

change the subject. "That'll be why Davies planted 'em, back when Binnie were a girl."

"I'd think George Crocker would have had some in his yard, then," I said. "He was scared to death of you people."

Joe laughed again. "Old George? He knowed the spells right enough, just like I do. And he didn't fear us old folk, it was them black arts he feared. But George didn't need rowans—he had that black cat that come from a witch's familiar. Little Jimmy Watson were a black witch, used the spells that bring on sickness and death, though nobody knowed where he learned 'em. When he vanished out of Far Wychwood, so did his cat. It left a kitten behind, and George Crocker were canny enough to take it in."

"Jimmy Watson was a poor handicapped child trying to get back at the kids who wouldn't accept him," I said angrily. "How can you talk such nonsense?"

"Well, he cursed Spencer's cow, everybody seen that, and in a week she was dead."

"I'm cold, Joe," the widdershins expert grumbled. "Are we going to bind vicar or talk all night?"

As he turned to put her in her place, I thought of something else.

"Was it you guys who put a circle of yew on George's doorstep one night, not long before he died?"

They looked at me blankly, then at Joe.

"Yew circle's a warning to keep your gob shut," he told them. "Why'd we want to leave one for old George? He didn't know nothing. Hardly knowed his name, by that time."

"How about two or three nights ago—was it you kids wizarding in the woods, laughing at me when I was in George's backyard?"

They looked even more mystified.

"We were at Joe's the past three evenings," Luke said. "That's when we made our plans for laying the spell on vicar."

"Then if you didn't do those things," I said slowly, "there must be others who believe in this stuff, and mean no good with it."

Joe leaned toward me confidentially. "Best not to pry, missus. Like I said about the doctor, you don't know what you might be dealin' with. Now," he straightened up and fixed his apprentices with a fierce glare, "I want a straight line there! Think ye can straggle about and cast a proper binding spell?"

I left them to it and sloshed back home, admitting reluctantly that, in this case, I'd love to see the magic work.

The next day was a beauty, but my feelings were better suited to last night's storm. I kept thinking about Emily and Archie, and puttered around in a hopeless way most of the morning. Then the part of myself that had no patience with self-pity bullied the other part into some clothes and out the door for a good long walk.

I followed the back lanes for miles, turning down any that looked inviting, climbing over stiles, sitting by a stream to watch the tadpoles and dragonflies, and mulling over this latest crisis.

Emily was right, of course, I was rash and impulsive. And somehow I always seemed to be surrounded by cautious people. As Billy had said, Dad and my brothers hadn't understood me. I had a feeling, though, that shy, self-effacing Mother had vicariously enjoyed the scrapes I'd got into. One of her quaint expressions came into my head, something she'd said when she'd had to come to school because I'd skipped classes and ridden the street-cars all day, exploring the city. She'd been properly grave and apologetic in the principal's office, but when we got home, before she disappeared into her kitchen, she'd quickly whispered to me, "I do glory in your spunk, honey!" As far as I knew, she was the only one who had.

Only someone Emily's age could believe it was possible to make oneself perfect—or someone as steeped as she was in psychiatric dogma. I had long ago given that up and accepted myself as I was, but there was no way I could make other people do that. I'd had to come to terms with the painful fact that I wasn't what Quin wanted after all. But I realized I hadn't been tormented by memories and regrets for at least a week. Since I'd never have to see him again, they ought to go on receding now, further and further to the back of my mind, until finally they would never surface again. All it had taken was distance and time, and two murders, to get him out of my system.

But now I had to deal with the more painful fact that I wasn't the kind of mother Emily wanted, either. If she really did cast me off, how would I ever get over *her?* I would do anything in my power to keep that from happening, but it was not in my power to change into the sensible, amenable woman she wanted me to be.

I came within sight of my cottage tired but still depressed, until I caught sight of Emily's car parked by the gate.

She was sitting alone on the steps, looking forlorn. She got up, smiling uncertainly, when I came through the gate, and I hurried over and took her in my arms.

"Mom, this is so awful!" she moaned. "I don't want us to fight."

"Then by all means, let's don't," I answered. "Come on in and have a cup of tea and we'll talk everything over calmly."

"No, I can't. I have to get to group."

She stepped back and started twisting her hair up. She was dressed for work in a chic but severe black pantsuit. She took a clip from her pocket, opened it with her teeth the way I had been telling her not to do since she was twelve, and fastened her hair.

"I've been sitting here almost half an hour. I thought I was going to have to leave without seeing you."

"I'm so glad you didn't. But why didn't you bring Archie with you? Then he could have stayed here today, instead of my going into Oxford and coming back. I know he'd love running around in the garden, and it's a great day for it."

"Yes, he would," she said, looking rather nervous. "And I will bring him, lots of times." She took a deep breath. "Only— Well, that's another thing I want to talk with you about. Don't you think I've been unfair to you?"

"Unfair about what? Well, whatever it is, I don't think so, no."

"You see, I'm well aware that Archie's a handful, and I've seen how tired you look after a whole day trying to keep up with him. And I know you get bored staying in with him."

"Oh, darling, is this going to be another lecture about not letting him be stimulated? Because I have to say—"

"No, just listen!" She closed her eyes for a moment, making a commendable effort to remain calm and tactful. "I haven't the right to tie you down to my schedule. I mean, expecting you to make yourself available three days a week, that's what's unfair. I've thought it over carefully, and what I've decided would be better is that, in future, you'll still see just as much of him as you like, but only *when* you like. I can bring him out here whenever you'd like to spend time with him, or you can come in, only you won't have to be there on certain days, doesn't that sound like a good plan?"

"But what about your work? He still has to be cared for."

"Do you remember Rose Voile?"

I nodded. How could I forget Rose?

"Well, she's been without a job since she left Dr. Crocker. She's had to move out of her flat because she couldn't pay the rent. I feel so sorry for her, and she absolutely adores Archie—so we've hired her as his live-in nanny! We have that extra bedroom, you know, where Peter's been storing all those books until we can get shelves built. She's moving into it today. She's such a quiet person, perfectly happy to stay at home. I think it's the perfect solution. You're not offended, are you?"

She watched anxiously for my reaction. It sounded to me like a nicer way of saying what she'd said last night, but I wasn't offended, now that she was so obviously trying to soften the blow. In fact, I was surprised to feel a certain relief. I did want to play a big part in my grandson's life, but those full days chasing him around really *had* been too hard for me.

"Not as long as this isn't just a way of keeping me away from him, in case I get him run over by a train or something," I said.

"I was afraid you might think that. But I really do want you always to be close to Archie, to all three of us. What about having him here tomorrow? He can run around your nice garden for as long as you'd like to have him. Will that prove to you that I don't want to keep you apart?"

"Of course, I'd love to have him tomorrow, and I promise to return him in one piece."

Her face clouded, and she looked away uneasily.

"There is something else I ought to tell you—" she began. Then she looked at her watch and exclaimed, "Oh, Lord, I've got to run!"

I followed her down the path, trying to ask what else she had wanted to tell me, but she only said, "Of course, I know he'll be all right out here, I mean, it's not as if there were any traffic or anything. I won't be worried at all about anything happening to him out here in the nice quiet countryside."

I shook my head as I watched her drive away. She hadn't added, "the way I would if he were with you in town," but I knew that was what she had meant. And I still wondered what she had been unwilling to tell me at the end.

Still, we were friends again, that was the important thing. She would be happier with her child in the care of placid little Rose. Archie, of course, would be bored stiff, but he was a tough baby. He would figure out how to get what he needed from those overprotective adults.

Walking back up the path, I had to smile at Emily's certainty that she was helping Rose to stand on her own feet. It looked to me as if the poor girl was just exchanging one demanding employer for another.

The postman came by, as usual, on his red bicycle at ten o'clock, and today he brought a letter from Jack and Sara, two of my oldest friends in New York. They told me about all the use they were getting from my cornstick pan, passed on some library gossip, reviewed a new production at the City Ballet, and reported on the latest political fight over the condition of the West Side Highway.

It was fun to get the news, and I promised myself I would answer after lunch. But it didn't make me homesick. I realized that I had stopped thinking of New York as home. Strangers were living through their joys and crises in the apartment on West Eighty-third, and the library was no doubt humming along the shining highway to total electronic conversion without the nuisance of my complaints.

I looked around my cottage, at the shelves put up by another book-lover some time in the past, at the blackened stone fireplace where Elizabeth Davie must have warmed her toes on winter evenings, at my clock above it preparing, with a visible shudder, to chime the hour, and I knew where home was.

I spent the rest of the morning cleaning and doing laundry. After lunch, I was writing my letter to Jack and Sara, trying to keep it down to half a dozen pages in spite of all that had been happening, when a knock came at the door. It was John Bennett and Dan Vincent.

"I wanted to see where those bones were buried," Dan explained. "So John drove me out, and since we were near we thought we'd drop by and see how you're doing after yesterday."

"I'm fine now. You were right, Emily came out to make up today. Come in and sit down, and tell me what you've found out. Do you really think those bones could be your friend's?"

They sat on the sofa and I curled up in the wing chair.

"I think they could," he said slowly. "From the little the police have figured out, it sounds like him."

"What little *have* you figured out?" I asked John.

I could see he was reluctant, as usual, to tell me anything. I doubted he had been the one to suggest stopping by.

"Very little beyond what I've already told you. Except that he was probably American. That, of course, would explain why nobody's claimed his remains or reported him missing."

"How can you tell he was American?"

"Enough of a label in the scraps of an overcoat survived for forensics to be sure it was of American manufacture."

"I *know* that manufacturer," Dan said excitedly. "I run a chain of men's clothing stores on Long Island, and that line of coats is in my stores solely because of this guy I've been looking for."

Before I could ask him to tell me more, he turned to John and said, "You haven't told her about those letters on the card."

"Yes, well, that's much less certain. There were scraps of paper in what had been a pocket. One piece had been laminated, and so it was not completely destroyed. At a guess, it was probably his driving license. Only a few letters could still be made out, but among them, at the top where one's name would be printed, were the letters 'J-A-M.' A few scattered letters and numbers can be seen on other parts of the thing, but nothing that makes any sense."

"I'm sure it was the name," Dan put in, "and how many names start with 'JAM'? Doesn't the most common one have to be 'James?' "

"And your friend's name was James?"

"Right. I knew him as Jim—Jim Cobb."

Cobb. The same name as the village shopkeepers. But the first name interested me more.

"You know, when I was talking to old George, he went on and on about somebody named 'Jimmy.' He said he'd never tell anybody where Jimmy was, and then when he was dying, his very last words were 'Jimmy' and 'church.' He could have meant Jimmy was buried in the churchyard. And a 'Jim' could also be a 'Jimmy,' couldn't he?"

"Thank you for that information, Catherine," John said drily. "It would have been nice to have had it earlier."

"I'm sorry. I didn't think of it when you questioned me, and after that I guess everything else just pushed it out of my mind. But if George kept this Jimmy's whereabouts secret, and that skeleton was Jimmy, then George must have known about his death and where he was buried!"

"I must say," John answered, "all this speculation is quite without any foundation in evidence."

"Maybe Jimmy was the mysterious visitor who helped George rob the Manor, and there was some sort of thieves' falling-out, and George killed him—over the loot, probably." I turned to Dan. "Do you think your friend could have turned burglar?"

"I wouldn't think so, but then I didn't know him all that well. I call him a friend, but I only saw him every few months over a period of about two years. He was a salesman for this line of overcoats, the same manufacturer that made the one your skeleton was wearing. He'd come by on his rounds, try to sell me on the product, maybe we'd go out for a drink. He finally talked me into stocking the coats, and they were pretty good sellers.

"This was while my wife was dying. My family's on the West Coast, and I needed somebody to talk to. We kind of hit it off. Then, just after Ruth died, he told me he'd found out his mother had terminal cancer, too. Well, I knew what it was like, and I tried to help him the way he'd helped me."

"That was good of you," I said warmly. For the first

time, I noticed the lines of suffering around his mouth and eyes. "So what was this Jim Cobb like?"

"Kind of a sad guy. Coming into middle age, never married, never made a success of any job he'd had. In fact, he finally lost his job with that coat company. Poor guy asked me for a loan, and I gave him a couple of hundred bucks. Never thought I'd see it again. Then a month or so later, he came by and said he had a chance of getting in on a sweet deal in England, in this place called Far Wychwood. If it panned out, he'd send me my two hundred with interest, he said, and he'd start out new over here. I'd never seen him so happy. He said he'd send me a card when he got settled, and I should visit him if I got a chance. I said sure, but I never did get that card.

"This year I decided to give myself a vacation and do a little business at the same time, look into stocking some of those great English raincoats. I buried myself in the business after Ruth died, but it pretty much runs itself now. I'd always wanted to see Westminster Abbey and Stratford-on-Avon and all. I figured I'd look Jim up while I was here."

He shook his head. "I don't get it. He'd never been overseas, so how would he know that guy Crocker? How would he get word in the States that this Manor house was an easy score? Unless there was a lot more going on behind the scenes in his life than I'd ever have guessed. I don't know, maybe those aren't his bones after all. I've just got this funny feeling they are. You know how you get feelings sometimes?"

"Oh, yes. I get them all the time. But maybe it's better not to act on them," I said, thinking of Arthur Crocker.

John had listened silently to all this, looking interested, although he must have heard the story before. His guard seemed lower now.

"We have checked with Immigration Control," he put in, "and a James Cobb did enter the country ten years ago, an American national. But there's no further record of him. Do you know, the thing that most strikes me about our skeleton is the way it was buried. I mean, right against the churchyard cross like that. Why would a murderer not just bury his victim in the wood somewhere, or in his own back garden?"

"Well, nobody thought the cross would ever be disturbed," I said. "After all, it had stood in the same spot for hundreds of years. Who could have predicted ten years ago that somebody like Ian Larribee would one day decide to dig it up?"

"True. Still, it's an odd choice for a killer, I think. I've developed a theory that the murderer wanted to put him in sacred ground. If the victim couldn't have a funeral and the vicar's blessing, at least, lying up against that much-revered cross, his soul would be safe from malign forces."

"Like witches!" I exclaimed. "There you are, that's George again. He was scared to death of them."

Dan shook his head. "I can't see that. It's not the way a murderer would think. If you hated somebody enough to kill him, why would you care what happened to his soul?"

"I've no idea," John admitted. "And certainly I see your point. It just seems odd to choose that place, with all its associations. I'm probably reading too much into it," he said with a shrug.

I offered them tea, and although Dan would have accepted happily, John was doing the driving and he was ready to leave. I had to admit that Dan Vincent showed every symptom of being attracted to me, old and undesirable though I saw myself. But he had definitely met me at the wrong time. Trusting another man with my happiness was not even a remote possibility.

After they left I finished the laundry, folded and put the clean clothes and linens away, then sat down in the corner of the sofa with *Lark Rise to Candleford*. Flora Thompson's beautiful evocation of old village England spoke to me much more directly now I was here. Along with a select group of mystery writers and my weekly doses of "Masterpiece Theatre" and "Mystery," she had kept my dreams of England alive for years.

It was a luxury finally to have a few hours to myself. After a solitary dinner of salad, bread, and Stilton, I took a turn around the back garden to admire the crocuses and cowslips.

I would have to go to Cobbs' soon, to see what kinds of flower seeds they stocked. Funny, Dan's friend having the same name as the village shopkeepers. I certainly wasn't going to start suspecting *them* of being involved in the murder! There must be thousands of people named Cobb.

The evening was clear and warm. I went out with the can of cat food just as the sun was setting. A chorus of birds greeted me, and I spotted a new nest among the blossoms in the apple tree by the front wall.

For the first time, Muzzle was sitting on the road side of the burned-out building, looking across at my cottage. It was nice to think that he might have been watching for me. I didn't go over, but opened my front gate and put his food inside the potting shed again.

He thought about it for a while as I watched him from the doorstep. Finally, he got up and stepped stiff-legged across the road, tail in the air. When he reached the open gate he stopped, and we looked at each other.

"Oh, come on," I said. "You don't really think I'd hurt you."

As if he understood me, he crossed the grass and walked into the potting shed. I left the gate open, so he could leave if he wanted to, but when I looked out before going up to bed, I saw his green eyes glowing just inside the doorway of the shed.

The next morning was warm and beautiful again. By now I knew that there was no predicting English weather. A sunny morning with singing birds was quite likely to be followed by an afternoon of rain, so the only thing to do was to bask in the sun and listen to the birds while you could.

That was pretty much my plan for Archie's visit. Emily left him with just a barely discernible note of apprehension in her voice as she said goodbye. He immediately set off exploring on his unsteady legs, without a trace of fear at being in a new place.

I followed him up and down the stairs, into the fireplace, under the sink, finally out to the garden. He squeaked and babbled enthusiastically about this different world of trees and flowers. I brought out my graph paper and tried to plan borders while he explored, but it was no use. I had to jump up and rescue him so often that I gave it up.

He was tired and fussy by lunchtime. After we had eaten, I planned a walk while he napped in the stroller. He passed out so fast once we were on the road that he didn't get to see Muzzle stalking around George's backyard like a little panther while the birds squawked warning calls from tree to tree. I made a mental note to look for him after Archie woke up. It would be a big thrill for him to see a cat up close.

I was smiling down at my grandson, slumped in perfect relaxation, one round arm hanging out of the stroller, as we turned into Church Lane, on our way to the greatest danger we had been in yet.

CHAPTER SEVENTEEN

I soaked up the sun's warmth and the scents of mown grass and blackthorn blossom in St. Etheldreda's churchyard, as I pushed the stroller along by the stone wall. The same robin was singing again from a tombstone, warning the others off his nesting ground. Funny little thing, I thought, making such a beautiful sound only to say, I was here first, this ground belongs to me.

It was hard to believe that, only the other night, I had come across a lesson in white witchcraft right here. But of course, it was at least as hard to believe what the police had found in that hole by the cross, the yellow tape gone now from around it, or that the unmarked mound by the far side of the wall covered an old man killed by a vicious blow to the head. Not in this world of spring flowers and sun.

I had planned to walk around the churchyard and read old graves, especially the Crockers'. But as I started through the gate I caught a glimpse of the Manor at the end of Church Lane, and remembered I had meant to apologize to Alan and Philippa for that rude remark at the police station. It must have confirmed all the stereotypes about Americans.

So I walked up the lane and across the circular drive to the mansion. I climbed the steps with some difficulty because of the stroller, and pressed the brass button at one side of the door. A set of chimes echoed inside.

It was only a couple of minutes before the door was opened by the portly butler who had admitted me to the party. But this time, when I asked for Mrs. Damerel, he didn't open it wider.

"Both Mr. and Mrs. Damerel are out of the house at present, Madame," he said stiffly.

"Oh. All right, I guess I'll have to come back another day. Will you tell them I called? "

"I am to inform you, Madame, that you will not be admitted to the house again at any time," he said, lifting his chin.

"What? Oh, for heaven's sake!"

I was first flabbergasted, and then angry. What I had said was surely not all that unforgivable, however inflated Philippa's opinion of the respect due her.

"And are you to tell me why?" I demanded.

"No reason was given," he answered shortly.

"Well, I would like you to tell Mrs. Damerel that I *will* speak to her, somewhere else if necessary, and clear this up. It's simply ridiculous to act as if I'd committed a crime!"

"I shall tell her, Madame," he said, "although I doubt that anything will change as a result."

Someone had come up behind him, and now actually

pushed him aside, making him sputter indignantly. It was Rupert.

He was barefooted, wearing jeans and a plain t-shirt, his blond hair mussed up as if he had just gotten out of bed. His eyes lit up and he flashed a brilliant smile when he saw me.

"My mate, Catherine Penny!" he exclaimed. "Come right in."

The butler looked at him with intense dislike.

"I have had orders, Master Rupert, that I am not to admit this lady to the house."

"Right, I can bloody well believe that!" he burst out, his face turning bright red. "The only person in this one-eyed village who's ever said a word on my be-half—of course the bitch would refuse to let her in the house."

He turned back to me with that excessive smile.

"Do please come in," he said. "Pay no attention to this jumped-up pot boy."

"You may be sure, Master Rupert," said the butler, al-most strangling with outrage, "that your parents will hear about this as soon as they return!"

"You think you have to tell me that?" the boy sneered. "Go on, get out of it, Haines. Go and write up your re-port for Mummy."

The butler turned and left us. Rupert waggled his fin-gers at me, still grinning.

"Come on in. I really want you to."

"Thanks, Rupert, but I have to—"

"Oh, come in, for God's sake! What's the matter, have

you heard what the police think about me? Are you afraid to be alone with a killer?"

That sent a little chill down my backbone, but I assured myself he was only showing off. Why would he want to hurt me? He actually seemed grateful for what I'd said to his parents.

"I'm not afraid of you, Rupert," I said steadily.

"Prove it by coming in." He held the door open wider. I hesitated. I didn't like that smile.

"Well, it was actually your mother or father I wanted to see, so I'd better—"

He looked surprised. Had he really thought I'd come to hang out with him, maybe share a joint?

"You could wait for them in the drawing room. I'd even give you tea. I know *she*, at least, will be back soon. She's only gone into Oxford to have her hair done or something. I don't know where my father is, but he never goes very far."

Oh, why not? I asked myself. He was really no different, except in accent and affluence, from the street kids who used to hang around the library in New York. I'd always talked to them, although most of my colleagues were only interested in getting them out of the building. I'd hoped I might say something that would help one of them get his life straight. I had never seen any evidence that I'd been successful, but you can't tell. At any rate, I hadn't been afraid of them, and they had been a lot scarier-looking than Rupert.

"All right," I said, "if you act like a regular person, and don't try to scare me."

I pushed the stroller through the door. It slammed closed behind me. Noiseless on his bare feet, he was immediately beside me.

"You seem like a nice woman," he said. "I can't figure out why anybody nice would want to see that bitch, Philippa." The smile was gone.

"Don't call her that," I said, annoyed. "What I said at the police station was rude. I wanted to tell her I only said it because I was so upset."

He stepped back from me, with the look of a child whose promised treat has been snatched away.

"Oh, hell. You're just like the rest of them, worrying about your bloody social niceties! I thought *you* were willing to stand up to the bitch."

And I complained about Emily's attitude! I should count my blessings, not to have been landed with a child like this one.

"Because you were quite right, you know," he went on, "about them not listening. Every time I try to tell either of them how it is—"

His voice trailed off and he looked away, suddenly despondent. His mood shifts were unsettling.

"Stop feeling sorry for yourself," I said briskly. "You've got everything going for you, money, position, things a lot of kids would use to make themselves and other people happy, if they had a chance of ever getting them. And how do you spend your time? Burglarizing old people!"

He scowled. "Philippa won't give me the money I need. She's got her own, you know, but it all goes on her back or into this house. She doesn't like the way I spend it, she says. The other day she even said she was afraid I'd run off and marry Patty if I had enough money!"

"And she couldn't be right about that?"

"Of course not. Patty's a little peasant. I don't have to *marry* her to have her."

Maybe he was more like his mother than he realized. I'd had enough. I started to wheel the stroller back to the door.

"On second thought," I said, "I don't think I'll wait."

He jumped in front of me, close enough that I could see the traces of acne on his cheeks and the wild light that glittered at the back of his blue eyes.

"What makes you think I'll let you go?" he asked softly.

That definitely made me nervous, but I wouldn't let him know it.

"Stop playing the fool, Rupert," I said. "Get out of my way."

Now his crazy smile returned. "You *are* afraid to be alone with me. And maybe you should be. But you're thinking we're not really alone, aren't you, that Haines is still around? Oh no, he'll have gone off to his pantry to brood. That's what he always does when he's offended, as I should know better than anyone. And while he could hear the bell there, if you could ring it, he'd never hear a scream."

Why had I come in? That was definitely my dumbest move yet. I didn't know what to do now, except that I was sure I shouldn't let him see fear in my eyes.

So I focused them over his shoulder, on the staircase

where the portraits of his ancestors stared back at me disdainfully. Then a sensation like electricity shot through me. There was somebody new on the stairs, somebody I recognized.

It was a splendid portrait in the deliberately rough style of thirty years before, when to leave off the sitter's feet or arms was the height of artistic fashion, and so he faded out at knees and shoulders, leaving the handsome face dominating the canvas, emerging out of a swirl of black brushstrokes.

The painter must have been a major artist, one I should know, to have rendered with such insight the slender face with its rakish mustache, smaller than Arthur Crocker's, the lopsided, charming grin, and what lay beneath, a cruel narcissism the camera had not perceived.

Rupert saw my shocked expression and looked over his shoulder.

"That's your grandfather, isn't it?" I breathed.

He put his head on one side and studied me, puzzled.

"That's right, old Julian. They only rehung him a few days ago, after he'd been cleaned. What about it? Oh, right, I see! You're trying to change the subject, throw me off my guard. Well, it won't work, Catherine Penny."

Now, with a new insight pounding at my brain for admittance, I was able to dismiss his theatrics and see him as he was, just a neglected kid trying desperately to get some adult attention.

"Look, I have to go now, Rupert. Come and see me

some time, when you want to talk without putting on the act."

He was thrown off stride. He muttered a few obscenities after me, but didn't try again to stop me.

Maneuvering the stroller down the steps and following the drive out to the road, I was completely absorbed by my discovery. I knew now why the butler wasn't supposed to let me in. There would have been no excuse for not hanging the portrait, once Philippa got it back from cleaning. Everyone would have thought it extremely odd, as she would say.

But I couldn't be permitted to see it, because I was the only one who had seen that photograph of Julian embracing Annie Crocker.

Archie slept on as I pushed him past the churchyard. I could see the photograph vividly in my memory, and now I wondered how I could ever have thought that young man was Arthur. It was just another example of my jumping to the most likely conclusion. I had even imagined an incestuous relationship, because instinct had told me the emotion those two had been feeling had not been sibling affection, but passion.

George had buried the picture in his cat's grave, where nobody would look for it. He must have known, then, about the romance between his daughter and the heir to the Manor, and for some reason had wanted to keep it secret, but not to destroy the evidence entirely.

Could he have been blackmailing Julian with it? But

love affairs between upper-class men and female servants had never been all that great a scandal, as I knew very well from watching "Upstairs, Downstairs." There had to be more to it. Why would an old love affair have to be concealed, even years afterward?

She might have had a baby. That could be why she'd left the area, too. I knew it was common practice in the past to bribe a servant girl with an inconvenient pregnancy to go away, since there could be no question of marriage. It was depressing to think how much heartache must have been caused by the British class system. Say what you like about today's world, at least that sort of cruelty is a thing of the past.

Or is it? I had just heard Rupert, who everyone said was a charmless version of his grandfather, talking about his own girlfriend in words Julian could have used about Annie: "She's a little peasant, I don't have to *marry* her to have her."

But if Julian had been the same sort of boor as Rupert, it occurred to me, Annie had been nothing at all like Patty Jenkins. A prig, Fiona had called her, and Alice had agreed that Annie had been adamantly against non-marital sex.

Suddenly the key to the whole problem fell into my hand. What if he *did* have to marry her to have her?

I sat down on the side of the hedgerow, under a hawthorn bush. I didn't smell its new blossoms, or hear the birds singing in its branches, because the implications of that thought amazed me so.

Everyone agreed that Julian could not deal with frustration. Fiona said he'd had to have what he wanted and hadn't cared what he had to do to get it. If Annie had guarded her virginity so fanatically, she would surely have held out for marriage, even from the closest to a romantic hero she would ever meet in Far Wychwood.

It would have to have been done secretly. Old What's-His-Name, Julian's dad, would hardly have sprung for a gala wedding between his son and the parlormaid. And it would have had to be kept secret, especially if Annie got pregnant. A legitimate child would have had actual legal claims on the Damerels, however low-born its mother.

My heart pounded as I leaped from one possibility to another. Maybe Julian had killed her! Maybe she had threatened to expose him and—

"Wait, wait, wait!" I said aloud.

There I was going off half-cocked again, making up yet another murder that I had no reason to think had ever happened. Two murders were plenty. If I could understand why either of them had happened, I'd be accomplishing something, never mind inventing a third.

But couldn't those two murders have some relation to the secret marriage? Okay, and to the burglary, and to Arthur trying to run me down, and to the circle of yew—

"Oh, dear," I sighed. I was never going to be able to connect everything.

I closed my eyes and forced my mind to slow down, relax, and just float. Julian, with that devil-may-care smile and that Errol Flynn mustache, was what it floated to. His loss of interest, they said, was always as total as his passion had been, once he'd gotten what he wanted.

So Annie would have waited, I mused, putting up with furtive sexual encounters, expecting any day to be presented to his parents. Instead, he had finally informed her that he'd had all he needed from her. He was now in love with a beautiful, accomplished woman of his own class, one who also demanded marriage.

I thought back to George's babblings about his daughter. It was hard to remember the exact words, but I knew he had said, "She made it right in the end." That didn't sound like murder.

Had she agreed to a divorce, then? They were much harder to get in England fifty-some years ago, and impossible to keep secret. Julian would have been in big trouble with his parents, who Fiona said scared him. And the disgrace, as it was considered in those days, might even have cost him the beautiful Cordelia.

So maybe Annie had agreed just to go away and keep quiet, for money or for love. And then? Then she'd had her baby, somewhere far away, while Julian danced at his sumptuous, illegitimate wedding?

And when the baby grew up she told him the truth—of course, when she was dying of cancer!—and he came to Far Wychwood to claim his rights. And his name was Jimmy.

I jumped up, squelching that annoying little voice inside that repeated John's favorite phrase: "pure speculation." I remembered the smoky room in the vanished hovel, and George's old, cracked voice rambling on. He had talked about some "papers" he had cleverly hidden away where they'd never be found—"not unless they're needed." A marriage license could be "papers," couldn't it?

I looked up the road at the ruins. Papers would have been destroyed in the fire, unless George had been really clever and put them in the place I was thinking of, a place he'd guarded jealously, where his anger had scared me the night I first stumbled on it. Where I had found the photograph.

I hurried to my own front garden. In the potting shed, I found the set of super English hand tools I'd bought at Debenham's. Trowel in hand, I crossed the road and bumped my sleeping grandson over the rubble to George's backyard. I put the stroller's foot-brake on and unbuckled the seat belt to keep him comfortable and, I hoped, asleep. Then I dropped to my knees and started digging Malkin up.

In a few minutes I was below the cat's skeleton, and the trowel hit something hard. I alternately pulled and dug until I got it half out of the ground. It was the kind of cheap metal strongbox they sell at Woolworth's, the key still dangling from the lock.

Inside, I found what I had expected. It was a faded document with an official seal, still legible as the marriage license of Julian Aubrey St. John Damerel and Anne Crocker, issued in Birmingham on May 16, 1954. My impulses had been right this time.

And underneath it, almost as faded, a document issued in New York City on June 15, 1955. It was the birth certificate of James Cobb Damerel.

"Good work, Catherine," a familiar voice said above

me. "I knew once you saw the portrait you would make the connection, but I didn't actually expect you to find the documents for me."

I looked up and saw Alan Damerel standing just a few feet away, wearing his usual friendly smile. His right hand was in the pocket of his tweed jacket.

CHAPTER EIGHTEEN

I sat back on my legs, and sighed. My first reaction was not fear but disappointment. Fear of such a decent English gentleman did not come automatically, even knowing what I knew.

"I didn't think it would be you," I said. "Philippa, that's who I was beginning to suspect. The Manor and the Damerel name mean so much to her. You never seemed to care much."

His voice was as amiable, as civilized as it had always been.

"Ah, well, Catherine, you're an American. You would never have completely understood our English mores. You see, one simply doesn't boast of one's class or pedigree. That is, my sort of people don't. Only the vulgar middle classes, descendants of tradesmen, like my wife, engage in that sort of thing." His lip curled scornfully when he mentioned her.

"It's the worst sort of bad form," he continued. "But, under the circumstances, I don't mind admitting to you that the house, the land, the family are all that have ever mattered in the end. Why did you suppose I'd married that woman, and continued to perform sexually with her until she produced an heir? Only because death duties would have forced me to sell up. As it was, when my father died I had to sell woods and fields I'd loved all my life. But it didn't all go, because I'd had the foresight to marry money, as quite a few of my ancestors had done before the Inland Revenue came to rule over us. And the woman has been willing to spend any amount on the Manor, thank God, to feed her delusions of grandeur.

"You can't understand all that, of course—any more than your countryman could when he came looking for us, ten years ago. The pathetic specimen my father got with the parlormaid, paunchy and balding, in an appalling off-the-rail suit, with an accent like Kojak's— some sort of commercial traveler, actually thinking he'd a right to this estate!"

"But legally," I couldn't help saying, "he *was* the rightful heir."

He laughed harshly. "How could my father's youthful lust for the Crocker girl be allowed to decide the fate of possessions that go back to the Conqueror? Well, she did at least go away when he came to his senses. Of course, he couldn't file for divorce without risking his father learning what he'd done. He was generous with her, according to their son, gave her money to emigrate and set herself up in a trade, and then, do you know, I think he simply forgot about her. He did that. When a thing became boring he simply moved on. He found me, for example, rather amusing in my earliest years, then once I was off at public school he always seemed surprised, even confused, when I put in an appearance at holidays. As if he had quite forgotten he had a son."

The bitter edge to his voice gave me a moment's glimpse of another needy boy, long ago.

"I feel sure he had no idea she was pregnant when she left. She almost certainly didn't know it herself. When this 'James Damerel' arrived, waving about the papers you now hold, he actually seemed to expect me to welcome him as a long-lost brother! Went on with some nonsense about our sharing the estate, wanted to go up to see Father on his deathbed, put on some sort of maudlin reunion scene. Extraordinary.

"I excused myself for a moment, went to my bedroom—"

"Stop, Alan. Don't tell me any more. Here, take the damned papers and destroy them if you want to. But don't tell me."

I held the papers out, but he made no move to take them.

"I got the gun from my bedtable. When I came back, he was turned away, looking out at the grounds, no doubt planning how he would change them. I put the gun to his head and shot him as I would a vicious dog that had wandered onto my property."

Lulled by his urbane voice, I had not yet been afraid. Now a shaft of fear shot through my chest.

"But then," he went on, as if we were discussing cricket scores, "of course the fool of a gardener walked in."

"Gardener? You mean George Crocker?"

He nodded. "He had come along with the fellow, you see, and had been waiting outside. Crocker was always out for the main chance. No doubt his only interest in his newfound grandson was the money he could get out of him. He never cared for anyone but that randy son of his.

"Well, you see, I knew I could get away with killing a stranger to the village, but not Crocker, one of our villagers, in fact an employee. That would have attracted attention. So I offered him a fair amount of money to keep quiet. He bargained for more, offering to get rid of the body and those papers for me. Obviously he was not too grief-stricken over 'James Damerel.'

"I gave him all the cash I had in the house, the wages and more, and left him to take care of the dirty work. His family had always served ours, you see. They were noted round the village for keeping their words, and, of course, he did. He never bothered me for more money, and he backed up the burglary story I concocted to account for the missing wages. But when that damned skeleton was dug up, I knew what had happened. The fool couldn't bury him out in the wood somewhere, it had to be beside the churchyard cross!"

"Maybe he felt more grief than you thought he did."

He shrugged. "Once the body was discovered, I had reason to worry. And at that drinks party my wife put on, when you said he had been nattering about 'Jimmy' and 'money' and 'papers,' I knew it was time to do more than worry. In his senile condition, he was apt to reveal everything. You were the first person actually to sit down and talk with him for years. I realized he must have kept those papers as leverage over me, in case he should ever need it. But I couldn't get at him without risking your seeing me, so I took advantage of his superstition and left a circle of yew on his doorstep, to stop him talking until I could act."

"How did you know what the yew meant?"

"It's not only Dr. Barry who collects books on folklore. My grandfather had a few. It was easy to find a symbol meaning 'keep your mouth shut.' If I scared him into doing that, I could wait until the next Tuesday, when you said you would be in Oxford until the evening."

"But I came back early, didn't I, and ruined everything?"

"You have been an annoyance, Catherine, one way and another. I have some idea how Arthur Crocker must feel. But in point of fact, your interference in that fellow's affairs served me rather well. Everyone found it easy to believe Arthur would try to run you down."

"That was you!"

"Of course. I knew Crocker spent most mornings with his latest conquest, a married woman. He's hoping she'll recoup his lost fortunes. Things intertwine in small communities, you know. She's actually one of my wife's silly friends, and I'd overheard them giggling in their common way about the affair.

"I'd been to his surgery for some reading glasses a few months before. I remembered seeing his keys hung from a hook near the front door. He was in the habit of leaving his car and walking to the woman's house, so it was easy to grab the keys and the car, when I saw you starting up St. Aldate's. A cheap fake mustache was all it took to convince you that Arthur was behind the wheel, at the speed I was going."

"You'd been watching me?" The thought gave me a chill.

"I couldn't let them bring my son to trial, now, could I? Worthless though he is, he's the only heir to the Manor. Believe me, not even family loyalty could force me back into Philippa's bed now. I had to divert the police away from Rupert and back to Arthur. If not for yet another interfering American, I'd have eliminated you and your snooping, as well as incriminating Crocker in another murder. Two birds with one stone, as they say. But I've been forced to wait until now, and employ a second stone in the form of this excellent pistol which my grandfather liberated from a German officer in Hitler's war."

He took his right hand out of his pocket, and raised the Luger to point directly at my face.

I froze with terror, but only for seconds. I forced myself to say, in a voice I didn't recognize, "Somebody will hear the shot."

He was smiling. "Oh, I think not. We're surrounded by the wood. There are no other houses nearby. In any case, in the countryside it would only be put down to poachers. I'm sure you know that, clever as you've been in figuring out the meaning of that photograph. I wasn't sure you'd remember my father's face after I slipped the photo into my pocket, the evening you served us that frightful American stodge. You wouldn't credit how amazed I was to see it lying there in plain view on your mantelpiece!

"But after Philippa rehung the portrait, I couldn't take the chance. That's why I instructed Haines not to admit you to the house. When he told me my idiot son had let you in anyhow, and the boy said you seemed to be struck by Father's portrait, I knew you would have to be eliminated, too."

I looked around desperately. No one would see us from the road. The front wall of the ruin was as high as his head. On the other three sides there were only woods.

It was no use begging for my life. I realized that the primacy of their perceived needs over lesser beings' lives was like a strain of madness that ran through the Damerels. In Julian his fleeting passions, in Alan the house and the land.

Then I saw Archie. He was awake, sitting quite still, gazing up at the gun in fascination. My heart seemed to twist in my chest. Alan wouldn't listen to pleas for my life, but surely—

"You won't hurt the baby?"

He shrugged. "It will make a noise and attract attention."

"No, Alan—if you have to kill me, at least don't hurt him. He can't give you away, he hasn't said his first word yet! Please, please, don't hurt him."

I was on the verge of tears, but I held them back with all my strength. Something told me he would only despise tears.

"Just let me move him over by the road," I begged,

"where he'll be found, where he won't have to see me die!"

"You do think me a fool, don't you, Catherine? No, you'll both stay where you are."

He lowered the gun and looked down at me earnestly.

"Look, I'm really sorry to have to kill you. I rather liked you, but I'd never be able to trust you, not as I could George Crocker. You can't begin to understand the code of service that bound the Crockers to the Damerels for so many centuries, that made George and Annie obey our will as their ancestors had. And of course, the idea of a murder trial, dragging our name through the mud, showing myself before a mob of boors, and then prison— You must see that I can't risk that?"

"But the baby—"

I don't think he even heard me. "Of course, I'll have to handle this burial myself. You may be sure I'll lay you in an inconspicuous grave, back in the wood where no presumptuous priest will dig you up.

"You know, Catherine, it's a pity you crossed the ocean and became involved in my affairs. You could have gone safely on into old age in your own country, couldn't you? Ah, well, perhaps this was your fate. Do you think so?"

He leveled the gun and aimed it at my forehead.

At the same instant, through the chaos of images and sensations roaring through my brain, I was aware that Archie had pulled himself up, holding onto the tray of the stroller with one hand, pointing the other at something behind Alan. His eyes were enormous. Inadvertently, mine followed them.

Muzzle was sitting at the edge of the little grave, staring back at him.

Archie opened his mouth as wide as it would go and, with what seemed the approximate decibel level of a factory whistle, his first word exploded from him.

"Cat!" he shrieked.

I saw Alan freeze for a split second in surprise. But the effect on Muzzle was astonishing. He leaped straight into the air, then ran for cover in his usual projectile fashion, skidding in confusion right between Alan's feet.

The gun wavered as Alan looked down. The cat scrambled, more and more panicked as it found itself trapped between his legs. It ran over his shoe, he tried to step away and trod on its tail and, yowling, it clawed at his trousers and pushed him backward.

Alan staggered and fell, barely missing Muzzle, who had found his way out and streaked for the woods. I heard Alan hit the ground hard and grunt as the breath was knocked out of him. I saw the gun fly into the air, and I heard it go off as I was running for the road, Archie under my arm and the papers clutched in my hand.

I would never have imagined I could move so fast. I cleared the rubble as if it had been flat ground. I crossed the road, I would estimate, in two strides. I didn't look back to see if Alan had recovered and started after me. I ran through my cottage door, slammed it, and turned the lock.

Of course, it was not much of a lock, because people in Far Wychwood had never worried about strong locks. He could easily break it if he applied some force. But it would delay him while I called the police.

I set Archie down, ran to turn the lock on the back door, too, and then got Oxford City Police Station on the phone. They put me through to John Bennett immediately, and I told him everything in one breath.

All he said was, "We'll be there directly. Don't leave the house."

"Are you serious?" I retorted.

After I hung up I grabbed Archie again and took the steps two at a time. I shut us in my bedroom with a chair under the door knob, and that was where John and a couple of constables found us, about twenty minutes later.

Archie already had my chest of drawers emptied, and was wearing my good satin nightgown. I sat on the bed, writing at top speed inside the cover of my bedtime mystery.

John's face was even more solemn than usual when I let him into the room.

"Here," I said, "I've been writing down everything he told me, in case I forget things." I gave him the book, the marriage license, and the birth certificate. "These are what it was all about." I exhaled a great sigh, feeling as if I'd handed him a hundred-pound weight. "Did you get him?"

He took my arm gently and led me to the bed, where he sat down beside me.

"I'm afraid we were too late," he said. "He's lying over there in the ruins of Crocker's cottage. He picked up the gun and shot himself in the head."

CHAPTER NINETEEN

On an afternoon three or four days later, I sat with some of my best friends at tea while the rain drizzled down outside, coaxing flowers out of the seeds I'd been planting.

Fiona and John, Dan Vincent, and Emily and her family were seated in front of the fire in my living room, drinking Lapsang Souchong tea and eating my freshly baked chocolate chip cookies and Fiona's scones with clotted cream. We all felt we deserved something really fattening after what we'd been through.

Archie, of course, wasn't exactly seated. He was toddling around, chattering to himself incessantly, more interested now in naming things than in grabbing and banging and chewing them. He returned every little while to find a lap, greeting "Mummy" or "Papa" or "Nana" as he climbed up, demanding "bikkie" or "milk," then sliding down to point to something and ask urgently, "Dat?"

"Books, darling," I replied to his latest demand. "You see, I said he'd start talking when the right time came. And he certainly couldn't have chosen a better time!"

Emily reached over to squeeze my hand.

"If he hadn't sung out like that and scared the cat, I don't think I would have been able to bear—"

She broke off as her eyes filled with tears.

"I wish we could find that little moggy and give it a big bowl of cream," Fiona said. "I'll never credit that old saying again, about black cats bringing bad luck!"

"Poor thing," I agreed. "I thought he was coming to trust me, before that awful scene scared him off again. I've been finding the cans of food empty every evening, so I know he's still around, but I haven't seen hide nor hair of him. I hope he's all right."

"Oh, Peter," said Emily, dabbing at her eyes with a tissue, "please go and stop him pulling all Mom's books out."

"It's all right," I said. "As long as he isn't tearing them, I don't mind picking them up after. In fact, I enjoy rearranging them. You know, you can take the librarian out of the library—"

"But he has to learn," Emily began, and then stopped. "All right, Mom, it's your house." We smiled at each other.

"He's a pistol, isn't he?" Dan said admiringly, raising himself several notches in my estimation.

"He's a holy terror," Peter laughed, and went after Archie, who had opened a picture book of Britain and was rumpling the pages rather badly as he turned them, shouting, "Dog! Twee! Baby!"

"Speaking of holy terrors," Fiona said, recklessly spreading clotted cream on a scone, "is Rupert really out of the running for the Manor, now it's established that Julian's marriage to Cordelia was bigamous? I mean to say, that's pretty hard on him."

"I doubt it bothers him much," John said. "He doesn't care for the estate or the family. And he's certainly not the type of young man who would feel it's his duty to take on all that responsibility. Quite the opposite. He'll turn eighteen in a few months and can do as he pleases. My guess is he'll move as far from his mother and the estate as he can. I'm told Philippa has set investigations in train for any distant Damerel who might be in line to inherit after Rupert. If she finds them, she'll buy the estate. She has pots of money, and she loves the Manor."

"Exactly the two reasons Alan married her," I said.

"What a dreadful specimen he was all along!" Fiona exclaimed bitterly. "And we all thought him such a perfect gentleman. It's very sad, really, for the village as well as for his victims. There's been a Damerel at the Manor since 1066, and now the succession will come to an end. Damn Julian for starting all this!"

"Neither Damerels nor Crockers at Far Wychwood any more," John mused. "Hard to credit."

"One may regret that," Fiona said, "but as far as Alan is concerned, I can't find it in my heart to pity *him* at all."

"The one I pity most," Dan said sadly, "is Jim. From what Catherine says, he came here not to steal the place from Alan Damerel, but to share it with him and to finally meet his father.

"You know, he tried to tell me, the last time I saw him, how his mother had given him some old family papers when she was dying, and told him who his people were. But I was having business problems then and I sort of cut him off. I just didn't have time to listen. I'm always going to feel bad about that."

"One thing that occurs to me—" said Fiona, "how can we be sure he's the same man, since when you knew him in America his name wasn't Damerel, but Cobb?"

"The Cobbs were Annie's grandparents," John explained. "Her mother, Emma, was our shopkeeper's cousin. Annie was so anxious to cause no trouble for the man she loved, she not only left the country at his behest but changed her name and her child's name. It's only luck that she put the legal one on the birth certificate."

"She named her boy after her grandfather," I said. "Jim Cobb had always been good to her when she was growing up, better in fact than her own father."

"Poor Annie," Emily said, "I wonder if she did go away out of love, or just the age-old instinct of Crockers to obey Damerels. What a sad life she had."

"Bit of a floormat, I'd say," Fiona scoffed. "Catch me fading quietly away if I'd married a man as rich as that! Well, I suppose one shouldn't be too hard on her, although submissive women like that always irritate me. Still, we're not all the same and it's probably a very good thing in the long run."

"Bikkie," said Archie firmly, climbing into his mother's lap. As she reached for the cookie plate I opened my mouth to say he'd had too many already, then quickly closed it. I caught Dan watching me with some amusement.

"Have you heard about Donald Barry?" Fiona asked. I shook my head. "Well, after his televised up-and-downer with Ian, he went home feeling quite ill. Being a doctor, he knew what the symptoms meant and got Louisa to take him right to the hospital, where they confirmed that he was on the verge of a major stroke. They were able to lower his blood pressure enough to prevent it, but he's still in hospital. He's on the mend, but when I popped over to see him yesterday, I could see how much his little crusade has taken out of him. So much that he and Louisa have decided to retire to Brighton as soon as he's released, and just live a relaxing life. He'll pass the time writing a history of occult practices."

"Poor man!" I said. "He ruined his health, but he did save our churchyard cross."

"Yes," said Fiona, "and Louisa told me the antiquarian society has voted him an award for his efforts!"

"The cross won't be moved after all?" Peter asked.

"No," Fiona said, "in point of fact, it's Ian Larribee who's going to be moved. I heard *that* just this morning from Enid, who had it from Jilly. All that embarrassing publicity and cameras thrust into his face displeased the bishop no end, so he decided to calm us down by transferring Ian to Manchester. I'm sure he'll be much happier there, doing social work among people who actually need it."

"He'll probably try to pull down half of Manchester and replace it with 'worship centers' and high-rises," I said tartly.

"Oh, I think Manchester's pretty well supplied with

such things already," John said with a smile. "He'll either be terribly frustrated, living in a place that doesn't need to be dragged into the twenty-first century, or he'll slip in happily among the city's extreme progressives."

"Anyway, we're safe for the moment," Fiona said. "We can go right on poking along in our own way without anyone trying to make us change to fit the fashion."

"I wouldn't be too optimistic," I answered, "not until we know what sort of vicar we'll get in his place."

"Haven't heard anything about that yet," she said, "except that it's generally expected the new vicar will be here in time to perform Audrey's wedding."

"Audrey—" The name sounded familiar, but I couldn't place it.

"Friend of Jilly's? Nose ring? Baby, name of Diana?"

"Oh, right! I met her in Cobbs' store, right after George's death. So she's getting married?"

"Yes, well. Since she already had the one baby, her mum was determined she wouldn't have another, so she wouldn't let her date. Of course, that meant she and her fellow, young Harry Ames from the petrol station, have been having to sneak off to the witch-wood on a regular basis, the result being that the second baby's due in the autumn, and the wedding's to be at the end of Lent.

"Actually, she told me they were eavesdropping on you a few days ago. They found it quite funny to hear you talking to George's cat about the murder."

"Cat," said Archie, through a mouthful of cookie.

"I'm more concerned about replacing the doctor than the vicar," John put in. "Doctors are not anxious to settle in country villages any more. There's not enough money about. It could be we'll just have to do without local medical care from now on."

"I want to come along when you visit him again," I told Fiona.

"Of course. I only didn't ask you yesterday because I thought you'd be done in by your brush with death. Alice and I thought we'd go tomorrow. Do you think you'll be up to it?"

"Listen," I said, a little irritated, "I'm not going to take to my bed just because I've looked down a gun barrel!"

"Right, then, why don't we go up to London, too, say on Friday?" Fiona proposed. "We can do a round of the shops, eat somewhere, and take in a matinee. I've been longing to see that outrageous new play that all the critics hate."

"Sounds wonderful," I said happily.

"I wish I could be around to buy your lunches," Dan put in, "but my flight home's booked for tomorrow. Maybe I'll catch that play tonight. Then we can compare notes on it, when I write to you. If that's okay."

He looked down, his face flushing. Everybody smiled knowingly, and I was mad at myself for being embarrassed.

He was such a nice guy, but I knew I was never going to let a man get close enough to hurt me again. Still, it seemed too ungrateful to say he couldn't even write to me, after he'd saved my life and Archie's. But I only hoped it wouldn't encourage him too much.

"I'll be glad to hear from you," I said primly.

The look of relief on his face made me determine to limit any correspondence to strictly impersonal topics.

Emily and Fiona helped me to clear away, and Emily lingered in the kitchen afterward, while Fiona went to get her belongings together.

"Mom," she said hesitantly, "I have to tell you something. I meant to the other day, but I didn't want to bring it up when we'd just made friends again, because you probably won't like it."

"What on earth is it?"

"The day we quarrelled, there was a message from Dad on the e-mail when I got home. He asked if he could come for a visit, and this time he suggested a date. I was so mad at you, I fired an answer back saying we'd be expecting him. He answered the next day. So he's going to be here for two weeks the end of next month."

"Look, best beloved, I've told you a hundred times I don't mind if you see your dad. Just give me the dates, and I'll avoid Oxford until he's gone."

But a sudden shortness of breath surprised me.

"The worst part," she went on miserably, "is he's bringing his Barbie doll. I'm sorry, Mom. I was so mad at you that I said it was fine with me. But he's not playing Barbies in my home, I promise you. She can stay at a hotel."

I turned away to put the cups in the cabinet. Why did the thought of those two on my side of the Atlantic make my heart pound so? There was a sense of foreboding, too, that I couldn't explain. I was afraid something very bad was going to happen.

"It's odd," Emily was saying, "and if I didn't have Archie I probably wouldn't see it, but this has all been about parents and children, hasn't it, all this tragedy? George who spoiled his son rotten and left his daughter hungering for love, the Damerels who cared so much more for 'the family' than for its individual members, and poor Jim Cobb, searching for the father and the relatives he must always have longed to know—not realizing he was threatening the only thing their father had ever given Alan—his land."

She was shaking her head sadly as I turned to her. "And yet I'll bet they all meant to do right by their children, the same as I do, the same as Dad meant to." She gave a little shrug. "Things just happened."

"Listen, we're all playing it by ear," I said, "despite those books of yours that claim to have it all figured out. Nobody starts out meaning to fail his children. We have needs, and those needs keep changing, and all we can do is try to get the kids through it whole. You're right, none of those people intended a tragedy, but that's what they created."

We put our arms around each other. "Even if I'm critical sometimes, I never get over my amazement that Dad and I did it so well. We couldn't keep it together in the end, but we did the hardest part right."

I walked to the gate to see everybody off, ignoring the drizzle like a real Englishwoman. Turning back, I pushed away the premonitions of trouble. So, he was coming. I didn't have to see him, or even acknowledge his existence. I had my new life and I was going to get on with it. The first thing to do was to get a piece of paper and make a list of all my plans for next week. I knew I could only trust my memory so far.

There was the trip to the hospital tomorrow to see Dr. Barry, dinner with Peter and Emily the next evening, when they had promised to actually cook something, then Friday a whole wonderful day in London with Fiona, and I must allow time to get over to Cobbs' for more flower seeds and the latest gossip about the new vicar.

As I stepped through my front door, something brushed against my ankle. I looked down and saw a narrow black streak cross the room and stop.

At first I hardly recognized Muzzle. He was soaked through, exhausted and desperate for shelter. His green eyes were very wide but for the first time I saw no fear in them.

"So," I said softly, "here you are at last."

He turned and wobbled toward the fire, stood gazing into it for a moment, then sank down on the hearth rug and curled his tail around himself as I closed the door.

POCKET BOOKS
PROUDLY PRESENTS

Slaying Is Such Sweet Sorrow

PATRICIA HARWIN

Coming in Fall 2005
from Pocket Books

Turn the page for a preview of
Slaying Is Such Sweet Sorrow. . . .

It was no use lying to myself, the baby was not in the house. I had searched every nook a sixteen-month-old boy could fit in, and my Tudor-era cottage had far more nooks than most houses. He was gone.

And it was my fault. What kind of grandmother leaves a toddler sleeping on the sofa and goes out to dig a damn perennial border, just because a sunny April day is a rarity in England? Although Archie had never shown any ability to reach, let alone turn, a doorknob, I knew how determined he was to figure things out. Emily was right, I wasn't fit to watch him.

I went to the front door and grabbed hold of the lintel, weak with apprehension, looking out at the one road through Far Wychwood, a two-lane that connected a mile beyond the village with a main route to Oxford. People went down our little road pretty fast, although there was a four-lane several miles away that got most of the traffic.

The scruffy black cat that had adopted me peered around the door of the potting shed by the stone wall. It was his favorite place of refuge when Archie visited, though I had known him to simply disappear for days. He was so easily spooked that I hadn't yet been permitted to touch him. I had no doubt he deeply resented my having gained his trust with tuna fish and then brought in a toddler on him.

"Where's he gone, Muzzle?" I murmured.

I stepped out into my front garden and he came toward me warily, tail in the air. The scar on my right arm throbbed dully at the sight of the old man's property across the road, raising subconscious memories of the day I'd been caught in the blaze that destroyed the cottage.

A few seconds later a shock went through my whole body at a screech of brakes and a shout, off to my right. I ran into the road, my heart knocking the breath out of my chest, knowing what I would see.

A tiny shape lay unmoving on the shoulder of the road, by the waist-high stone wall in front of the old village schoolhouse. I knew it was Archie by the overalls and the ringlets of yellow hair, and despair slumped like a sinkhole into my brain.

Running toward him, I was vaguely aware of some kind of car sitting slantwise across the road and a male figure, with something red about him, standing there looking down at Archie.

I stopped a few feet from the man and screamed, "Stupid, stupid— Couldn't slow down, could you?"

"No, no!" he stuttered. "I didn't hit him, he fell—"

I sank to my knees beside Archie. His quicksilver presence, incessantly searching and questioning, seemed utterly stilled. He was sprawled on his stomach with his blue eyes closed, his soft pink lips open, even the curls seeming to lie lifeless against his head. My faithless husband, my brilliant Emily—it seemed to me at that moment I'd never loved them or anyone except this child lying like a piece of refuse beside the road.

I heard the man babbling on, "I was driving along, at the speed limit, I assure you, and I saw the little boy standing on the wall there, and then as I reached it I saw him lose balance and fall. He hit his head against that large rock, do you see? I stopped to help him—"

Then, incredibly, Archie made a little moaning sound and turned on his side. His features puckered into a frown, his eyes still shut.

Relief flooded through me. The man exclaimed, "There, he's not— He's knocked himself out, that's all! Best to take him round to your local GP. Let me carry him for you."

"There's no doctor here any more," I answered breathlessly. "The one we had's been gone ever since the murder."

"Murder?" he repeated, startled.

"But somebody has to examine him," I went on. "Look where his poor little head's starting to swell, behind his ear. Concussion, it must be, oh, Archie, oh, God—"

"Oxford's less than half an hour away," he said. "We'll take him to the main hospital." He slipped his arms under Archie and lifted him from the ground. "If you'll just hold the door," he began, stepping toward his car. I scrambled up and jerked the passenger-side door open. "No, best let him lie on the rear seat—" he began, but I broke in.

"I'm going to hold him, don't try to stop me."

"Very well, get in and I'll give him to you." We accomplished this, and I sat cradling Archie while the man got in beside us and started the car. He glanced over and said reassuringly, "There, his color's coming back, isn't it?"

"Just drive!" I snapped.

But as we headed through the village I had to admit that Archie's cheeks were pinker now, and he had started making mewing noises, scowling, closing his fingers around the bottom of my cardigan. After a few minutes he tried to sit up, pulling on the sweater. His eyes popped open as he got nearly vertical. He grabbed the right side of his head, where the swelling was increasing rapidly, stared at me indignantly and said, "Ow!"

"Be quiet, baby," I said. "I know it hurts, but we're going to make it all better."

His face scrunched up and he wept in soft whimpers, knowing another outcry would hurt just as that one had.

My panic had begun to subside and now I felt sorry for my rudeness. It hadn't, after all, been the man's fault. I glanced at him for the first time. He was, at a guess, in his early twenties, thin and lanky, dressed in jeans and a red sweater under a tweed jacket. His straight brown hair kept flopping over his forehead, so he had to push it back every few minutes. If I were his mother I'd make him get a decent haircut, I thought fleetingly.

"Sorry," I said. "I shouldn't have jumped to conclusions, but I tend to do that."

"Not at all," he said with that embarrassed air the English get when accepting an apology. "Quite understandable. I'm Tom Ivey," he added shyly.

"Catherine Penny. And Archie Tyler." I nodded toward my grandson.

"Oh, I say, is *that* who—" His amiable young face was filled with amazement. "Peter Tyler's son! Of course, and you're the American mother-in-law. Peter has often mentioned you, said you lived in Far Wychwood, but somehow I never connected— I'm Peter's colleague, well, that's to say, I'm only a post-graduate student, a Junior Research Fellow, while Peter of course is a Lecturer and, we're all sure, will be named to the Headship tonight, as our current head's retiring at the end of this term. If anyone at Mercy College would be an excellent Head of Faculty, he would. And of course you'll be there to see the presentation, I mean to say, I'm sure the little chap will be completely recovered well beforehand—"

"I'm not going," I said brusquely. "Can't you drive any faster, Mr. Ivey?"

"Call me Tom. 'I hold he loves me best that calls me Tom.' Sorry, couldn't resist, that's from Thomas Heywood, one of the minor Elizabethans. But you probably don't know of him. Frightfully irritating habit we all have, coming up with these quotations, but our heads are simply stuffed with them. Did you say you're not coming to the ceremony? Oh, do reconsider. Peter thinks the world and all of you, he'll be—"

"Before you go any further, I'm telling you I *won't* be at the ceremony, and before you ask why, I'll tell you it's nothing to do with Peter, who I'm crazy about. I'd have to be in the same room with my ex-husband, Emily's father, and his—dolly-bird, isn't that the expression? The woman he left me for a year and a half ago, in America. They're visiting Peter and Emily for a couple of weeks, and I'm not going near Oxford during that time, not for anything. Well, except an emergency, like this."

"Oh, I do apologize for prying," he said, in an agony of embarrassment. "Peter hadn't told me— I didn't mean—" He fell silent.

We were soon climbing a steep hill to the enormous white rectangle of John Radcliffe Hospital, in a suburb of Oxford. Then down a driveway to a door labeled "Accident and Emergency." Inside, about half a dozen people in various stages of misery occupied a row of uncomfortable chairs in a narrow hallway near the reception desk.

"Yes, may I help you, Madame?" inquired a young black woman behind the desk, in a crisp Oxbridge accent.

"The baby fell and hit his head on a rock," I told her. "He's got a big swollen place on the side of his head there—"

"He's on our records, is he?" she asked, turning to her computer.

"Yes, Archie Tyler. Can't somebody see him right now?" I begged. "Just look at that swelling!"

"Must follow proper procedure, mustn't we?" she said coolly, typing.

Another woman, dressed in nurse-white, came through a set of swinging double doors, consulted the list of names, and shouted, "Thatcher!" An old man got up and limped after her through the doors.

"While you wait," Tom Ivey said behind me, "mightn't I ring Peter up and let him know what's happened? He said he'd be at home today."

I nodded distractedly and he set off for a bank of phones down the hall.

"Do you know Emily Tyler?" I asked the guardian of the gates. "She's on the psychiatric staff here."

She smiled for the first time. "Oh, I know Emily very well indeed."

"Well, this is her boy. She should be here this afternoon, seeing a private patient. I've really got to go and tell her about this."

"You'd be best advised to remain here, Madame," she replied. "They might call you and you'd miss your turn. But I'll ring her consultation room if you like."

"No, no, I have to see her face-to-face to explain how I let it happen. Somebody else told her the last time, and it was awful."

"Very well. Any of the chairs in the corridor."

I gave up and carried Archie to a chair. During the ten or fifteen minutes we waited, his weeping subsided and he succeeded first in sitting up, then in scrambling to the floor, uttering an absentminded "Ow!" every few minutes. When he crawled down the line of chairs to start untying the shoes of a woman too sunk in discomfort to notice, I dragged him back.

"Feeling better, I'd wager!" said Tom, beside us again, and I had to admit the boy was recovering at a rate I'd never expected when I'd seen him lying by the road.

When my name was finally called the nurse took Archie from me, assuring me firmly that I'd be allowed in after the doctor had finished his examination. So I went back to the reception desk and got the directions I needed, took the stairs to the next level two at a time, and burst into my daughter's consulting room. She was sitting in a leather wing chair, dressed severely as she always was at work, in a plain black pantsuit with her long blonde hair pulled tightly back in a chignon, horn-rimmed glasses perched on her nose. Despite her best efforts, she still looked like a teenager although she was a licensed psychotherapist as well as a wife and mother.

My lingering apprehension must have showed, because as soon as she saw me she jumped up from the chair and her face went white.

"Oh, God, what's happened to him now?" she cried.

There was another woman in the room, sitting opposite Emily, but I hardly noticed her as I stuttered out an account of the accident.

"Now, it's *okay!*" I finished. "He's conscious, he's crawling around and causing trouble already. And the swelling will go down, I'm sure, bad as it looks—"

Emily was already headed for the door. The other woman came after her, protesting in a voice stretched taut as a bowstring, "You can't leave me now. You can't draw those terrible memories out of me and then just walk out on me!"

Emily turned to her for a second. "We will reschedule, Mrs. Stone," she said shortly. "It's my child!"

"What about *my* child?" the woman called after her as Emily went out the door. Her curiously deep voice broke with desperation. She grabbed my sleeve and stopped me as I hurried past her. I saw now that she was tall, thin, with jet-black hair piled on the top of her head in a messy bun, and piercing dark eyes that held me almost as irresistibly as her fingers.

"He killed my child," she said. "That's what she has to help me deal with. He killed Simon! And I think he's planning to kill me, too—"

A shiver went down my spine. I had never encountered any of Emily's patients before, and of course she never talked about them. This woman was speaking to me from another realm of consciousness, one I hoped I would never understand. I pulled loose and hurried down the stairs after Emily.

We went down a hallway, all gray linoleum and white walls in need of repainting like the rest of the hospital, and into a windowless cubicle furnished with an examining table, a sink, and a metal cabinet with lots of shallow drawers. Archie was on his feet now, a stethoscope hanging around his neck, pulling open one drawer after another and exploring among the sharp instruments inside. A young man in a white coat was trying frantically to pull him away from the cabinet, but Archie was small enough to dodge him and, obviously, well enough to enjoy the game.

Emily approached from behind and swiped him up before he saw her. She looked him over, and gasped at the swelling behind his ear.

"Good afternoon, Ms. Tyler," the doctor said, lifting his stethoscope off Archie.

"Dr. Barnes," she said with a distracted nod.

"I don't see any sign of concussion," he told her. "Young children easily develop these startling swellings, but they recede quickly. I think you're quite safe taking him home now. In fact, as quickly as possible."

People were suddenly crowding through the door behind us, filling the little room. I turned and saw Tom first with my son-in-law, Peter, beside him. Rose, Archie's young nanny, trailed behind them, and then I caught a glimpse of the man I had loved and trusted for thirty years. A curving, green blur was now attached to his left side, and that was all I wanted to see of the woman who had broken up my marriage. I quickly fixed my eyes on the far wall. I had never seen her, didn't even know her name. Emily and I always referred to her as "Barbie," knowing she had to be the kind of sexpot the dolls were modeled on.

Archie leaned out from his mother's arms and enumerated, "Papa-Danda-Zanny-Vofe!" He pointed at Tom and said, "Dat?"

Rose ran over to embrace him, tears running down her cheeks. He ignored her, still pointing at Tom and demanding, "Dat? Dat?" until Tom realized what was needed and said, "Oh—Tom."

"Ta," said Archie with satisfaction.

He started squirming, trying to get down from Emily's arms. Her father stepped over and took him, raising him way up over his head. Archie shrieked with delight, Emily gave a strangled cry, and I yelled, "What the hell are you doing, he's got a head injury!"

Shock and anger forced my eyes to Quin, although I'd sworn I would never look at him again. There was the same cocky grin I knew so well, the thick, wavy hair, not yet all gray like mine, but grayer than the last time I'd seen him, the sharp blue eyes that met mine with an expression I'd never seen in them before, like a challenge he wasn't sure that he could carry off or that I would meet. He lowered the baby against his chest.

"Calm down, Kit," he said quietly. "He's okay. When Emily hit her head on that swing it swelled up just as big and it went away within an hour. Remember?"

That damned overconfident grin, the nerve of that demand that I share a memory with him, and, most of all, that blur of green attached to his side, filled me with poisonous vapors that threatened to explode and take the whole room out, until I released it in a voice that betrayed me by cracking: "Shut up!" I shrilled.

"Shup!" Archie echoed with delight.

"Archie!" Emily cried. "No, no, nice little boys don't tell people to shut up." She glanced at me indignantly.

The doctor, obviously anxious to be rid of the lot of us, broke in, "As I was saying, it will be quite safe to take him home so long as he's watched for signs of concussion. Those would be excessive drowsiness, confusion—"

"That's ridiculous," I interrupted, driven into a fury at everybody, myself included. "You haven't had him x-rayed for a fractured skull, and *something* has to be done about that swelling! How can you say people with no medical training can recognize symptoms of concussion? He needs to be here, with proper medical supervision!"

"I assure you, this child does not have a fractured skull," the doctor said with growing annoyance. "He is anything but lethargic," and he gestured toward Archie, now bouncing up and down in Quin's arms, chortling, "Shup! Shup!"

"He shows no sign of dizziness or disorientation, his pupils are normal—in short, he doesn't require an x-ray and, as we do have other patients waiting to be seen, I feel quite confident in releasing him."

"What are you, an intern?" I demanded. "I want him evaluated by a specialist."

"Come along, Catherine," said Peter, obviously embarrassed. "You're making too much of a bit of a bump. I'm sure we can trust the doctor's diagnosis."

"Yes, Mother," Emily said. "He *is* our child, after all, and if Peter and I are satisfied that he's not seriously hurt, that's an end to it."

"We'll be with him till it's time to go to Peter's award ceremony," Quin had to put in, "and we'll watch him all the time. And of course little Rosie will call us if there's any problem later." Rose, standing across from me, blushed and smiled shyly. "You can even come back with us, Kit, and help us watch him. How about that?"

I hadn't thought the level of anger inside me could rise any higher, but now I felt the way Krakatoa must have just before it leveled Sumatra.

I shouted, "Don't you tell me what I can do! And don't call me Kit!"

"Mother, stop it!" Emily commanded.

"I really must ask you to take your discussion to some other area," the doctor said stiffly, "as this room is needed. And *should* you require a consultant—"

Blundering out the door, I heard Emily saying earnestly, "Certainly not, Dr. Barnes, and do let me apologize—"

The woman who had been with Emily upstairs was now standing beside the reception desk, tearing a tissue to shreds as she watched the door to the examining rooms. Her hair had come loose and was falling around her face. Her black eyes kindled, looking over my shoulder, and then I heard Emily again, her voice soft and steady: "Have you been waiting all this time, Mrs. Stone? Everything's all right, we'll be able to finish our session after all."

She came around me and took the woman's arm, deftly removing the shreds of tissue from her hands and putting them on the desk. Mrs. Stone's tense face relaxed and she clutched Emily's hand as if it were a lifeline. They moved toward the doors.

"Mrs. Tyler is such an excellent therapist," the young black woman behind the desk said to me, and a smile again softened her ultracompetent manner. "She has a real gift for coping with disturbed patients. But of course you know that."

I hadn't known. Her profession had always been a bone of contention between Emily and me. I believed neurosis was just another name for self-indulgence, that a no-nonsense attitude and plenty of outdoor exercise were of far more use than complaining to a psychologist. But it was good to hear that people who worked with her thought she had "a real gift."

"Now," I heard Peter say softly, "you've got it over with, you've seen and dealt with him, so you'll be able to come to the presentation of the Headship tonight, won't you?"

I turned and saw him looking down at me with genuine eagerness in his intelligent brown eyes. He was a tall, angular young man, rather good-looking once you got past his scholarly stoop and self-effacing manner. I had always been fond of him, and I was touched to see that he really did want me there at his big moment.

"Oh, Peter," I sighed, "are you sure you want to take the chance of another scene like that one? I knew if I was forced to be in the same room with them, I'd behave badly."

"You'll not need to go anywhere near them," he assured me. "There will be nine people there besides you and them. Please say you'll come. It means a lot to me."

How could I refuse that? It was true, the first encounter had to have been the worst. I vowed silently that I'd stay on the other side of the room and prove to everybody that I *could* control my emotions.

Agatha Award nominee for Best First Mystery

ANTIQUE PRINT MYSTERIES

BY LEA WAIT

SHADOWS AT THE FAIR
0-7434-5620-3
For antique print expert Maggie Summer, the Rensselaer
County Spring Antiques Fair is normally full of friendly
colleagues and customers. But when dealers start dying,
she wonders—could someone in the cozy antiques
business be a cold-blooded killer?

"Cannily draws on its author's professional experiences
in the antiques trade…beckons like a weekend in the
country." —*The New York Times Book Review*

And now available in hardcover

SHADOWS ON THE COAST OF MAINE
Maggie Summer finds her old friend's new home in Maine
comes with a history—and when a series of accidents,
ghostly crying of an infant, and hostile neighbors lead up
to a body in the backyard, Maggie finds herself embroiled
in a murder investigation once again.

Available wherever books are sold.

POCKET BOOKS
A Division of Simon & Schuster
A VIACOM COMPANY

www.simonsays.com

09481

First in the brand new

Poetic
Death Mystery
Series

By Diana Killian

High Rhymes and Misdemeanors
0-7434-6678-0

American English teacher Grace Hollister comes to England's Lake District to tour the homes of her beloved Romantic poets. What she gets is tangled up with a charismatic ex-jewel-thief-turned-antiques-dealer who apparently has something worth killing for—if only he and Grace knew what it was.

"Witty and winsome. I was won over. You don't have to know Lord Byron to read and enjoy."
— G. Miki Hayden, author of the Macavity Award-winning *Writing the Mystery*

A Selection of the Mystery Guild

Available wherever books are sold.

POCKET BOOKS
A Division of Simon & Schuster
A VIACOM COMPANY
www.simonsays.com

09482

POCKET BOOKS
MYSTERIES
are to die for!

Curl up with a cozy...

Arson and Old Lace by Patricia Harwin	0-7434-8224-7
Misery Loves Maggody by Joan Hess	0-671-01684-9
murder@maggody.com by Joan Hess	0-671-01685-7
Maggody and the Moonbeams by Joan Hess	0-7434-0658-3
Alpine for You by Maddy Hunter	0-7434-5811-7
Top O' the Mournin' by Maddy Hunter	0-7434-5812-5
High Rhymes and Misdemeanors by Diana Killian	0-7434-6678-0
A Lady Never Trifles with Thieves by Suzann Ledbetter	0-7434-5747-1
Shadows at the Fair by Lea Wait	0-7434-5620-3
Star Struck Dead by Sheila York	0-7434-7046-X

Available wherever books are sold.

POCKET BOOKS
A Division of Simon & Schuster
A VIACOM COMPANY

www.simonsays.com

09483

NATIONAL BESTSELLING AUTHORS

Meet savvy sleuths so intriguing they have their own series...

STEPHEN BOOTH

*British Detectives
Ben Cooper and Diane Fry*

Black Dog
0-671-78604-0
Dancing with the Virgins
0-7434-3100-6
Blood on the Tongue
0-7434-5783-8

JAN BURKE

*California reporter
Irene Kelly*

Goodnight, Irene
0-7434-4451-5
Sweet Dreams, Irene
0-7434-4452-3
Dear Irene,
0-7434-4449-3
Remember Me, Irene
0-7434-4450-7
Hocus
0-7434-4453-1

JOHN DUNNING

*Rare-book dealer
Cliff Janeway*

Booked to Die
0-7434-1065-3
The Bookman's Wake
0-671-56782-9

NANCY PICKARD

*True-crime writer
Marie Lightfoot*

The Whole Truth
0-671-88794-7
Ring of Truth
0-671-88796-3
The Truth Hurts
0-7434-1204-4

BARBARA SERANELLA

*Female mechanic
Munch Mancini*

Unfinished Business
0-7434-2209-0
No Man Standing
0-7434-2033-0

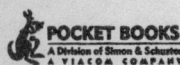

POCKET BOOKS
A Division of Simon & Schuster
A VIACOM COMPANY

AVAILABLE WHEREVER BOOKS ARE SOLD.

09548